DAVID H

TOMORROWS WORLD

Medallion Press, Inc.
Printed in USA

DEDICATION:

To dad, mum, Audrey and the Pattersons.

Published 2008 by Medallion Press, Inc.

The MEDALLION PRESS LOGO
is a registered tradmark of Medallion Press, Inc.

Cover Illustration by Adam Mock

Typeset in Baskerville
Printed in the United States of America

ISBN#978-193383646-1

10 9 8 7 6 5 4 3 2 1
First Edition

TABLE OF CONTENTS

010101000100000101000010010011000100010100100000010011110100011000100000
0010000011010011110100111001010100010000101010011100101010001010011

CHAPTER 1

Footprints in the Sand, Lost World in the Mountains

Most citizens take time travel for granted, the way people a hundred years ago were blasé about splitting the atom, breaking the sound barrier and sending men to the Moon. For me those trips through time aren't simply a novel form of entertainment, though—they're a way of ecaping from a world that has lost its heart and soul.

When I stand on the threshold of a timesphere I know life is about to come alive in a way it doesn't in the soulless apartment blocks and windswept concrete canyons of the community. I feel like Marco Polo, Christopher Columbus or Neil Armstrong, except that my excitement is an order of magnitude higher than theirs because I can travel through time as well as space.

Of course, there's a trade-off. You can go wherever you want, but when you get there all you can do is look. The spherical capsule that's my *Santa Maria*, my *Rocinante* and *Apollo,* that gives me the freedom to go where and when I want, becomes my prison cell once I'm there. That's because the sphere doesn't really hurtle through time and space. Rather, it simulates a destination so vividly you think you're there. Images are projected in every direction and sounds fill the air. As you take your first steps the sphere spins in synchronicity with your movements, and the scenery changes as if you were walking wherever it is you want to be. It's easy to believe you're actually there—until you reach out and try to touch something, because your hand keeps on going. But that doesn't stop me reaching out, or being disappointed when there's nothing to feel with my fingertips.

Hollowed out by a sleepless night remembering a woman I'm trying to forget, I was standing on the threshold of a timesphere raking in the hip pocket of my dark blue coveralls for the ID card that's payment, passport and ticket for the trip. It's only a little piece of plastic but you can't even get into your apartment, let alone a timesphere, without one. It contains every piece of information about a person that can be expressed in words and numbers: from height to fingerprint pattern, academic qualifications to criminal record. And it tells how you earn your pleasure points, where you spend them and how many you have left.

I held my breath as I fed my card into the slot at the side of the timesphere chamber, hoping I had enough credit. The spheres use a lot of computing power, which has to be paid for with hard earned points. My weakness for such virtual trips means I go through points almost as fast as I earn them, so I was half expecting the infuriatingly neutral Voice of Reason to tell me: "You have insufficient credit for this amenity. Have a nice day."

However it said, "Welcome, Citizen Travis. State your desired time and place. Alternatively, select Random and the Ecosystem will choose for you. Or select Favorite to program your most frequently visited destination."

I suppose I should try the Random option, but there's a place I love so much I keep wanting to go back there. So I said what I usually say: "Favorite."

"You have sufficient credit for 15 minutes at your requested time and place," The Voice of Reason told me.

Each timesphere is housed in a chamber. The doors to those chambers are the same neutral gray as everything else in the community. Like every other door, they slide open if your ID has sufficient credit and security clearance. The door that opened in front of me now revealed a blackness so complete I hesitated before entering. I always do, because it feels like you're stepping into space. I suppose in a way you are; to all intents and purposes you're entering another universe, or at least a little world.

Then, heart pounding and pulse racing, I stepped over

the threshold.

The electromagnetic sphere, which is a little under three meters in diameter, is generated by particle projectors in the chamber walls. Information drawn from the Ecosystem's databank colors the charged particles to simulate your desired destination. When you're inside the timesphere you're not aware of the technology, though. At least, I'm not. All I'm aware of are the sights and sounds.

The trips begin with a crackle and buzz from the surrounding blackness, dying away to a barely audible hum that's felt as much as heard. There's a slight increase in temperature, a faint smell of burning, and the air itself is transformed into a shimmering, spherical envelope not quite as dark as the blackness preceding it.

After a pause when nothing seems to happen, the sphere lifts far enough off the chamber floor to rotate freely. The shimmering increases, and suddenly you're in the midst of a kaleidoscope of colors so bright you have to blink. Then one of the times when you open your eyes after blinking, the colors are no longer a confused blur. You're wherever it is you want to be.

Where and when would you choose, if you could take a trip to any place on Earth, at any time? I say 'on Earth' because simulating space travel makes such high demands on the Ecosystem. Our lack of knowledge about what's out there in the vastness of the cosmos means the Ecosystem has to do so much interpolation that the cost is prohibitive, as it was for the real space program back in the Old Days. Anyway, back to my question: where and when would you choose? Not easy, is it? I suppose it's a classic case of being spoilt for choice. It's easier for me to decide than it is for most people, though, because of that place I love above all others.

When I opened my eyes, I was there.

To my right was a curving beach, to my left the breaking waves of an ocean. Up ahead, the sun was sinking behind a couple of fantastically shaped mountains—one a sugar loaf, the other flat-topped and looking like the stage for a movie about a lost world. I don't know the name of the mountains, but I know the ocean is the Atlantic and the beach is called Ipanema. I'd learned about this place from a travel article written in the Old Days. That's the sort of thing I love reading in my spare time: accounts of explorers, discoverers and travel writers. The article was called *Footsteps in the Sand, Lost World in the Mountains.* It was written more than sixty years ago, when it was safe to go Outside; when people could visit places for real and didn't have to rely on second-hand accounts and virtual trips. The article described Rio de Janeiro, and even before reading it I fell in love with the city because of the photo that went with the words. It was taken from where I was standing, and showed a couple walking hand-in-hand along the water's edge toward a sun setting behind those fabulously shaped mountains.

When I first saw the photo I wished with all my heart

that I was the man silhouetted against the breaking waves, holding the woman's hand, and the woman was Jen, and that she hadn't. . . The sadness in the pit of my stomach—the awful sense of loss and longing that's become a part of me—had been so overwhelming I'd had to look away from the photo. I'd started reading the words that went with it:

Other cities have buildings more beautiful than those of Rio de Janeiro, streets more pleasant, and a richer past. But it doesn't matter. Rio has no need of beautiful buildings and boulevards in order to take your breath away—it does it with curving beaches like crescent moons fallen to earth, and magnificent ocean waves breaking with a beauty which eclipses the beaches; it does it with enchanting mountains in the distance, and fantastic views from those close at hand. It doesn't need the romance of ruins, remainders and reminders of some glorious past. Rio lives for the present, and is full of people who want to make the most of each moment through music and dance.

I turned to my right and looked at the beachside hotels lining Avenida Atlantica, thinking about how the travel writer, Calum Tait, had described the scene:

Walking down the avenue one afternoon I heard music from beneath a cluster of parasols and saw half a dozen middle-aged men and women sitting around a table. They had cold drinks in front of them and tambourines, guitars and tom-toms in their hands. A small crowd had gathered to listen, but the friends weren't playing for an audience. They were playing for each other and the joy of making music. They were communicating with sound and song rather than token spoken words punctuated by awkward silences. As I watched, another friend joined the circle. She didn't simply walk up to the table, she danced all around it before sitting down. I don't think I've ever seen a happier group of people or a more perfect picture of friendship, and I don't think I ever will.

I longed to join one of the groups sitting under the parasols that lined Avenida Atlantica, but there was no point approaching them because they were pixels rather than people. I couldn't talk to them, make music with them or partner them in a dance. Still, I drew comfort from the sound of their laughter on the summer evening breeze. Watching them, I wondered what they'd be talking about if they were really there. Maybe they'd be discussing the latest Chaplin movie, *Modern Times*, little realizing the future would be far more frightening than the most nightmarish predictions in any film or book.

The time I'd picked for my virtual trip was 1936, almost 70 years before Calum Tait visited the city. In my imagination it was a golden age. The war to end all wars had been fought and won, and the next one hadn't yet begun. The worst of the Great Depression was over, and the Lost Generation was finding itself. It was the age of grand ocean liners and propeller-driven aeroplanes; art deco and film noir; jazz and cocktail parties. Technology had shrunk the world, making it safer and more comfortable, but hadn't yet taken all the mystery and adventure out of it. The planet hadn't been homogenized, polluted and finally poisoned to the extent plants and animals and people could barely survive Outside. It was a time when people could do for real what I can only do in a timesphere, in dreams or my imagination—gaze at a far horizon made of a romantic meeting of sky with land or sea rather than the desolation of ruined buildings shrouded in a choking haze.

I don't know how long I gazed at the make-believe horizon, but it was long enough to wonder what lands lay beyond it, what people walked its distant shores.

It was long enough to wonder what ships floated upon the ocean, where they'd come from and where they were going; and what lay beneath the surface—ancient wrecks and sunken treasure chests; coral reefs of amazing colors, and bottomless chasms that swallowed light and harbored mystery.

I thought about whales that sang haunting songs of love and loneliness, dolphins leaping from the water with joy unconfined, and seahorses drifting on the tide with their tails entwined like lovers.

Then I walked down to the ocean, and the movements of the little world around me were so synchronous with my own I felt I really was on the beach.

But, when I reached the water's edge and looked back, there weren't any footprints in the sand. I could only imagine what the warmth and give of the beach would be like beneath my feet, and what it would feel like to let the cool water wash over my toes.

All I could do was stand there looking and listening. But even that was better by far than anything I could do for real in the community. Gazing out at the far horizon I found myself thinking again about what Calum Tait wrote all those years ago. I'd read the article so many times I knew it word for word:

Ipanema and Copacabana are beaches as long as a day. You can spend a morning walking along them, and an afternoon just standing there with nothing in front of you but waves that have traveled a third of the way around the globe to break at your feet. The height and sound of the surf leaves you in no doubt you're at the edge of not a sea but an ocean. You feel small as you stand there, but not diminished; quite the opposite. For all the restless, roaring power there's something seductive about the sight and soothing about the sound, so that soon your heartbeat slows, your breathing deepens and your thoughts drift with the tide, carried away as vague notions and brought back as something more by the ocean. It's as if you've had the chance to talk with Mother Nature, listen to Father Time, and they've answered questions you weren't aware you'd asked.

Listen hard enough and you hear not only the roar but a whisper that seems to be telling the secrets of time and tide: where the wind and waves come from, where they're going and why they want to get there. You hear a wealth of knowledge, the wisdom of ages, and for a little while you feel you understand.

But only for a little while. For about as long as your footprints last in the sand.

Somehow not all the wealth is lost with the knowledge, though. You remember the roar if not the whisper, the feeling if not the thoughts. Like the tide that carried it, the richness you gain from leaving your footprints in the sand is never wholly spent.

I was in the middle of a wistful sigh, thinking about far horizons, lost worlds in the mountains and footprints in the sand when I got the call that changed my life forever.

And everyone else's.

CHAPTER 2

The Perfect Partner

Like all citizens I wear a hear-ring in my ear and an i-band around my wrist, and they're not fashion accessories. The ring is a microspeaker and the i-band is, among other things, a voice-activated transmitter. Together they take the place of the clumsy cell phones people slavishly carried everywhere sixty or seventy years ago.

It was a voice from the hear-ring that interrupted me in mid-sigh as I looked out across the ocean of my dreams. The Voice of Reason, saying, "Flatliner in apartment 331. Respond ASAP."

My sigh, which started wistfully, finished up as one of resignation because the Ecosystem was telling me somebody had just become some body.

Not the best start to the day, but I'm used to it. I'm a LogiPol Blue, the equivalent of a police officer from the Old Days. My beat is the apartment block known as Haven Nine. It's where I used to love and laugh, but now it's just where I live and work. It's by no means an unpleasant place, but it's too confined, colorless and predictable to be my whole world. I can escape it for a little while in the timesphere, or by donning a filtermask and going Outside, but before long the credit on my card ran out or the filter in my mask choked up and I ended up right back in the place I longed to leave.

My hear-ring crackled into life again: "Flatliner in 331. Respond ASAP."

As well as a tiny transmitter, the smartfabric i-bands are laced with sensors which monitor all your physiological signs and relay them to the Ecosystem. Just as the flatline from the i-band in 331 had caused the Ecosystem to call me, so my own biometric relay would have betrayed my lack of movement and brought about the reminder. Even though the voice was system-generated, there was a hint of irritation in it now; the only time there's any trace of emotion in the voice is when it's repeating a message you haven't acted on. The Voice of Reason has been scientifically calculated to make it difficult to ignore, to command obedience and respect. In short, to be so *reasonable* you'll want to do what it tells you. That's the theory, but it falls down somewhere because I often deliberately ignore directives first time around. I know the resulting irritation in the Voice of Reason is nothing more than a sound effect, but I derive a perverse sense of satisfaction from hearing it.

It doesn't pay to make the voice repeat itself more than once, however. It's not just that it gets incrementally stroppier, it also starts deducting credit from your card. So I took a last look at the far horizon, the ocean waves and the fabulous mountains. Then, speaking to the faceless Ecosystem that's everywhere and nowhere, controlling all aspects of my life and everyone else's for The Common Good, I said, "Exit."

Nothing happened for a second or two. As always in such moments I had the heart-stoppingly wonderful thought that maybe the beautiful scene around me wasn't an idyllic re-creation of the past, but rather the community was a nightmarish vision of the future.

Then the golden colors of the sky dimmed, and so did my hope. The mountains faded into darkness and the breaking waves receded into a silence broken only by the hum of electro-magnetic energy. Within seconds the blackness was even more complete than when I first entered the sphere. I tried to brace myself for the drop of a couple of centimeters that would follow, but as usual I had to throw my hands out for balance when the force field dissipated. It's the most disconcerting feeling, like when you're going down a flight of stairs and misplace a foot and know you're about to stumble but can't stop yourself. Maybe it isn't possible to make the timesphere lower you that couple of centimeters gradually. Maybe the energy field forming the sphere is either strong enough to completely support you, or not strong enough to support you at all. However I have a sneaking suspicion the Ecosystem, with the same flawless logic it applies to every other aspect of existence, has engineered the end of timesphere trips in a way that literally jolts virtual travelers back to reality.

Whatever, the timesphere always brings me back to earth with a bang.

The darkness slowly faded, allowing my eyes to adjust to the light levels of the haven at large, so that when the chamber opened I left it without blinking.

There was someone waiting to use the timesphere. We studied each other, and I knew he was asking himself the same thing I was. It's the first question people in communities everywhere ask themselves when they encounter a stranger: *us or them? Name or Number?* Somehow *we* can answer the question almost as soon as it's asked, and the thinly veiled contempt I see in their eyes tells me *they* can, too.

The man in front of me had crew-cut white-blond hair, cold and knowing pale blue eyes, and the slightest hint of a sardonic smile about his thin-lipped mouth. He was a shade under 190cm, neither light enough to lack strength nor heavy enough to be muscle-bound. Although he wasn't *that much* taller than me, he managed to give the impression of looking down on me from a great height.

I was tempted to bang into him as I passed, and ashamed of myself for wanting to. As a LogiPol Blue, I should be preventing that sort of behavior, not indulging in it.

Having said all that, I couldn't walk by without doing something to upset him. So I said, "Have a nice trip," enjoying the confusion my unnecessary words caused. Pleasantries and spontaneous conversational gambits always bewilder *them*.

I smiled at his confusion, and knew he was glad when the Voice of Reason said, "Welcome, Citizen 320978," and engaged him in the sort of formal exchange he could understand.

His kind feel more of an affinity with machines and computers than they do with people like me, I thought as I walked away.

"Please state the time and place of your desired destination," the disembodied Voice of Reason said to the man standing on the threshold of the timesphere.

Putting words into his mouth, I said to myself, "You choose."

I smiled moments later when the Number said those very words.

Numbers always say 'You choose' when they're about to enter a timesphere, because they lack the imagination to pick a time and place for themselves.

I automatically headed for the stairs from the basement to level three, then remembered why I was going there and made my way to the elevator instead. Usually it pays to take the stairs. The credit card which gives you pleasure points for every act that enhances The Common Good also debits you for each action detrimental to society—like using power by taking the elevator rather than the stairs. But, given the nature of my business, the Ecosystem wouldn't debit me for this elevator ride. It knew where I was going, and why.

It knows everything.

"Come on, come on," I said as I waited for the elevator doors to open. I have to admit my haste to get to apartment 331 wasn't a reflection of any great dedication to duty, but rather a childish desire to get there before my partner, Perfect Paula. That's not her real name. Well, not the Perfect bit. Perfect describes her much better than Paula, though. Like the man who'd taken my place in the timesphere, Perfect Paula brings out the worst in me, and I want to beat her in some way, in every way I can. Except for physically—though there are times when only the fact she's a woman stops me wanting to do that. The fact I rarely manage to put one over on her makes me try all the harder. I hate myself for being so childish, and I hate Perfect Paula and those like her even more for making me hate myself. My one consolation is that I'm not alone in being this way. Ask any Name how they feel about a Number and, whatever words they use, they'll say pretty much the same thing. Unless they're the most pathetic kind of Name—the sort who want to be Numbers, who dress and talk and act like *them* but don't fool anybody except themselves.

Waiting for the lift, I weighed up the odds of getting to apartment 331 ahead of Paula. She'd have been deep in a dreamless sleep, but would stir at the first crackle of the hear-ring and be wide awake by the time the Voice of Reason finished speaking. She wouldn't waste a moment or a movement, but she'd still have to get dressed and make her way down from her apartment on level six.

The odds seemed slightly in my favor, but then Paula is, well, Paula.

It's pathetic, I know, but we can't help trying to score points against each other. Or, at least, I can't help trying to score points against her. She doesn't have to try, but I know she keeps count. I can tell from the hint of a sneer that's never far from her perfectly proportioned mouth and from those coldly beautiful silver-blue eyes that are slightly upswept at the corners. The sneer constantly challenges me—and mocks my efforts when I attempt to meet the challenge and match the impossibly high standards she sets. If I had to characterize our relationship, I'd say the word 'competitors' is closer to the mark than 'partners.' Except it's not really much of a competition, because Paula always wins.

"Come on," I said again, willing the lift to reach me.

At last there was a soft *Bing!* and the doors opened. I stepped inside and said, "Level three, please." I could imagine Paula's expression if she'd been at my side—a mildly bemused and contemptuous look that asked the unspoken question: *Why are you saying 'please' to a machine?*

The doors closed and there was a tug in my guts as my stomach caught up with the rising elevator. Impatiently I watched the red neon counter above the doors change. It started at F3. The F stands for foundation. There are three foundation levels, housing the non-residential components of the haven: from clinic and classroom to canteen, gym and timesphere. The idea is that each haven in the community is as self-sufficient as possible. Spending too much time Outside literally takes years off your life.

The F faded out when the lift reached 1, the first of the ten residential levels. There's no point building much higher than that, or the superstorms are likely to knock down whatever it is you've constructed.

With a sense of shame I realized I'd hardly given a thought to the flatlined occupant of 331. In a belated attempt to make up for that, I tried to fit a face to the apartment. It's not easy, because two thousand people live in Haven Nine. Two thousand people live in each of the twenty identical havens that make up the community. I'm sure Paula could put a name and face to every apartment in Haven Nine. I can, too, but because my mind isn't like a supercomputer I'd have to call on the Ecosystem in order to do it. Raising my wrist, palm up, I spoke into the tiny microphone woven into the fabric of the i-band: "I need a basic background report on 331." I didn't have to identify myself or who I was addressing. The Ecosystem can tell who's speaking and assumes you're addressing it, and not another citizen, unless you say differently.

The Ecosystem that controls all aspects of life in my community is also at the heart of every other community on Earth. That's 10,000 communities, and close to half a billion people. Its processing power is so great, however, that if you have sufficient clearance it can tell you almost anything about anyone within a second of being asked. As the lift rose from level one to two, the basic facts about the occupant of apartment 331 were relayed through my hear-ring: "Douglas MacDougall. Caucasian male. Age 44. Height 189cm. Weight 75kg. Long brown hair—" I thought I heard a trace of disapproval, but knew it was only in my imagination—"Green eyes. Widowed. One daughter—" now I was sure I heard a hint of censure. "No history of corrective counseling. Positive credit rating. Ran plant store in Community Central."

The last bit of information let me put a face to the name, because I knew the shop. It was a little oasis of green—and occasionally, if you were lucky, blossoms of incredibly beautiful colors—in a desert of gray. Like most Names, I keep a plant and love it dearly. It's only a common-or-garden prickly cactus of the kind you find all over most of northern Europe. But to me it's something special, at once an object of affection and a source of wonder. It's a symbol of inherited guilt because it reminds me of what previous generations reduced the planet to; and it's a beacon of hope because, despite all the dreadful things done to the Earth, Doug MacDougall was still able to find that plant surviving Outside.

I've spent many a contented hour in Doug's shop, looking at the exotics—the geraniums and dandelions and daisies—and wishing I could afford one. He usually had half a dozen different exotics, flowers that were once found in every garden in this part of the world but are now so rare only licensed bio-prospectors can source them. There's only one license per community, and the holder has a quota carefully calculated by the Ecosystem. The quota ensures the species has a chance to survive in the wild—and that some examples will live on in the communities in case the toxic haze, acid rain and sterile soil of the Outside prove too much.

Numbers walk past Doug's shop without a second glance; Names browse around it and lose all track of time, or stand gazing in the window, lost in wonder. I'm sure many Names go out of their way to pass the shop, like I do, to check on how a plant they can't afford is progressing; whether a bud has appeared, a blossom opened. You can tell when one of the plants has come into flower because there's a queue to get into the shop, and a crowd outside the window. Most people can't afford anything but the kind of prickly cactus I've got, but Doug MacDougall didn't mind them coming into his shop and looking around. He wasn't into earning credits; he just loved to share his knowledge, his joy and wonder. His reward was seeing someone's face light up at the sight of a new leaf, or watching their eyes close in ecstasy and their breath catch as they stooped to smell the fragrance of a blossom. He was happy talking to you whether you had credit to spend or not, and I'm certain he got more satisfaction from answering a question than making a sale. The Plant Place was more like a natural history museum or a living shrine than a shop, and to me the man who ran it was everything that's good about people, all in one person. If there had been more men and women like him a few generations back, the world would be a very different place—and I'm sure all the differences would be for the better. He was good-natured in the same way as Je—

Everything came back to Jen.

I let out a long sigh. I usually do after thinking about Jen.

The lift came to a halt. The slight judder brought me back from my thoughts of Jen, just as the jolt in the time-sphere had brought me back from Rio de Janeiro. Number 3 lit up and the doors opened.

As I walked down the soulless gray corridor of identical doors I wondered what had happened to Doug MacDougall. He'd looked lean and fit, but then he spent more time Outside than was good for him. Any time spent Outside isn't good for you. His shop was closed each Wednesday afternoon and all day Sunday, and I've no doubt he spent most of that time plant prospecting. You can't spend that much time Outside without paying a heavy price somewhere down the line.

Now that I thought about it, I suppose Doug MacDougall had looked closer to gaunt than lean of late. I love old movies and have a habit of likening people to the actors who starred in them. I think of myself as a pocket Bruce Willis and Paula as Sharon Stone, circa *Basic Instinct.* As for Doug MacDougall, he was a ringer for an old country and western singer and movie star whose name escapes me. Anyway, maybe Doug had been sick and hadn't told anyone—he was that sort of guy. In the Old Days I suppose a heart attack would be the first thing that sprang to mind in a case like this, but myocardial infarctions are practically unheard of now. I-bands monitor everything from heart-rate to perspiration, and the combination of early intervention and advanced medical techniques usually nips any problem in the bud.

Doug was bound to have some extra special plants in his apartment, so it could have been a robbery gone wrong. The trouble was, I couldn't imagine anyone wanting to hurt him, even to get their hands on something as precious as a rose or a crocus, a tulip or a daffodil.

I checked the door number on my left, figuring I must be getting close. It was apartment 323.

Walking past the next door my thoughts turned to Paula. I decided if she wasn't in 331 already I'd call and ask what was holding her up, mimic her impatience and—

"Travis?" I heard that impatience through my hear-ring, and stopped in my tracks outside the door marked *331: Doug MacDougall.* "I'm in 331," Paula said. "Where are you?"

I might not be able to get one up on her, but at least I could wind her up. I did it by ignoring her call.

"Travis?"

I smiled with satisfaction at the aggravation my silence would be causing her. Paula doesn't have a fiery temper. Her kind rarely do. But they don't suffer fools gladly, and patience isn't among their many supposed virtues. Trying her limited patience is one of the few ways I can get back at her in our constant low-key guerrilla war, because the odds are so heavily stacked in her favor.

Finally she cracked and said, "Damnit, Travis!"

My smile broadened at having forced her to show emotion, utter an unnecessary word—and an expletive at that. *That's what you get for never calling me by my first name*, I thought. Travis is my second name. My first name is Ben. Paula never uses my first name, and always says my second one with thinly-veiled contempt. It's a habit they have when talking to us. We can't reciprocate because they don't have second names; they don't have parents. At least not ones who actually conceived them in a moment of bewildering passion, gave birth to them, and nurtured them with selfless, devoted love.

Instead of a second name they have a serial number that identifies the pool of 'optimal' genes their X and Y chromosomes were selected from, and the date of their production. The only reason they have first names at all is that it's more logical. 'Paula' is easier to say than a six-digit number. The names certainly don't reflect any desire to be more human. That's the last thing they want to be. You can tell that by a thousand little things, like their habit of calling us by our surnames. I have a theory about that habit. I have a theory about pretty much everything. This particular one says calling us by our surname serves as a reminder that we're different, makes them feel once removed from what they see as our contemptible weaknesses, our frailties and failings.

If that was their only motivation I could dismiss it as a genetic predisposition they can't help. But I think there's something else behind the surname thing: they know it annoys us, and it amuses them to make us mad and know we can't get even. When we try to press similar buttons with them it doesn't work because they don't share the same emotions, or at least not to the same degree.

The one exception is that they get impatient.

I considered making Paula say my name once more before I answered, or doing as I'd seen the great boxer Muhammad Ali do in archive footage from a hundred years ago, after he'd changed his name from Cassius Clay and an opponent mocked him by calling him by his old 'slave name' in the run-up to the fight. Once inside the ring, Ali gave him a lesson in more than boxing, pausing between punches to taunt him with the question: "What's my name?"

But I have to work with Paula, and she is one rank above me. We joined LogiPol at the same time, but Numbers generally do slightly better than Names in every measurable performance indicator and psychometric test. So I raised my hand to my mouth and spoke in the general direction of the i-band: "Yeah. Ben here."

"Is your hear-ring not working properly?" Paula said, her voice even more curt than usual.

I saw an opening to really get to her, and went for it: "I was daydreaming, that's all."

There was silence, as I expected. I gloried in it. Usually I'm the one who comes off worst in our war of words, but this time I'd scored a little victory. Numbers are faster, stronger, smarter and consequently more confident than Names. The differences aren't big enough to be embarrassing—sometimes the margin is so narrow it's barely noticeable, and sometimes it might not be there at all except in their mind and in ours. But, generally speaking, they have a slight edge in any given situation. It's a case of anything we can do, they can do better. They know it, and we know it, and we have to live with seeing the knowledge in their eyes.

There are a few things they aren't so good at, however. For some reason they struggle to dream and imagine and to wonder. A whole raft of scientific studies was done about it a while back, but the raft sank without a trace. Scientific studies have been done about everything you can think of, but not many were as unsuccessful as that one. Anyway, whatever the reason, their inability to dream and imagine and wonder is a fact of life.

That brings me to another of my theories: I think there's more than a little envy mixed in with the contempt Numbers have for Names.

To reduce it to a more personal level, I think one of the reasons Paula doesn't like me is that she has no idea what I'm seeing when there's a faraway look in my eyes. She has no idea where my thoughts take me when there's no task at hand to think about, but I'm sure she's desperate to go there, too. Numbers live in a world that's black and white; Names live in a world that's gray, but we dream in color. I get the feeling that deep down, even if they won't admit it to themselves let alone to others, Numbers desperately want to see those colors. They pity us because to them it's blindingly obvious we'll never get to the bottom of the rainbow; but, at the same time, I'm sure they envy us because at least we can see the colors making it up; we can dream of far horizons and feel their pull.

Whether as a result of envy or contempt, or more likely a mixture of both, Paula said, "Well, quit daydreaming because we've got work to do. Meet me in 331, ASAP."

I pushed the door open and said, "Okay," into my i-band.

Paula, who was standing in the middle of the apartment, facing the other way, turned around to look at me. She shook her head at my childishness, and rolled those silvery-blue eyes that are as beautiful as the blossom of any flower.

My heart skipped a beat. It's started doing that every time I look at Paula, which is strange given the way I feel about Numbers. I suppose it comes down to how achingly beautiful she is. All her kind are, but I'm beginning to think Paula's different. Her eyes aren't quite so cold, and she doesn't seem as certain about absolutely everything as the others do. Or maybe that's just wishful thinking on my part.

Whatever, I looked at Paula for longer than I meant to.

Then I looked past her. A lifeless arm dangled over the side of an armchair. I walked around my perfect partner to get a look at the head that went with the arm, hoping I wasn't about to see the face of Doug MacDougall.

CHAPTER 3

01000011010010000100000101010000010101000100010101010010

Daffodils

The head was slumped forward and the face hidden, but the mane of brown hair and grizzled beard told me all I needed to know. I've lost count of how many dead people I've walked in on, but I still feel something at the first sight of a body. I don't feel as much as I once did if it's a Name, but I feel more than I used to if it's a Number. I hate to say that what I feel if it's a Number is best summed up by the words 'good-riddance.' Doug MacDougall was everything Numbers aren't, however, and as I looked at him I felt a sense of loss and sadness. I let out another of those long sighs. I was aware of Paula looking at me. Numbers always look at us when we sigh, as if it's an alien sound they can't comprehend. I've never heard one of *them* let out a sigh of sorrow, longing or wistfulness.

Paula looked from me back to Doug MacDougall, and I looked at Paula. I hoped to see some sadness on her face, but all I saw was disapproval of Doug's long hair and beard. Incidentally, Paula also disapproved of my shaved head and designer stubble goatee. All Numbers do. That's one of the reasons I shave my head and design my stubble.

"What happened?" I asked.

"OD."

Not, 'looks like he took an overdose,' or he 'oh-deed.' Just 'OD.' Numbers rarely use idiom or metaphor or add any of the small words that perform no real function but add fluidity to a sentence. They have no grasp of the poetic, even when they're talking about subjects that lend themselves to poetry a little better than a drug overdose.

A drug overdose. I looked at the lifeless body and tried to relate it to the owner of The Plant Place. "No way," I said.

Paula pointed to a small tube on the couch beside Doug. A compressed-air syringe.

"He's the last person who'd touch drugs," I said.

"You knew him?"

"Just from his shop. He owned The Plant Place. If he wanted a hit he'd bend down and smell one of his flowers. He'd get more of a high from that than any drug."

"Apparently he wanted to end a low, not reach a high."

"You're trying to say this was suicide?" That was even more incomprehensible to me than the notion Doug

MacDougall had accidentally overdosed.

"He said it himself," Paula told me. "There's a note on his screen."

I walked over to the wafer-thin computer screen on the flat-topped carbon-fiber arch-desk in a corner of the room. Putting my hands on the back of the matching seat for support, I leaned forward to read the words shimmering on the screen: *I was cloud lonely and there weren't even any daffodils. Maybe the grass will be greener on the other side.*

I shook my head in disbelief. Paula must have been watching me, because she said, "I don't understand what you don't understand."

As I said, they've no sense of linguistic aesthetics.

"Doug MacDougall would never write something like this," I told her. "He mourned what was lost, but it made him appreciate what remained all the more. He saw beauty in even a thorny cactus. If you went in his shop on the day before a plant hunt he could hardly contain his excitement at the prospect of what he might find. Then, the next time you went in, he'd talk about his latest discoveries for as long as you'd listen."

"Apparently you didn't know him as well as you thought you did."

"I know that life, all life, was precious to him in a way you'd never understand."

I thought I saw a hurt look in her eyes. It was quickly replaced by a coldness I was more used to seeing. "I understand exactly what happened here," Paula said.

"Go on, then, explain it to me."

"You know as well as I do that Names often find it hard to cope. They act illogically, get themselves in situations they can't handle, and can't get out of them any other way than this."

"What you're trying to say is that we're pathetically weak and hopelessly flawed."

"Well put, Travis."

"I know you'd like to believe that, to console yourself at not being able to dream and laugh and love like we can," I said.

Again, I thought I saw hurt in her eyes, but it was quickly replaced by another of those cold stares. Just once I'd like to be able to out-stare a Number, make *them* blink or look away from *me*. However, I've come to the conclusion it's not physiologically possible. The one consolation is that I don't know of any other Name who can do it, either.

Come to think of it, that's not much of a consolation at all. In fact, it's the opposite.

"You honestly think I envy this?" Paula said, gesturing at the slumped body of Doug MacDougall.

I was desperate not to look away from her, because she'd take it as a sign she was right. I did my best to meet her gaze. When my eyes teared up and I couldn't go any longer without blinking, I reached a hand up and brushed the end of my nose. It's my 'go-to' play when all else fails in any confrontation with Paula. It might sound like an innocuous gesture, but my partner is somewhat sensitive about the fact her nose has a hint of an upturn. It's her token physical flaw: every Number is given a slight physiological flaw in their genetic profile, and a psychological one in their emotional make-up. At first the Ecosystem presumed the logical thing to do was to make genetically-manufactured people as perfect as possible. But experience soon showed Names found those perfect people impossible to get along with. Not to mince words, they were a pain in the butt. As a result, each Number from the second generation onward has been given a random cosmetic and emotional flaw. Paula's cosmetic flaw is her nose. I dearly wish I knew what her emotional flaw was—that's the one I could really push her buttons with.

Anyway, the nose is better than nothing. I actually think it gives her character and makes her look even prettier, but the important thing is that it bothers Paula. Maybe she's afraid it'll make people think she a Name. If so, I could put her mind at rest: with the coldness of her eyes, her thin-lipped mouth and perfect proportions there was no way she'd ever be mistaken for a Name. Of course I'd never tell her that, just as I'd never tell her I think her nose is even prettier than if it was as perfect as the rest of her.

It may appear odd that a system which is so logical pairs Names and Numbers in LogiPol teams when they find it so hard to get along. Well, the explanation's simple: it's a case of one and one making more than two. To continue the mathematical metaphor, pair a couple of Numbers and when they put two and two together they'll always come up with four. If the correct answer happens to be five, for some strange reason, they haven't a hope of coming up with it—and crimes tend to involve strange reasoning somewhere along the line. Numbers would have a one hundred percent clean-up rate for crimes involving only other Numbers. But most crimes cross the genetic divide, and as soon as a Name is involved, Numbers struggle. They lack insight, instinct, and the ability to form a hunch, let alone know whether it's worth backing.

Pair a Named LogiPol officer with a Numbered one, on the other hand—ideally a man with a woman—and you'll get a lot of friction but you'll also get a team that's more than a sum of its parts and capable of covering every angle.

That's the theory, at least.

"Travis, grow up," Perfect Paula said now in response to my nose rubbing.

I gave her a knowing sneer. I call it my 'taste of your own medicine' expression.

Paula reacted as she usually does in such situations—by giving me a command just to show who's boss. In this case it was, "Bag the syringe."

I have to admit, I kind of like it when she gets all bossy.

Anyway, I did what I was told like a good little boy, picking up the syringe with the bag to avoid contaminating the plastic tube with my paw prints, then fastening the seal and pocketing the evidence.

When I brought my hand out of my pocket there was a small digital camera in it. I was aware of Paula shaking her head and sneering, like she does every time I take out my camera. Her point of view is that the crime-scene team will shoot any photos that need to be taken; I'd rather grab some shots myself. That way I get exactly the ones I want, without having to rely on anyone else.

Besides, I find the challenge of taking photos an absorbing one. I first got interested in photography through the pictures that went with Calum Tait's travel articles. It's turned from pastime into passion over the years since then, to the extent I spend longer than I should Outside, taking photos of the ruins and looking for classic cameras and images of the Old World that were taken with them. Those antique cameras aren't any practical use; they stopped making photographic film back in 2010. Still, I love to collect them. Everyone—well every Name—likes to collect something from the Old Days.

Wishing I held an Olympus OM3 Ti or Leica M6 in my hands rather than a generic digital, and that I was taking a photo of those beautiful sugarloaf mountains at the end of Ipanema beach instead of the body of a good man who'd died before his time, I switched the camera from automatic exposure to manual mode and pointed it at the carpet; the omnipresent shade known as logica gray is exactly half an exposure stop lighter than the mid-tone all automatic exposures are based on.

"Why are you taking a photo of the carpet?" Paula asked with unconcealed disdain.

"I'm not," I told her. "I'm just getting an exposure reading."

"Can't the camera do that for you?"

"Yeah, but it gives an average, and clinically calculated averages lack heart and soul," I said, talking about more than camera exposures.

I don't know if Paula understood my dig, because I didn't look up to see the expression on her face. I was too intent on taking photos. First, I took close-ups of the slumped body and syringe. Something about the scene bothered me—I mean, besides the corpse—but I couldn't think what it was. I puzzled over it without success, then stepped back and zoomed the lens out, taking progressively wider shots to show the position of the body.

Then, from the doorway, I framed a shot that took in the whole apartment—including Paula, who stood shaking her head.

"Smile!" I said, and fired off a couple of shots of my partner scowling at me. After that I turned my attention to the personal possessions scattered around the apartment. I started with the biggest one: a bookcase. It was filled with oversized natural history titles. I switched the camera to panorama mode and took a shot of the shelves, then put it down and tilted my head to look at the individual books. I passed over the ones that obviously dated from the last days of old earth—*Cacti of The Amazon Desert*, *The Flora and Fauna of Subtropical Britain*, and *The Temperate Arctic*—and came to some even older volumes. I was drawn to one that must have been truly ancient, because it was called *The Amazon Jungle*. Curiosity made me take it out.

Flicking through the tattered pages, I was entranced in seconds. I forgot all about Perfect Paula and Doug MacDougall, all about Haven Nine and the community, about the ghost city it replaced and the ghastly world beyond. I was traveling back in time like I did in the sphere. I was exploring a world I could only dream about, with a pith helmet on my head and a razor-sharp machete in my hand. Each page took me deeper into that world and revealed a new wonder beyond my wildest imagining. It was a world of giant trees with shafts of sunlight slanting down between them, falling on flaming orchids, man-sized slotted ferns, and tangled vines and creepers. I heard the sighing of the wind through high branches, and the pitter-patter of rain falling from leaf to leaf; the chatter of a hundred monkeys, the songs of a thousand birds, the buzz of a billion beating insect wings. I saw monkeys with almost-human hands and faces; alligators that looked like creatures from prehistoric times, and snakes big enough to swallow them whole; butterflies of the most brilliant shades of blue, and humming birds whose brilliance put even the brightest butterflies in the shade. There were giant caterpillars and pygmy people, parrots as colorful as an artist's palette, and a dappled gold and black jaguar that was wild nature embodied. There was life in countless forms.

And now nearly all of it was gone. Thinking about it as I stood there with the dog-eared book in my hand, I felt as sick as when I realized the flatliner in 331 was Doug MacDougall.

I also felt what Calum Tait once called an end-of-summer sadness. It's what I feel when I think about Jen—a longing that's too powerful to put into words, that comes from losing something irreplaceable, and knowing it's gone forever.

And there was guilt, too, like I also felt over Jen. This time, however, the guilt wasn't mine alone. I wasn't to blame, like I was for Jen; it was an ancestral guilt, a knowledge of what the people who were part of my past, part of me, had done to the planet. As I do at some point nearly every day, I wondered how they could have been so selfish and short-sighted. I wondered how much of it was due to ignorance, and how much of it was down to knowing but not caring. How could anyone have believed the convenience offered by a motor car was more precious than the life of a single humming bird or butterfly?

Aware I was being watched, I looked up from the book to Paula. Her expression had no trace of the usual know-it-all look I'm used to seeing on the face of Numbers. Quite the opposite—there were a dozen questions in her eyes.

Just as I was bewildered by my heritage, I think Paula was bewildered by me, by the way a book could transport me to another time and place.

Putting the oversized volume back on the shelf, I turned my attention and my camera to the pot plants that sat on every flat surface.

I hesitated after the first couple of shots. Something wasn't quite right about the plants, just like something wasn't right about the body. But, again, I couldn't put my finger on it.

I moved to the nearest pot, containing a cheese-plant worth as many pleasure points as I earn in a month, and my unease deepened.

Aware of my puzzlement, Paula said, "What's wrong?"

"I don't know, but something's not quite right."

The arrival of a Community Police officer prevented Paula from quizzing me further.

The CP are the equivalent of the old FBI. Each haven has a couple of LogiPol wardens like Paula and me, first-responders who handle the-day-to-day law and order issues. But if anything big goes down, the CP usually check it out. Most of them are Paretos. I think Pareto was the name given in the Old Days to some product that was perfect. Whatever, Paretos are 'perfect people.' Their flaw is that they have no flaws. No, seriously. Flaws are randomly generated, and because not having flaws is a flaw, occasionally you get a perfect person. If somebody's perfect you'd think they'd be impossible not to like if you put your jealousy to one side.

But, take it from me, they are the biggest pains in the butt imaginable. They have every infuriating trait of your average Number, but to the nth degree (I'm sure they can give you the exact figure rather than having to make do with a superscript letter). Just in case anyone's in the slightest doubt about how cool and hard they are, they wear black jumpsuits rather than the dark blue of LogiPol. Paretos come in several varieties. This one was the blond male Caucasian model. There are a dozen of that type in our community's CP. I couldn't tell which one this was, because they all look identical to me: clean-cut, well-coordinated features; brush-cut hair the colour of white gold; eyes like sapphires; pearly white teeth, and a tight-lipped mouth that's never learned how to express anything except a sneer.

From the way Paula looked at this Pareto, *she* knew who he was. I wasn't sure how she knew, and didn't want to think about that for too long. My dislike of the Pareto increased exponentially, and with a shock I realized I was jealous. I was used to only feeling unadulterated contempt for Paretos. I wasn't used to being jealous of them. I had a feeling Paula was mentally undressing him. I'd never had the feeling she was mentally undressing me, which hardly seemed fair since I'd done it so many times to her.

The Pareto ignored me, which suited me fine, and addressed Paula, which I wasn't so happy about. "SitRep," he said.

So Paula gave him a situation report, if you can call two

words and an abbreviation a report: "Suicide by OD."

"Evidence for?"

"Note and syringe. No sign of struggle. No forced entry. Last authorized entry was by the deceased last night."

"Evidence against?" the Pareto asked.

Paula looked at me, like she was daring me to say something.

I looked at Doug MacDougall, trying to figure out what to say. If my formless doubts hadn't cut any ice with Paula, there wasn't the remotest chance they would impress the Pareto. He was sneering at me bigtime as it was, and would cut me down mercilessly if I voiced the mix of hunch and intuition that made me think there might be more to this than met the eye. Still, I was going to voice my doubts anyway. I opened my mouth, not quite sure exactly what I was going to say.

Paula beat me to it. No doubt scared my idiocy would reflect badly on her, given she's my immediate superior, she hurriedly said, "We can probably close the case with an autopsy."

"Good," the Pareto said.

So we could all live happily ever after.

Well, except for Doug MacDougall.

And, as it turned out, not-so-perfect Paula.

And, of course, me.

Not to mention all the other people in every haven on the planet.

CHAPTER 4

01000011010010000100000101010000010101000100010101010010

Slo-Mo

I HAD A SNOOP AROUND THE APARTMENT WHILE WE waited for the body to be bagged. I had no idea what I was looking for, but I was sure things weren't quite what they seemed.

By the time I got back where I'd started, Paula had rolled up the left sleeve of Doug's green coveralls and was checking for signs of previous drug abuse. That was when I realized one of the things that wasn't right about the scene we'd walked in on. "His sleeve," I said, thinking aloud.

Paula gave me a questioning look. That's the nicest thing I can call it.

"His sleeve should have already been rolled up," I said by way of explanation.

"What are you talking about?"

"He wouldn't have injected himself through his coveralls."

"Why not? He wouldn't have to worry about introducing textile fragments into his bloodstream if he was injecting enough drugs to kill himself."

That was perfectly logical, but I would roll up my sleeve before injecting anything into my arm, and I'm certain other people—well, other Names—would do likewise.

The arrival of the haven counselors saved me from trying to explain any of that to Paula.

We're supposed to brief the counselors in cases like this so they can break the bad news to the next of kin. They work in male and female Name and Number pairs—like LogiPol wardens, and for pretty much the same reasons. I sensed the same sort of antipathy between this pair as there is between me and Paula, and took a perverse satisfaction from it. The knowledge that these people, who are trained to get on with everyone, can't get on with each other made me feel less unreasonable and bigoted in comparison.

Paula related what we knew about Doug and his death, and passed on what she'd learned from the Ecosystem about his next of kin—a daughter called Annie, who taught in Haven Nine's school. Each haven has its own little school. Pupils who do well go on to the Learning Zone, a self-contained university in Community Central.

Normally I'm only too glad to let counselors break bad news to the next of kin. I find it hard enough coping with my own emotions, let alone helping someone else deal with theirs. However, the same instinct that led me to believe there might be more to Doug's death than met the eye made me think it would be worth accompanying the counselors to see if Annie MacDougall's shock and grief were genuine. While I was there, I could slip in a few questions about her father's state of mind and the people who made up his world.

Another callout, this time to a disturbance in an apartment on level eight, prevented me from suggesting any of that to Paula. The counselors headed off to break the news to Annie MacDougall, and Paula and I hurried for the lift.

We heard the racket as soon as we got to level eight, and it gave me a good idea what to expect. It sounded like the occupants of the apartment we'd been called to were watching a sexually explicit movie with the volume turned up and the tracking slowed down. I was getting used to such sounds—and no, that doesn't mean I'd started watching explicit movies on slow advance.

With barely veiled disgust, Paula said, "You people are so weak and pathetic, Travis."

I didn't say, 'How do you know they're Names and not Numbers?' because we both knew that Numbers don't get themselves into these sort of situations. The best I could manage was, "And you people are so likeable and compassionate."

There was no let-up in the ecstatic moaning as we

made our way along the corridor. If we hadn't been called, it would have gone on for days, if not weeks. We couldn't stop it, just ensure it continued in a sound-proof room in Community General. I was mortally embarrassed, not only because of the intimate nature of the moans but because they voiced so much more than desire. They proclaimed loud and clear the sort of pathetic weakness which Numbers never miss an opportunity to denigrate us for, and which we spend our lives trying to deny to ourselves and to them. That is, when we don't give ourselves over to it completely, like the couple we were about to walk in on. As the moaning grew even more abandoned, I resorted to a lame attempt at humor to cover my shame: "I bet you're just jealous because you're not getting—"

"Travis, don't go there."

Time for another in my series of pathetic confessions: I love it when Perfect Paula tells me off.

We paused at the apartment door, listening in horrified fascination to the sounds from within. There were seemingly endless groans and moans of ecstasy, and other sounds that might have been words but were so drawn out you couldn't even tell what the language was. I'm guessing there was a 'No' and a 'Yes' and a man and a woman, but I'd no idea who was saying what.

I looked at Paula as she listened to those sounds, and thought I glimpsed more than disapproval and disgust in her upswept eyes. I've started thinking I glimpse a whole lot of things in her eyes. I don't know how many of those things are actually there, all I know is that I like to think they are.

Paula caught me looking at her, and for once she couldn't meet my gaze. For a few moments I forgot all about the moaning from the other side of the door marked 826.

But only for a few moments. It was far too loud to forget for any longer than that.

I drew my knockdown—an air-pistol that fires gel-filled sacks. They'll stop the strongest man in his tracks without doing lasting damage to anything except his coverall; they leave a fluorescent dye-stain no amount of washing will remove. I wouldn't need the knockdown if the only people in the apartment were the ones I could hear, but if there's anything I've learned from fifteen years in this job it's to expect the unexpected. Plus, let's be honest, I like playing with my knockdown.

Paula rapped on the door and said, "LogiPol! Open up!"

The moaning carried on regardless. Even if the two people on the other side of the door had heard Paula, they wouldn't be able to react. Not for about a year, if they'd taken what I thought they had.

I reached for the door, threw it open, and stormed inside, waving my knockdown about like I'd seen actors do in the Olden Days detective shows I like so much. I was William Shatner's T.J. Hooker to Paula's Heather Locklear; I was Jimmy Smits' Bobby Simone to her Detective Russell.

If I looked anything like as impressive as I felt, Perfect Paula had to be impressed. I pointed my knockdown at each corner of the room in turn, holding the last pose long enough to let Paula get a good look at me being heroic.

"Travis, put your knockdown away," she said.

She's good at hiding it when she's impressed.

Reluctantly, I holstered my handgun. I've no desire to actually fire it at anyone, but I've got to admit I enjoy waving it around and pointing it at anything that moves. I'd like to say it was protecting the weak and putting away the bad guys that makes my job worthwhile, but in truth it's playing with my knockdown that gives me the most satisfaction.

The door to the bedroom was wide open, and the room beyond contained a man, a woman and some clothes as well as a bed. The clothes were on the floor, the woman was on the bed, and the man was on the woman. You'd think the amount of emotion being expressed would require quite a bit of motion to generate it, but the bodies on the bed weren't moving any more than the clothes on the floor.

Well, actually, that's not quite true. They didn't *seem* to be moving, but in fact they were dancing to the beat of a different drummer.

As I walked toward the room I saw a bedside cabinet with two tumblers and an empty sachet on it. Even without a four-year course in criminology at The Learning Zone I could have guessed what the sachet had contained. In a word, Slo-Mo. Or maybe that's two words. Whatever, it slows your metabolism down and, with it, your reactions and sensory perception. It's the latter quality people take it for. What would otherwise be a passing pleasure becomes a long-distance journey to the furthest realms of ecstasy. It becomes a trip to a place where the joy is so exquisite you cry out at the top of your voice and keep on doing so until your cries turn to moans, and your moans to groans, and you lose your voice altogether. And then your mouth stays open in a wordless expression of pleasure. Or so they say. I've never tried it. Listening to those two on the bed, I was wondering why I'd never tried it. And I was glad I'd squirreled away a syringe of the stuff from a similar call-out the week before, when my perfect partner had been playing the role of Miss G. Two-Shoes, taking fingerprints or a witness statement or something boring like that.

Paula joined me in the bedroom.

I'd love to be able to say *Paula joined me in the bedroom* in a sentence that didn't have anything to do with a crime scene or a daydream.

She shook her head with a mix of disapproval and bewilderment and said, "Why do they do it?"

"Are you kidding? Just listen to them. Look at them."

Only when you looked at them for longer than a moment could you see the man's hips pulling almost imperceptibly back and up, the woman's hands slowly dragging down his back, her nails gouging pink furrows that took a very long time to fill with blood because his metabolism had slowed down so much.

Get the dosage wrong and your body wears out before the drug wears off. Knowing how much is too much is a fine art, and part of the trouble is that Slo-Mo's such a new craze nobody's actually got it down to a fine art yet. Another part of the trouble is that the drug is addictive, and people keep upping the dose each time they use it because the pleasure's so intense they want it to last longer. They want it to last forever.

After a small part of forever the man's hips started to sink, and the woman's fingers began digging in. Her head turned ever so slowly to one side, and her eyelids gradually parted to reveal glassy eyes focused on somewhere a thousand miles away. Her pupils darkened and widened until they swallowed the irises, and her moans became louder and more intense, which I wouldn't have believed possible.

Remembering my partner's 'why do they do it?' I said, "If you can experience something like that without taking drugs, I'm going to look at you in a whole different light, Paula. You don't mind if I call you Paula, do you?"

"Sometimes I think you forget you're talking to a superior."

"I never forget I'm talking to someone superior," I told her. Without looking away from the couple on the bed, I said, "I feel like I shouldn't be watching this."

"I can tell you're forcing yourself," Paula said with the thinly disguised sarcasm which is usually all that differentiates a Number's voice from the Voice of Reason. She walked over to the cabinet to take a closer look at the tumblers.

"Any left?" I asked.

She shook her head.

"Damn." I said it as a joke, but if there had been any Slo-Mo left and Paula had asked me to split it with her, I wouldn't have hesitated. Suddenly I realized how much I longed for love, and felt as pathetic as the people on the bed. I just wanted to get out of there. "I'll call the medics," I said.

Paula nodded. She pulled up the sheet that had slipped down to the lovers' ankles. They didn't notice. I doubt if they would have noticed if the roof fell in. Listening to them, you'd think it already had and they were buried in the rubble.

We waited for the haven's medical team to arrive. They probably only took a couple of minutes, but time stretched almost as much for me as it did for the two people slowly writhing on the bed. I tried to shut out the sounds that went with the writhing, but didn't come close. I heard those sounds with my heart as well as my head. I was scared to look at Paula in case she was looking at me. When I finally did risk a glance, she was watching the couple on the bed. I got the strangest feeling she was as deeply affected by what she was seeing and hearing as I was.

I had to be imagining it, because one of the things about Numbers is that they're not only incapable of dreaming and of wonder, they're incapable of love.

And then at last the medics came in—a doctor and a nurse.

The nurse was called Carol Connor. We'd had a fling once, not long after Jen died, but it was obvious to us both that it was a case of coinciding needs rather than anything remotely resembling love.

The doctor was a brown-haired, brown-eyed Number.

While there was pity on Carol's face as she summed up the situation, the doctor's expression was one of contempt. He ignored me altogether and said to Paula, "Any indication of how much they took?"

Paula shook her head.

"No need to wait," he told her. "There's nothing you can do." He looked at me and said with more than a hint of a sneer, "Unless you want to watch."

All that stopped me from coming out with a scathing put-down was the knowledge my life might be in his hands one day. And the fact I couldn't think of a scathing put-down.

Since there was nothing more for Paula and I to do in apartment 826 we headed back to the station house. It's nothing more than an office with two desks and an adjoining holding pen. It's not really called the station house, but that's what they used to call the place where police officers went to play at being police officers back in the Old Days, so it's what I call the place I go when I'm not waving my knockdown around and trying to look heroic.

I sat down and went through my daily routine of fussily adjusting the framed photo of Bernard Russell that has pride of place on my desk. I 'accidentally' knocked it over to draw attention to it, like I do every morning, and Paula 'tutted' and rolled her eyes like she does every time I knock it over. I'm willing to bet there's a photo like it on the desk of Names everywhere. A balding, bespectacled man with a beaky nose, a soup-stained paisley-pattern tie, and a moth-eaten tweed jacket, Bernard Russell is an unlikely looking hero, but he's become an iconic figure to us. Back in 2012 he beat the most advanced computer on the planet in a game of chess. His victory passed largely un-noticed at the time—there was too much serious stuff happening, because the world was in the process of going down the toilet—but, with the benefit of hindsight, it was a seminal moment. It was the last time the mind of man outwitted the pure logic of a computer.

As I adjusted the photo I glimpsed Paula's reflection in the plexiglass that covered it. She was shaking her head in a mixture of disapproval and disbelief at my pettiness, and no doubt thinking how pathetic I was by scoring the same point every day. Still, getting her to shake her head and exhibit emotion was a triumph in itself.

By then it was time for our mid-morning coffee break. We're allowed two cups a day—like everything else, coffee and water are rationed. I always share my morning coffee with the small plant I keep in the corner of the room. I love watching Paula's face when I pour the last of my precious coffee into the plant pot. She looks at me like I've gone a little loco.

Maybe she's right.

While I waited for my coffee to cool I stared at the plant, thinking about the man who'd sold it to me. Actually, Doug gave it to me for nothing when he found out it was for the station house. In my mind I replayed my last few visits to The Plant Place, looking for some sign Doug MacDougall had a drug problem, or any other kind of problem. I couldn't remember anything to suggest he was wrestling with inner demons, let alone any indication he was on the brink of taking his own life.

All the while there was a monotonous BEEP . . . BEEP . . . BEEP . . . going on in the background. Finally it got on my nerves so much I turned from the plant to Paula and said, "Do you never get tired of those things?"

By 'those things' I meant logic puzzles. Numbers are obsessed with them. Theory time, again, folks. I think Numbers quickly get bored when they don't have a practical task to accomplish or a problem to solve. And, since they can't fill empty moments with daydreams and imagination, they fill them with logic puzzles—and Name-baiting.

"Why does my doing puzzles bother you so much?" Paula said without looking up from the screen, eliciting those infuriating BEEPs as she tapped various parts of it with the tip of an elegant forefinger that appeared increasingly sensual the longer I looked at it. "Is it because you can't do them?" she asked.

"I wouldn't swap," I told her.

"Swap what?"

"Daydreaming for being able to do a logic puzzle."

For once, Paula didn't have a put-down.

Winning our little exchange should have given me a warm glow of satisfaction. Instead it left me feeling ashamed, and like I should apologize.

An extra loud BEEP! signaled completion of the logic puzzle. There was no sign of satisfaction on Paula's face. I think her triumph over the puzzle was as hollow as my victory over her. While I watched over the top of my screen she cocked her head to one side, the way you do when a message is coming through on your hear-ring. After a few seconds she raised her i-band to her mouth and said, "Okay, I'll close the case."

"Let me guess, Doug MacDougall's toxicology shows he died of an OD," I said.

Paula nodded. "Pure R8XL. Death would be instantaneous."

Rush—or, as Numbers call it, R8XL—is the opposite of Slo-Mo. It's another drug that's recently appeared out of nowhere and is gaining a worryingly widespread following among Names. It speeds up the metabolism and amplifies adrenaline production to the extent that those who've taken it become a danger to themselves and anyone in striking distance. It's as if the drug generates more energy than the user can contain—and compels them to release it with total disregard for their own safety and everyone else's. Apparently it was developed to treat people who've taken Slo-Mo, but somehow it got out of the lab and found its way onto the dance floors. In the last month we've had reports of broken limbs resulting from frenzied disco moves, and people collapsing from dehydration and exhaustion after dances that would have made the whirling dervishes of old look like they were doing a slow waltz. There was even word of a couple of young lovers being found with their hearts stopped and faces frozen in expressions of awesome ecstasy, legs entwined and arms wrapped around each other like they were holding on for dear life. The man's back was apparently torn to shreds by the woman's nails, and her spine had been snapped in two by a spasm of pleasure-pain that was too much for her body to bear. I don't know if the thing with the lovers is apocryphal, but it's helped Rush achieve cult status in a couple of months, becoming the drug of choice among people who want to push back the boundaries and don't mind how much they abuse themselves and others in the process.

"Doug MacDougall doesn't come anywhere close to fitting the user profile for Rush," I said, thinking aloud.

"He wasn't taking it for recreation. He was taking it to kill himself. Which would explain why he took it undiluted and intravenously rather than orally."

"He'd no reason to kill himself," I said, giving voice to the thought that had been going through my head all morning.

"We've worked together for two years and four days, yet there are lots of things you don't know about me," Paula said. "I think it's safe to assume there's a great deal you didn't know about someone you only had occasional contact with."

I would have dearly loved to find out some of those things I didn't know about Perfect Paula, but now wasn't the time to ask. So, instead, I said, "Don't you feel the least bit curious about why Doug MacDougall would have taken his own life?"

"No," Paula said. "His reason was probably pathetic. It's certainly academic. The case is closed, Travis."

CHAPTER 5

01000011010010000010000010101000001010100010001010101010010

LOVE, OR SOMETHING LIKE IT

THE CASE MIGHT BE CLOSED FOR PAULA, BUT NOT FOR me. For the rest of the afternoon we had the usual mix of minor incidents and dramas to deal with, each demanding my complete attention. But, when I got back to my apartment at the end of the shift, my thoughts soon turned back to Doug MacDougall.

I tried reading one of Calum Tait's travel articles but the words didn't register, and when I looked at the photos they dissolved into Doug MacDougall's face or Paula's.

I put on a Meg Ryan film, but for once she didn't win my heart or make me laugh, and my mind kept straying to the scene I'd walked into in apartment 331 that morning. I switched the movie off halfway through and sat there staring at the blank wallscreen, projecting my own thoughts onto it. The result was a mystery that seemed insoluble. Doug MacDougall simply wasn't the sort of guy to mess with drugs. He got his rush from looking for plants and sharing his love of them with other people. To me, that made an accidental overdose a non-starter. If it wasn't an accident, then it had to be on purpose. Which meant suicide or murder. Suicide didn't make sense, either. The autopsy failed to reveal any life-threatening physical ailments that might have led him to end it all. His body had far more toxins in it than was good for him, as you'd expect in someone who spent so long Outside. But, although those toxins would have taken twenty or thirty years off his life, he'd still had a good ten years left before it was an issue. Meantime, he wouldn't have felt anything worse than a shortness of breath and recurring sore throat.

Of course there was always the other kind of ailment, the kind that afflicted mind rather than body. In my job you become a good judge of character. You notice things other people miss, tell-tale signs of stress and worry, guilt and shame, fear and doubt. I'd never seen any of those signs in Doug MacDougall's face or body language. I've been wrong about people enough times to know my intuition isn't perfect, but I'm right far more often than I'm wrong, and I'd back my judgment with my life. Those aren't empty words, because sometimes I've had to do exactly that. If I was wrong about Doug, then I could be wrong about anyone, and I'd never be able to trust my judgment with the same certainty again.

I'd lose faith in a whole lot of things if I was wrong about Doug MacDougall. I suppose he'd come to symbolize all that's best about people in my mind, and if he had a dark side of pathological proportions, then we all did. If he had a fatal weakness, a fundamental flaw, then all Names did, just as Perfect Paula believed. If she was right about that, I was wrong—and truly *human* beings had no future.

The trouble was that if Doug's death wasn't an accident or suicide, that only left murder, and the facts didn't fit a murder, either.

I used my computer screen to review the haven records one more time, checking the movements in and out of Doug's apartment. He was the only person to enter or leave it over the last few days. I tried to find ways around that, but there weren't any. Even if the apartment hadn't been on the third story, the windows don't open—they're sealed units to keep out the toxic atmosphere. As for the door, the only ID card used in it was Doug's. I've never heard of anyone getting into an apartment without a card, but there's a first time for everything. So, for the sake of argument, I imagined someone had found a way to sneak into Doug's flat. If they had, they would have left a trace of their presence behind somewhere. Without realizing it, people leave traces of everything they do in the Ecosystem database. We call them ghosts. Well, actually, I call them ghosts. Paula calls them EBTs, which stands for electronic bio traces, or something like that. Anyway, after all this time on the job, I have a good idea where to look for ghosts. I started the search by saying to my voice-activated computer, "Give me the thermal records for apartment 331."

Almost instantly a histogram appeared on the screen. The processing power of the Ecosystem never fails to astonish me. It has to monitor half-a-billion citizens in communities around the world, and yet it can tell you the most intimate details of any one of those lives in the blink of an eye. What it was effectively telling me now was when Doug MacDougall's apartment was accessed, and by how many people. The histogram showed temperature on the vertical axis and time along the bottom. To save energy—we've learned our lesson from the past—apartments are kept at the ambient temperature when no one's in them. The temperature is raised by body heat when someone enters, which in turn tells the sensors to provide cool air until the room reaches 23C if you're a Name, or 22.5C if you're a Number; *they* really are colder than *us*. The resulting chart is made up of characteristic spikes and plateaus. The more people who enter, the more pronounced the spike and the longer it takes to cool the room to its optimum temperature. "Indicate occupant entries," I said.

A series of red crosses appeared along the timeline. Each marked an insertion of Doug's card into the slot beside his door. Every cross corresponded to a spike, and each spike was the same height, indicating only one person entered. It confirmed only Doug MacDougall had been in the apartment.

I let out one of those long sighs that are punctuating my days with increasing frequency. Since I was getting nowhere, I decided to go somewhere. When things are getting the better of me I like to take out my frustration by beating up some prisoners in the station holding cell, so I headed there now.

Just kidding. I work out my frustration on an exercise bike, so I went down to the gym.

When I got there the first thing I did was look around for Paula, and my heart sank when there was no sign of her. I was surprised at that—not her absence, but how much it disappointed me. After all, I spend my working days with her, so her face is the last one I should want to see at night, especially since I don't even like her.

I headed for the only empty exercise bike. All the others were being ridden by Numbers, each pedaling faster than the next. It was as if they were being chased or were chasing someone. They're ridiculously competitive, and take as much pride in their physical condition as they do in their mental prowess. They also hate lying awake at night, because they get bored and restless, so they like to work-out to the point of exhaustion. That's one of the few things about them I can relate to—although I like to work to exhaustion because I think *too much* when I lie awake at night.

Making myself comfortable on the bike—or as comfortable as it's possible to be on a bicycle seat—I decided not to be childish, and just to go at my own pace.

But of course, once I got warmed up, I inevitably found myself going faster and faster in a futile effort to match the Numbers on either side of me. I never learn.

The Number on my right turned to sneer at me. It was a Pareto. I don't know if it was the same one who'd shown up in Doug's apartment that morning—they really do all look the same to me. He certainly had the same sneer. That sneer was like a challenge laid down, and I'd no choice but to accept it.

What followed was the work-out equivalent of a staring match. I'm in pretty good physical condition, but I couldn't live with him for more than five minutes. And I was only working at level eight resistance, while he'd be on level ten. They always work at level ten. With my legs turning to jelly, I had to slow down. In a pathetic attempt to save face I turned my head to one side and pretended I'd just got a call on my hear-ring. I went so far as to pant, "Okay, I'll be right there."

The Pareto was watching me and sneering big-time now. He knew there hadn't been any call, and he knew I knew he knew, and I knew—

Well, you get the picture.

I couldn't meet his eye any more than I could match his pedaling power. Feeling every one of my forty years,

I got off the bike and walked slowly to the showers. My little act should have involved rushing, but I couldn't have managed that even if Perfect Paula had been waiting for me in the showers, ready to cxpress a heretofore stoically suppressed love with enough passion to turn ice-cold jets of waters into clouds of steaming mist.

The shower cleansed the sweat from my skin but not the lactic acid from my muscles, so I had to take the elevator, although it cost me pleasure points I'd rather have spent on a timesphere trip. I was about to tell the lift to take me to level two, because that's where my apartment is, but on the spur of the moment I said, "Three." I wanted another look at Doug's flat to see if I'd missed anything first time around.

When I got there all his personal possessions were gone, which was a bit strange. It usually takes longer than that to clean out the apartment of a deceased. I tried imagining where everything had been. First I envisaged the body, then the plants.

And as soon as I thought about the plants I again had the feeling of something being not as it should be, just like when I'd looked at Doug's rolled-down sleeve. I don't know how long I stood there, trying to put a finger on what was bothering me, but it was long enough to realize I could stand there all night and not get any further forward.

And it was long enough to start thinking about Paula. Not about anything she'd said while we were in the apartment that morning, but how she'd looked as she stood there. I seem to have been ending every day by thinking about Paula lately. I used to think about her to stop thinking about Jen, because it hurt too much to think about Jen, and because Paula was an ideal object of desire—physically beautiful yet so emotionally cold I could never get close enough to be hurt by her.

However, somewhere along the line I'd started thinking about Paula in her own right, rather than as a distraction from Jen. I started looking for things in her eyes, signs that she had thoughts and feelings I could relate to. Most of the time I only saw the same gemstone coldness or mocking sneer that was present on the face of every other Number.

But increasingly there were times when I thought I saw something else—a look that might have been longing, though for what I don't know. Then again, it could have been a figment of my imagination. Whatever, it never lasted long enough for me to be sure it had really been there; it changed into that gemstone coldness the instant she realized I was watching her.

I thought about Paula's response to the Pareto that morning; the way her eyes moved over his body, and his moved over hers. There was no getting away from it. I was jealous. I felt a sliding sensation in my guts. The kind that comes from facing up to an unpalatable truth. I'd always had a crush on Perfect Paula, but it had been a purely physical thing. Now it was turning into something more, which frightened me for all sorts of reasons.

Firstly, I've had my heart well and truly broken once before, and I've no desire to go through anything like that again.

Secondly, if there's one thing I'm sure about, it's that a Name wanting anything more than a one-night stand of no-holds barred carnal knowledge with a Number is asking for a world of trouble. I've seen it so often in my work. I'd say 90% of crimes cross the genetic divide, and about 90% of those also cross the gender divide. It's a case of opposites attracting—briefly and unequally—and then repelling with far greater force than they attracted. The conventional wisdom is that, due to their superior physical condition, Numbers are better lovers. Because of that, and their physical beauty, they're sought after by Names. Where *we* score is in being far more emotionally responsive, which apparently never fails to amuse and strangely arouse Numbers. On the face of it, that should mean everyone is happy.

However, the resulting matches are made in Hell rather than Heaven. Numbers are apparently incapable of matching their lovemaking with affection, and their contempt and sense of superiority always show through. Once they've made love with a Name, the novelty wears off and they get bored. They're simply incapable of connecting emotionally—probably because they've no hidden hopes and dreams to share. So the morning after, while a Name might experience the kind of crush you can have for physical perfection, the Number is bored and ready to move on. The kindest interpretation is that Numbers don't care about whatever hurt the subsequent brush-off involves for their Named partner. But I'm pretty sure they actually enjoy toying with our emotions, which they can do with impunity as they can't be hurt this way in return.

I think it's another way in which they try to make themselves feel better for not having our capacity to love, dream and wonder—they try to make those things seem like worthless, pathetic self-delusions born of weakness and need, and so convince themselves they're better off without them. They build themselves up by constantly bringing us down, never missing a chance to find fault with us or mock us; to point out our illogicalities, frailties and foibles. In other words, the things that make us human.

And nothing makes us more human than love.

Whatever else we are, we're not stupid and we know it'll end in tears. But our hearts rule our heads—I suppose that's the difference between us and them in a nutshell—and we're capable of loving people who we know can never love us back. Sometimes I think that might even make them more attractive to us. I know it makes Paula more attractive to me.

And then it dawned on me: maybe Doug MacDougall had lost his heart to a Number. He had a lot of heart to lose, and maybe he hadn't been able to go on living without it.

Try as I might, I couldn't imagine Doug falling for a Number—he'd fall for a Jen.

But then again, I'd fallen for Jen, and was also on the brink of falling for Paula.

Go figure.

Unrequited love of a Number wasn't a satisfactory explanation for Doug MacDougall's death, but it was the only one I had. If it hadn't been for what happened when I got back to my apartment, I might have settled for it.

It's funny, you can bring all your experience and analytical powers to bear on a problem to no avail, and it's when you've given up and are doing something else completely that the answer finally comes to you. I'd made my final cup of coffee for the day and was about to pour the last of it into my pot plant when it hit me. Not the pot plant, but the thing that hadn't been right about Doug MacDougall's apartment.

CHAPTER 6

0100000110100100000100000010101000000101010001000101010101010010

Logic Puzzle

Doug hadn't watered his plants.

There was undoubtedly much I didn't know about Citizen MacDougall, but there was one thing I could be certain of—he would have watered his plants before killing himself.

Now I was sure it wasn't suicide.

Unfortunately, I was equally sure Paula wouldn't be convinced by my certainty. She wouldn't understand Doug MacDougall's love of living things. She wouldn't understand that, even if he was capable of harming himself, he'd never have harmed the precious plants he'd gathered around him. Not even by a sin of omission like failing to water them before he took his own life.

I was nowhere near establishing a case, let alone breaking it, but I came painfully close to breaking the only piece of evidence. The syringe. Paula had obviously dismissed it from her thoughts as an irrelevance. I'd simply forgotten all about it. I didn't remember again until I was getting dressed for work the next morning and put both feet in the same leg of my coveralls. I barely managed to get a hand out in time to break my fall and avoid crushing the little plastic tube in my pocket.

My excuse for forgetting about the syringe is that the call-out to the apartment of the Slo-Mo lovers came right after I put it in my pocket, and what we found in the apartment was enough to make anyone forget about anything.

My excuse for putting both feet in the same leg of my coveralls is that I'm not a morning person, even after a good night's sleep—and, instead of a good night's sleep, I'd had a dream that was nearly as messed up as the world at the end of the Old Days.

In the dream I was in Rio, going around the places mentioned in my favorite travel article. As so often in dreams, things had gone crazy somewhere down the line. For instance, the giant statue of Christ the Redeemer on top of Corcovado was in fact a statue of Doug MacDougall, and when I walked along Ipanema beach it was with

Paula, not Jen.

Jen did put in an appearance, as a mermaid washed up on the beach. Her hair was entwined with seaweed, and she stared up at me with sightless eyes that were like holes in the fabric of humanity.

Paula stepped over Jen as if she was a stranded jelly-fish. She tugged my hand to get me to follow, but I was transfixed by those sightless eyes that were seeing nothing and everything.

I don't know how the dream would have ended, because the imaginary Paula jerked my hand hard enough to wake me up.

When I got to the station house I didn't mention the dream to Paula. Or the fact I'd fallen over while getting dressed. I didn't mention the syringe, either. Since the case was closed she would have asked me to hand the syringe over for recycling, and I didn't want to do that until I'd had it checked for prints.

Because it wasn't strictly official business I had to conduct the check in my own time. Lunchtime, to be exact. While Paula headed to the haven canteen—all meals are served there, to simplify food rationing and distribution—I headed for LogiPol HQ in Community Central.

It's quite funny; I can remember hearing a line in an Olden Days movie where an office worker says he's stepping outside for 'a breath of fresh air.' Nowadays if you step Outside for anything more than a few breaths the air is so far from fresh you need a filtermask. There's a dispenser next to every Outside door. The dispenser looks like a box of paper handkerchiefs tacked to the wall, and the filter-masks are like ultra-thin tissues. You spread one out on the palm of your hand, put your hand over your mouth and nose as if you're about to sneeze, then breathe on it. The heat and moisture of your exhalation softens the mask and turns it into a translucent membrane that lets you talk and breathe but filters out the worst of the pollutants in the air. After about thirty minutes you notice an acrid smell and a metallic taste, and that tells you the filter's saturated with toxins. If you don't change it, the protective membrane darkens, dries out and falls off, and the same things that turned it toxic go straight into your body.

Prolonged exposure to those toxins does all manner of nasty things, from impairing your lungs to screwing up your immune system and DNA. That's why Numbers and the more sensible Names never go Outside unless they have to. It's also why the Ecosystem has designed havens to be as self-sufficient as possible, and laid out each community to make sure its central zone is within a short walk of all surrounding havens. These central zones contain all the things that won't fit in a haven. Like a hospital, university, pleasure dome, and the civil service building. The latter houses, among other things, the Justice Department, including the Community Police and LogiPol headquarters, and the forensic labs.

There was no queue at Haven Nine's filtermask dispenser. It's only at night, in the hour before the Pleasure Dome opens, that a queue forms. I slotted my card in the reader. Ten points came off my account and a filtermask came out the dispenser. I slapped the membrane over my nose and mouth, fought back the urge to gag at the antiseptic smell, then retrieved my card and waited for the first set of doors to open. When they did I walked through them. The inner doors closed behind me before the outer ones opened. There was a slight hiss as the pressure equalized; the havens are sealed units. There's only one air intake for each haven, and all of the air it takes in is purified before being circulated.

The filtermask had softened by the time I walked through the outer doors, and I'd all but forgotten I was wearing it.

Apart from the occasional hoverfreighter, the streets of the communities are almost as eerily deserted as those of their abandoned counterparts. I've read Olden Days travel articles about places like Hong Kong, Marrakech and Istanbul, and how you could hardly move for the crowds; how you smelled food being cooked on every street corner, heard buskers making music, saw color all around you in the clothes people wore, the displays in shop windows, the signs advertising every product under the sun. Now the only smell is the antiseptic of your mask and the acrid accumulations that build up in it when you've worn it for too long. The only sound is the wind. Most of the time there's little more than a breeze, and it's like the whisper of distant, ancient voices echoing through the concrete canyons formed by the apartment blocks. But, when there's a superstorm on the way, the whisper gets steadily louder until it's like the screaming of a banshee and you can hear it even inside the havens. As for color, well, there isn't any—everything's logica gray. Even the sky. Leaden, oppressive and suffocating, it looks like it might fall to earth at any moment. It's as if you can see an accumulation of all the toxic fumes spewed forth from car exhausts, factory chimneys and airliner engines during the Old Days.

As I walked up the hillside the city was built on, between the gray, ten-story blocks with their tiny, storm-resistant windows, I wondered what it had been like to live under a blue sky. The only good thing about the superstorms is they sometimes thin the haze enough to reveal a hint of what lies beyond. Word spreads when it happens and people—Names, that is—hurry down to grab a filtermask and gather outside the havens to get a tantalizing glimpse of the pale blue sky impossibly far above them. I can't help thinking if only people a hundred years ago had felt the tiniest fraction of the awe we feel when we look up at times like that, we'd be living in a very different world. A world of big skies, far horizons and bright colors.

I can't help wondering what it would have been like to lie in a field of tall grass with my arms and legs spread out and the stalks caressing my skin. If I'd lived back then I would have spent an entire day and night doing just that. I would have listened to the quiet, rhythmic language of living things all around me: the lulling susurrus of the growing crops; the chirruping of crickets; the scrabbling of field mice, and the lyrical songs of unseen birds wooing a mate or warning a fledgling. . . Feeling the planet turn beneath me; gazing up into the boundless blue high above and making shapes from pure white cumulus and high cirrus clouds. I'd turn the clouds into everything from far-off mountain ranges of the kind that might conceal Shangri-La, to ships that sail across the vast ocean of the sky.

And all the while I'd be vaguely aware of the rise and fall of the sun, and intuitively I'd understand why people in the past had worshipped it with awe and wonder.

Closing my eyes when the sun got too bright I'd soon doze off, and in my dreams I'd visit the Shangri-La in the mountains and sail on the ship of clouds.

I'd wake as the sun fell slowly from the sky, and watch blue change to the glowing red and amber that love would be if it was something you could see.

Then I'd let darkness and the night cast a spell over me, watching the stars come out one by one and feeling like I was looking at infinity and eternity.

At least, that's what I like to think I would have done if I'd lived back then. But in all likelihood I'd have done the same as everyone else: consumed conspicuously, polluted with carefree abandon, and not given a used filtermask about the moral high-horses I mowed down with my SUV and the little living things I trampled with my disproportionately large environmental footprint.

I felt a catch in my throat as the slope steepened: maybe a sign all the lonely Saturdays I'd spent exploring the old city with a camera for company were catching up with me. Filtermasks help, but they can't keep all the toxins out. The only way they could do that is if they kept all the air out, which would kind of defeat the purpose.

I know I've spent more time Outside than I should have over the years, but I don't regret a moment of it. For one thing, I'd go nuts if I had to live my whole life in the haven. It's comfortable enough, but dull and predictable. Life for me only comes alive Outside. You never know what you'll find when rooting through the half-flooded or storm-damaged ruins. Every building is an Aladdin's cave, every room a treasure trove. To a Number, the stuff those buildings contain is worthless junk—which is why you never find *them* in the old cities. But to someone like me that 'junk' is priceless. When I stand on the threshold of a building in the old city I feel like Heinrich Schliemann must have when he dug for Troy, or Howard Carter uncovering the tomb of Tutankhamun. I find fascination in everyday things, in picking up once commonplace objects that are now only found in history books—everything from tin-openers to telescopes. I leave most of the stuff where

I found it, for other people to come across and wonder at. I want someone else to pick up the telescope and think about who once gazed through it, and what they might have seen—from Halley's Comet passing overhead, to a distant star going supernova. There are two things I keep, however. The first is cameras. It's crazy, I know, but I love to collect old cameras even though you can't get film to take photos with them any more. Every Name I know wants to collect something or another. Usually the things we collect are completely useless, but that doesn't make our desire to possess them any less powerful. Maybe we draw comfort from the link they provide to the past; or it might simply be that looking for such objects gives us something to do. Whatever, they give us a disproportionate amount of pleasure.

My other weakness is for diaries. This is a whole lot easier to justify than collecting old cameras. By adding diaries to the Ecosystem database I'm increasing The Sum Total of Human Knowledge, so I earn pleasure points to supplement the ones I get from working with LogiPol. That's not really why I go looking for diaries, though; I just love to find out what life was like for ordinary people during the Old Days. I learned about the big picture at school, like every youngster does; but to my mind history is way more vivid and engaging when it's seen through the eyes of people who were alive while it was being made.

I was nearing Community Central, which is something

of a misnomer. It's not physically at the center of the community—its buildings are near the top of a lee slope, safe from flooding and sheltered from high winds, and the apartment blocks radiate down the hillside—however it's the center of the community in every meaningful way. It's where the power that heats and lights the havens is generated, and where the civil service administers the Ecosystem directives which determine the details of daily life. It's where you'll find the university and hospital; the retail zone with its little luxuries like plants, priced so high consumption can never be conspicuous; and the Pleasure Dome.

The dome is meant to be a place where movement to music melts away the distinction between Names and Numbers. In reality, it's anything but. Numbers only get up for rhythmic synth and drum tracks. The rest of us request hard-driving rock to dance to, or schmaltzy power ballads of the kind that apparently used to make 'tired and emotional' bikers weep into their Budweiser at the end of heavy metal discos back in the Old Days. The last time I was in the Pleasure Dome *they* made us listen to the same electro-techno track a dozen times. But it was worth it, because one of *us* got to choose the last song and picked a stone-cold classic from the Old Days—*Winds of Change* by the Scorpions. Just thinking about what happened that night makes the hairs on the back of my neck stand on end. *We* stood around the dance floor, linking arms and swaying from side to side as one while we belted out the words to

Winds of Change like an anthem to something we've lost and might one day find again; *they* sat there looking totally bemused. For once they'd no idea what was going on. A few of them laughed at us. A lot of them sneered. Most of them looked on in bewilderment, knowing they were witnessing something spiritual that moved us deeply—and probably wishing they could feel even of a little of it themselves.

The Pleasure Dome caps the hilltop and seems to grow out of it, like a rounded summit of granite stripped bare of the heather scrub covering those parts of the lower slopes that haven't been built on. The other buildings follow the contours of the hill, using the slope to shelter them from the wind. Those higher up, starting with my destination—the civil service building, known as C-Serv—are lower and longer and more curved than the havens.

You can't actually see the most important part of the community, the power plant, because it occupies a chamber quarried into the rock. I'm not sure if the safety of its location reflects human paranoia—the rapid breakdown of society caused by power-cuts resulting from the floods and storms that became such a feature of early 21st century life must have been truly terrifying—or if the plant's position was determined by some survival instinct in the Ecosystem itself. After all, energy is its lifeblood.

I'm much more interested in history than science, but even I'm fascinated by the way the aforementioned energy is generated. There's not enough sunlight for solar power to be an option, and either too little or too much wind to harness. The jagged stumps of wind farms dotting the horizon bear mute testament to that. As a result, an entirely different approach to generating energy was taken in the wake of the Hydrocarbon Holocaust. The process has its origins in a phenomenon called sonic fusion. As far as I understand, it involves passing sound through liquid, generating bubbles which give off incredibly intense bursts of light as they implode or explode or, well, burst. Like so many scientific discoveries, this one was apparently made by chance. In the 1930s someone came up with the idea of putting an ultrasound device in a tank of photographic fluid to see if the resulting agitation would speed up the development process. Examining the negative afterwards, they saw it was covered in curious marks which indicated light had been produced by the waves of sound.

Nothing much came of this chance discovery for the best part of a hundred years. But, as the need to find alternative sources of energy became increasingly urgent, scientific advances led to better understanding and control of the phenomenon, and allowed the development of what's come to be known as sonic fusion. I'm no expert, but it seems that passing sound through liquid generates bubbles which are continuously expanded and compressed by the motion of the sonic wave. Each bubble contains gas—I suppose that's what makes it a bubble—and, under the right conditions, the compression of that gas generates a heat matching the temperature at the heart of the sun. The heat is released in ultra intense flashes as the bubbles expand. You can control the process by varying the frequency of the sound, the composition of the liquid, and the shape of the container. Doing so allows you to harness the heat, providing a safe, endless power source. However it's not the sort of technological miracle men dreamed of back in the early 21st century, because it only provides relatively small amounts of energy. That's why the Ecosystem has energy thrift down to a fine art and rewards you with pleasure points for doing things like taking the stairs rather than the lift.

Having said that, by the time I got to C-Serv my legs felt pretty much the same as when I got off the exercise bike the night before—so, after passing through the airlock and ditching my filtermask in the recycling bin, I headed for the lift.

A minute later I was in the forensic lab, and ten minutes after that I had the results of the fingerprint test.

Common sense had told me we'd find Doug MacDougall's prints on the syringe.

A mix of instinct and wishful thinking made me hope we'd find someone else's.

The one thing I hadn't figured on was what we actually found.

In light of what I'd learned I had to make my pitch to Paula just right. I used the walk back from C-Serv to Haven Nine to think it over. I'd get a flat refusal if I asked her straight out to reopen the MacDougall case. I had to be a bit more subtle. Unfortunately, subtlety's not my strong point. Come to think of it, I'm not sure what my strong point is. That's what working so closely with a Number does—destroys your self-confidence.

There were ten minutes of the lunch break left by the time I got back to the haven, so I headed for the canteen. Without time for a proper meal, I grabbed a protein bar. It's the sort of food Numbers usually favor. They take nourishment in its most easily digestible forms. They don't have much appreciation of things like flavor, texture, smell and color. I pulled a face as I bit into the off-white bar. It wasn't that it tasted bad, it didn't taste of anything at all. Nitrogen, sulphur and carbon compounds collected from filters in the community's air-purification systems are used to synthesize sugars and amino acids, which feed cultures of meat and plant life in the food factories of the Outer Limits at the foot of the hill. The food situation is similar to that with power generation—the supply is inexhaustible, but there's a limit to how much can be produced at one time. As a result, food and fluids are rationed to the optimum daily amount. Your allocation in its most basic form—the sort of bland protein bar I was struggling to swallow now—doesn't cost any pleasure points. But if you want it in a more appetizing guise, you have to pay for it.

I looked around the canteen for Perfect Paula as I munched away on the food bar, and tried to think of what to say if I saw her.

There's a de facto segregation in the canteens—as there is in every other aspect of community life, even though the Ecosystem has done everything it can to lessen the genetic divide. Numbers always choose the nearest empty seat at a table with no Names, and sit an exact distance apart from each other. They silently cut their food into precise mouthfuls—which they quickly chew and swallow with no sign of relish or distaste—and leave whenever they've finished eating; whereas we chat and laugh, complain, argue and sometimes even agree. We hesitate with fork or cup halfway to our mouth, let our food go cold or eat it while it's too hot. We stay at the table long after our meal is finished, exchanging opinions or chat-up lines, or just listening to the conversation around us and drawing comfort from the presence of other people.

Looking around the canteen, I saw that half the tables had animated figures sitting around them: gesturing with their hands and talking louder than was necessary to be heard—two things Numbers never do; or leaning back in their chairs and laughing—another thing Numbers hardly ever do.

The rest of the tables were either empty or hosted

solitary figures, each spaced at a spookily regular distance from the next, chewing away and looking like they couldn't wait to be doing something else. There were several dozen women with hair the same color and style as Paula's. And eyes like hers. And the same perfect posture. But none wore LogiPol blue coveralls. I wasn't surprised. Paula wouldn't hang around after eating lunch, and the sort of lunch she favored didn't take long to eat.

I found her in the station house, dictating a report on the morning's call-outs. She looked up when I came in.

I gave her my most charming smile and offered her a bite of my protein bar.

She gave me a disapproving look for eating outside a designated food-consumption area. No doubt my next credit card statement would include a deduction for a conduct violation, with this precise time and date next to it.

Paula finished her report at the same time I finished my bar. Well, she finished just before me, so my mouth was half full of food when I said: "I've got a present for you."

Say that to a Name and they'll smile or look suspicious or at least a little curious. Paula merely gave me the sort of withering look that made me think I'd find another deduction on my next statement, this time for talking with my mouth full. I waited for her to ask what the present was.

When it became obvious she wasn't going to, I said, "I missed out on my lunch to get it for you."

She looked pointedly at the remains of the protein bar in my hand.

"This isn't real food; it doesn't count," I told her. Wanting to get in her good books, I waited until I'd swallowed the last bite before carrying on with my pitch: "Go on, ask me about your present."

She kept looking at me with an un-nerving stare. I wasn't sure whether her silence was due to lack of curiosity, whether she'd guessed what I was up to, or if she was simply enjoying letting me squirm. I suspect it was the latter. Finally, she said, "Just tell me what's on your mind, Travis."

"I've got a logic puzzle for you."

"I've already got the latest one, and I've done all the others."

"You don't have this one. Nobody has this one. Except me."

She didn't exactly gasp in surprise and move to the edge of her seat in anticipation, but she didn't turn back to her screen, either. I took that as a good sign and carried on. "What's more, I'm willing to bet it's a puzzle you can't solve."

"I'm willing to bet this has something to do with Doug MacDougall," she said.

I shouldn't be surprised at the way her kind can read our minds, but I always am.

"The case is closed, Travis," she told me.

"You might want to reconsider that once you hear about my logic puzzle. That is, unless you're scared you won't be able to solve it."

She knew she was being manipulated but was powerless to resist. Numbers pride themselves on their mental prowess and logicality. It seems to be at the core of their being. Maybe that's because they lack the ability to dream and imagine and wonder; take away their awesome powers of logic and they have nothing. "I suppose you think you're being clever," she said.

"I'm just interested to see if you're as clever as you think you are. And I'm interested to find out what really happened to Doug MacDougall."

"He killed himself, Travis. End of story."

"Then how come he didn't water his plants before he died?"

"That's your big mystery?" she asked, mocking me with her eyes and her words and the way she said them.

I didn't tell her it wasn't my big mystery. For once I knew something she didn't, and I wanted to savor the feeling of superiority.

"Hasn't it occurred to you that if he was too messed up to look out for himself, he probably wasn't in any fit state to take care of some stupid little pot plants?" she said.

"There's nothing to suggest he was too messed up to look out for himself."

"Apart from the fact we found his body slumped next to an empty syringe."

I went over things in my mind one more time, looking for an innocent explanation for what I'd learned at the forensics lab, scared I was setting myself up for a much bigger put-down than the one she'd just sarcastically delivered. When I couldn't come up with any explanations that weren't sinister I said, "The syringe is the really puzzling bit."

"How come?"

"Doug had too much love of life and living things to kill himself with what was in it."

"Maybe he loved some living thing that didn't love him back, and that's why he killed himself."

"What would you know about love?" I said. For a moment I saw such hurt in her eyes I was sorry I'd said it. Quickly moving on, I said, "I decided to get a couple of tests done on the syringe."

"Which you'd no right to do without my authorization."

"Which you wouldn't have given me. Anyway, the residue inside the syringe matches the Rush in Doug's body."

"Where's the puzzle in that?"

"The puzzle is in what we found on the outside of the syringe."

"Other fingerprints beside MacDougall's?" she asked. They can't resist the temptation to show how clever they are by guessing what you're about to say.

I shook my head. I love it when they guess wrong. "There were no suspicious fingerprints on the syringe," I told her.

"You're not making any sense."

"There weren't any fingerprints on the syringe at all."

For once, Perfect Paula was lost for words.

Her silence didn't last long. "They must have been accidentally wiped off somewhere down the line," she said.

I shook my head. "The chain of evidence couldn't be more complete. I lifted the syringe from Doug's apartment with a non-rub bag, and the next person to handle it was the forensics technician at LogiPol HQ. He did the tests while I waited, and I watched him do them."

And now I watched Paula as she tried to figure out the little puzzle I'd posed.

"I'm trying to work out how he could have injected himself without leaving his fingerprints on the syringe, and I'm not coming close," I said. "The only way I can solve the puzzle is by having someone else inject Doug. Someone who either wore gloves or wiped the syringe after sticking it into him. If you've got another explanation I'd love to hear it."

Her silence spoke volumes, which I greatly enjoyed reading.

Rather than admit she was stumped—Numbers hate that nearly as much as admitting they're wrong—she finally said, "If someone wanted to make it look like suicide, why not press MacDougall's fingers against the syringe after killing him, to get his prints on it?"

I'd already asked myself the same question, so I had some answers ready: "They might not have had time. Or maybe they thought the scenario looked so cut-and-dried there wouldn't be an investigation. They could be too dumb to have thought of it, or so arrogant they think they can get away with stuff like that because they're so much cleverer than us. Maybe they get a kick out of knowing there's a risk of being caught. Or maybe it's something else entirely, something more bizarre than I'm able to think of. All I know is that I'd like to find out what really happened. Doug deserves that much. Besides, justice demands an explanation. And so does my own curiosity."

"Without a motive you don't have a case."

"I only have no case if you have an explanation for the lack of prints on the syringe," I said. "Do you?"

I wanted her to admit she was stumped. But, of course, she didn't.

I let the silence stretch for long enough to be awkward, then gave her a way out by saying, "I think it's at least worth having a word with his daughter, finding out if she had a motive or knows of anyone who does. What do you say?" I asked, knowing my perfect partner couldn't say no.

CHAPTER 7

01000011010010000010000010101000001010100010001010101010010

The Last Days of Old Earth

"WE'LL COME BACK LATER," PAULA SAID TO ME. WE were standing outside one of Haven Nine's classrooms, looking through the clear panel in the door. The lights were off and one wall of the room was alive with dramatic images from the Old Days; an audiovisual presentation was in progress. I watched the pupils. They were little more than silhouettes and shadows. Some leaned forward over their carbon-fiber desks, obviously fascinated by what they saw. Others sat back and stared at the wallscreen with little interest, fidgeting restlessly. You can see the difference between *us* and *them* even at this age and when it's too dark to make out faces.

Annie MacDougall stood to one side of the wallscreen,

dividing her attention between the images and her class. The sound-proofing was so good we couldn't hear her words, but the pictures told me she was giving a history lecture. I love learning about the past. So, ignoring what Paula said about coming back later, I quietly opened the door and entered the classroom.

"Travis!" Paula said in an angry whisper that turned every head in our direction.

We were saved by an atomic bomb exploding—a giant mushroom cloud filled the wallscreen, its awful beauty drawing all eyes to it. All eyes but the teacher's. She stared at us, her face illuminated by the nuclear blast. She had her father's dirty blond hair, but her features were pretty and feminine. They didn't hold my attention, however; it was drawn by her left arm, which was less than half the size it should have been and ended in a hand not much bigger than a toddler's. I guess she'd paid the price for the damage done to Doug's DNA by his lifelong love of prospecting for plants. Whatever, instead of getting a limb graft, Annie MacDougall had tailored her coverall to fit her arm. It must take real guts to stand up in front of a class that's more than half full of physically perfect people when you have a disability of that nature, and I found myself full of admiration for her.

The screen went black. I used the cover of darkness to sit down in an empty seat, and Paula hurriedly sat next to me. She gave me a dig in the ribs to express her anger at the way I'd ignored her order. Since we were in a classroom I figured it was okay to act like a child, and stuck my tongue out at her.

A young Name behind us laughed at my clowning but the sound died in his throat when the wallscreen came to life again, because it showed footage of badly burned, bewildered figures stumbling through the ruins of Hiroshima. Annie MacDougall let the image speak for itself, then said, "The Second World War was followed by the so-called Cold War, with the United States and Russia locked in a ruinous arms race and the entire world living in fear of atomic Armageddon."

Images of missile silos and nuclear submarines flashed across the screen.

"In the end, it was market forces rather than military might which ended the Cold War." The screen showed a picture of American fast-food franchises within sight of the Kremlin, followed by images of the Berlin Wall being torn down.

I sensed Paula fidgeting beside me. For some reason Numbers can't relate to the past and have no interest in it. If you asked them to explain why they feel that way, they'd no doubt say the past is gone and time spent thinking about it is wasted. They'd say it's more logical to think about the present and the future because you can do something about them. I think there's more to it than that, though. I think their lack of interest in the past stems from the fact they don't feel connected to it in any way. Sometimes I envy them because they have no sense of shame and guilt over what was done to the planet. But most of the time I pity them, because they can never know the excitement of finding out about their forefathers. They can never uncover ancestral acts of heroism and romance and kindness, take pride in knowing a part of all of that lives on in themselves. Numbers learn the important dates from the past and remember them long after we do, but they don't understand the stories behind them. They could tell you when the Taj Mahal was built, but couldn't hope to understand the love that led to its construction.

"Capitalism was now king," Annie MacDougall said. The backdrop changed to a stock exchange in London or New York. Traders frantically waved pieces of paper to get attention, while above them a neon ticker-tape conveyed the latest share prices, telling of fortunes made and lost in the blink of an eye. The classroom around me was filled with the frenzied bidding of jostling brokers from a bygone age, each shouting louder than the next. A bell rang to signal the close of business, the brokers fell silent, and Annie MacDougall said, "You're witnessing the collective madness of unbridled individual greed, of people who know the price of everything and the value of nothing.

"Perhaps it's human nature to never be satisfied with what you have. Over the ages this desire for more was a great asset. It drove men to the ends of the earth, firing their imaginations and fuelling their ingenuity, leading them to risk their lives and make great discoveries in the process.

"But, by the end of the twentieth century, people had developed the technology to actually satisfy an unhealthy amount of their desires. You could say they'd gained a great deal of knowledge without acquiring the wisdom or self-restraint that would have made it a blessing rather than a curse. Completely failing to recognize that there's a balance between living standards and quality of life, they single-mindedly strove to improve the former without due thought for the latter.

"Nothing illustrates the folly of this time better than attitudes toward the motor car. It became commonplace for households in the developed world to have two or three—"

The screen filled with an aerial view of a city gridlocked by eight lanes of nose-to-tail traffic, accompanied by a soundtrack of bad-tempered horn-honking.

"And when traffic became unmanageable the 'solution' adopted was the worst one possible—the building of more roads.

"As with cars, so with other things. Each household had two or three television sets, three or four computers. Technology made consumer goods obsolete within months rather than years, and everyone wanted the latest model, the next big thing.

"And, thanks to the onset of the information age and the power of advertising, people in the underdeveloped world became increasingly aware of what those in the west had, and wanted such things for themselves."

Her point was made by shots of a hillside favela where every second shanty had a satellite TV dish.

"Those growing expectations effectively had a multiplier effect on the environmental footprint left by a global population which was doubling in less than a lifetime, with over a million more mouths to feed every week.

"The inevitable result was the rapid depletion of resources far beyond Earth's ability to replenish them—" An aerial view of an isolated patch of rainforest in a windblown plain of dust flashed across the screen.

"And the pollution of the planet beyond its ability to recover—" A lake filled with scummy water and dead fish made further words unnecessary.

"Mankind was living on borrowed time, lulled into a false sense of security by Earth's amazing resilience and our own extraordinary selfishness and short-sighted—"

"*Their* extraordinary selfishness and short-sightedness," one of the students said.

Annie MacDougall paused and looked in the direction of the bored, know-it-all voice.

I didn't have to do likewise to know the speaker was a Number.

"You said 'lulled into a false sense of security by *our* own selfishness and short-sightedness'," the student said, as if he was the teacher. "You should have said *their.*"

Annie was either very good-natured or simply resigned to dealing with obnoxious smart-asses, because she managed to keep her cool. "You have a point," she conceded. "However, if I'd said *their*, someone could have told me that I should have said *our*. Perhaps I should have said simply 'lulled into a false sense of security by selfishness and shortsightedness'."

"It's more accurate and concise," the student said snottily.

I'd had enough and was about to turn around and tell the know-it-all to shut up, but Paula covered my mouth with her hand before I could get the words out.

For a moment Annie MacDougall looked like she was going to rebuke the smartass student, but she thought better of it and clicked the tiny audio-visual controller in her good hand to bring up the next image. It showed a city being lashed by a hurricane. Trees were uprooted, roofs ripped off buildings, and cars floated down streets that had been turned into waterways by torrential rain. "There were warning signs that we were doing irreparable damage to—" Annie stopped to correct herself—"that irreparable damage was being done to the planet. But those warnings were initially dismissed as aberrations or arbitrary acts of God.

"As the warning signs increased in frequency and intensity, so they became harder to dismiss. However, efforts to tackle the global warming that lay behind these catastrophes were completely ineffective."

"Really?" another of those arrogant voices said sarcastically.

"Perhaps you'd like to tell us why they were ineffective," Annie MacDougall said.

When her offer wasn't taken up, she said, "Then maybe you'll show enough manners to keep quiet while *I* tell *you*." A click of the AV controller filled the wallscreen with a picture of a wind farm. "The early efforts to counteract global warming took the form of mainly token gestures in the developed world, where countries struggled merely to reduce the *increase* in harmful greenhouse gas emissions.

"Meanwhile there were vast increases in such emissions from the developing world, especially China and India.

"Remedial action was hindered by the impossibility of producing a definitive model to predict the threat being faced; global warming is a complex function of an almost infinite amount of interlinked variables, each of them responding with different sensitivity, and each affecting all the others. As a result, the early models ranged from the idea that big increases in greenhouses gases had a small effect as the Earth would find ways to compensate, to the notion of an unknown threshold—a point beyond which drastic changes would take place. People tended to believe the former as it was what they wanted to believe, and because the latter prospect was so frightening.

"Policy-makers and populations at large either regarded the people who issued warnings as scaremongers, or thought the problems belonged to the far distant future.

Researchers who said a point of no return was being reached were dismissed as cranks and lunatics. People preferred to listen to the mouthpieces of vested interests who said things they wanted to hear, rather than heed warnings that the end was nigh unless they accepted major lifestyle changes.

"In the end, something had to give: Earth or Man. Since people were too selfish and short-sighted to limit their lifestyles, it was the Earth that gave. A tipping point was reached, a point of no return. Can anyone tell me what provided the final push?"

Looking around, I had no difficulty picking out Names from Numbers despite the dim lighting: the Names either sank down in their seats, trying to make themselves as inconspicuous as possible because they were shy or didn't know the answer, or else they had their hands raised as high as they'd go and waved them about, eager to impress and hungry for a word of praise in a world where they were constantly made to feel slow and dumb and second-best.

Before Annie MacDougall could pick out a pupil, the know-it-all who'd corrected her earlier said, "The Hydrocarbon Holocaust."

It had to be a Pareto. I turned around to see if I was right. Sure enough, I found myself looking at a younger version of the smug face that had sneered at me as I got off the exercise bike in the gym the night before. A few desks away was another face just like it, displaying an identical sneer. I don't know if it's my imagination, but there seem to be more Paretos than there used to be. My heart went out to Annie MacDougall—two in one class.

When I turned back to Annie, she was nodding. "Can anyone explain how the Hydrocarbon Holocaust came about?" This time, before either of the Paretos could answer, she looked at a small boy in the front row who'd been begging to answer the previous question, and said, "Frankie, would you like to try?"

He nodded. Although I was looking at the back of his head I could picture his face. It would be a mask of concentration. The silence stretched out long enough to become awkward, and then embarrassing. It was filled by a snigger. I imagined the boy's face turning bright red. Finally he said, "It was the bomb in the beefburger place and the Americans getting mad at the Muslims and the Muslims getting their own back and. . ." the words dried up.

More sniggers, then one of the Paretos piped up: "What he's trying to say is that tensions between Christians and Muslims over the treatment of the Palestinians and the terrorism it spawned were worsened by the policies of a US government which was increasingly a puppet for multinational companies who manipulated it for their own ends, principally to meet their growing demand for increasingly scarce resources, especially oil."

I shook my head in disbelief. The Pareto was no more than fourteen years old, and yet talked like an adult. And history is their *weakest* subject.

He wasn't finished yet. "United by a sense of injustice and double standards, a Muslim Coalition was formed. The first thing it did was increase oil prices. This caused great hardship in the developed countries, especially the US, and ratcheted up racial and religious tensions even further."

"Thank you, Paul, or is it Mark?" the teacher said sweetly.

Someone sniggered. It was me. I was sniggering because I knew Annie was having a dig at the Pareto's lack of individuality. Although I'd laughed, it wasn't really all that funny. I'd seen enough of Annie MacDougall to know that, like her father, she was as good as people get—yet even she'd been driven to launch an attack across the genetic divide.

"I'll take it from here, because I've got some more pictures to show you," she said. With her good hand she clicked the audio-visual control, and the wall behind her became a city of skyscrapers seen from ground level. All the shop windows were blown out, and a cloud of smoke hung heavily just above the debris-strewn street. People emerged coughing and choking from the dust, their clothes torn and bloodstained. Some held handkerchiefs to their mouths, many looked like they didn't know where they were. A few people, mostly wearing fire and police and paramedic uniforms, rushed toward the cloud to help those who came staggering out of it, but they had to fight their way through panicked crowds pouring from the surrounding buildings. The classroom around me was filled with the screams of pain, fear and panic of long-dead people, and the wailing of a hundred sirens. I'd seen the footage many times before but it hadn't lost its power to shock me, and I found myself caught up in the heroism and sheer terror of the events portrayed. I stole a glance at Paula. She only looked mildly interested, as if she was watching an old Hollywood movie rather than a turning point in history.

Annie MacDougall froze the image. The dust cloud appeared to billow out of the wall. A mother carrying a baby was emerging from its midst. She'd tripped over a briefcase dropped by some fleeing businessman. She was about to fall, and her face was frozen in helplessness and horror.

Annie stared at that face. I saw how much she was moved by the mother's plight, and heard it in her voice when she said, "Things came to a head with the dirty bomb attack in a fast-food restaurant in Lower Manhattan. The blast was blamed on Muslim fundamentalists, but one theory is that the bomb was planted by the government to provide an excuse for what was to follow. It's unlikely the truth will ever be known, and it's academic, anyway. What matters is the incident led to the Third Gulf War."

Now the screen was filled with a succession of striking images:

A squadron of bat-like stealth bombers streaking across a dusky sky.

Fireballs erupting in a city of minarets.

A desert highway littered with burnt-out tanks.

"Intent on tackling terrorism and securing oil supplies, the west invaded much of the Middle East," Annie said. "It created the secular United States of Arabia puppet regime, outraging Muslim fundamentalists. Unable to match the military might of what they saw as corrupt infidel invaders, the fundamentalists struck back by targeting oil production at all stages—"

The screen showed thick clouds of smoke belching into the air from a hundred burning oil wells; then a massive oil tanker, its back broken, sinking below the surface of an ocean darkened by a spreading slick.

"Weren't the fundamentalists spiting themselves by doing that?" The question, in a naïve voice, came from a young Name to my left.

Annie MacDougall turned from the screen to the teenager and said, "Indeed they were, but they reasoned—and I use the term loosely—that if they couldn't benefit from the oil, they could at least deny it to their sworn enemy and burden them with the crippling costs of cleaning up the mess.

"Of course the mess wasn't so easily cleaned up, and the resulting environmental catastrophe came to be known as the Hydrocarbon Holocaust."

There were more images of burning oil fields and dense black smoke blotting out the sun.

"In a way the entire planet came to resemble a battlefield, as if a no-holds-barred war was being waged against Mother Nature. While that wasn't the intention, it was the result—the catastrophic 'collateral damage' that comes from overdevelopment, strident nationalism and religious strife. The planet was under attack from all sides: from the Hydrocarbon Holocaust in the Middle East to the smogs of the great conurbations of the west; from a holed ozone layer to melting polar ice caps; from oceans overfished to the point of extinction, to rainforests being slashed and burned beyond regeneration. Pollution increased at the same time as the ability of the planet to cope with it was diminishing and, as a consequence, the problems worsened exponentially. The so-called tipping point had been reached."

"What exactly does that mean?" Frankie asked.

The question was greeted by sniggering from the Numbers, which made me wonder how many questions went unasked for fear of ridicule. A lot of people favored segregation in classes, but I hadn't been one of them. Now I was having second thoughts.

Annie MacDougall ignored the sniggering. No doubt she'd had plenty practice, even before becoming a teacher. "Imagine you have something balanced on your outstretched finger," she said. "A food bar, say. If you give it a gentle push it'll rock up and down but return to its resting point. If you push it too far, however, it'll fall right off your finger."

She looked from Frankie around the rest of the class and said, "A good way to understand what was happening is to look at the polar regions. As the climate warmed and the icecaps began to melt, so less heat was reflected—

vegetation and bare rock absorb a lot more of the sun's energy than snow and ice—and the pace of melting increased. The melting of the ice created its own terrible momentum. Self-accelerating processes like that were going on all over the planet.

"Take the tundra: methane which had been trapped in frozen organic matter was released as the permafrost thawed. It's a much more harmful greenhouse gas than carbon dioxide, so the more of it that was released, the warmer things got—melting more permafrost and releasing yet more methane.

"Likewise with the forests: as they were cut down and burned, more carbon dioxide was released—and of course there were fewer trees to help with its absorption.

"Then there were the oceans: vast and powerful, yet deceptively sensitive to changes in temperature."

"In what way?" a Name asked.

"The warming of the surface shut off the circulation that brought nutrients up from the depths. Without those nutrients, the algae that absorb carbon dioxide from the air died off. It was a double disaster: the dying algae released methane and carbon dioxide into the atmosphere, and at the same time reduced the ability of the ocean to soak it up."

"What date was the tipping point reached?" Frankie asked, to more sniggers.

Annie allowed herself a not unkind smile at the naiveté

of the question. "It's not something we can put an exact date on, because we're dealing with continuous processes, and a great deal of them," she explained patiently. "But it's generally agreed the point of no return was passed in the mid-2020s. Before then the consequences of man's abuse of the environment were just beginning to impact on everyday life, but they were felt as irritations and minor inconveniences. There was only the occasional catastrophic event, like Hurricane Katrina."

"The one that flattened New York?" Frankie said.

"Wrong!" one of the Paretos crowed.

Annie ignored the Pareto, and said, "It was Hurricane Zena that devastated New York. Katrina hit New Orleans. They were both warning signs—and perhaps if they'd been heeded, it wouldn't have been too late.

"But people chose to treat the symptoms rather consider the root causes, and by the early 2030s the symptoms were too severe to treat—and so was the cause."

"What sort of things do you mean when you talk about irritations and symptoms?" a student somewhere behind me asked. I guessed it was a Name: we love the details that give color; Numbers are just interested in facts and figures.

Annie said, "I'm talking about things like how breathing unfiltered air began to result in respiratory problems; how exposure to even modest amounts of sunlight, washing in untreated water, or getting caught in showers of rain started causing skin problems. Not to mention the long-term health concerns associated with drinking untreated water and eating unprocessed, unpurified food. The lifespan and fertility of people, plants and animals markedly declined, while the incidence of mutations increased."

"Things like your arm," one of the Paretos said with undisguised mockery. I could quite happily have choked him for his callousness. Worryingly, I could quite happily have choked the other Pareto, too.

Annie evinced no such malice. "Yes," she said quietly. "Like my arm."

"Why don't you get a graft?" a Number sitting a couple of desks along from me asked.

Annie looked him straight in the eye and said, "If you don't know, nothing I can say will make you understand."

I sensed the Number's quiet seething. Even at that age they hate to feel there's anything they don't know or are incapable of learning.

"Anyway," Annie carried on, "as I suggested, the initial response to the mounting problems was superficial and cosmetic—" The screen was filled with a shot of a busy high street where every shopper wore a crude face mask.

"The prophylactics were marketed as fashion accessories—"

The next shot showed three pretty women, each in a differently colored ensemble with a matching shade of mask.

"The protective measures people had to take to go outside became increasingly extreme—higher-factor UV creams, face masks with primitive filters in them. Even then, they weren't enough to stop people feeling unwell if they were outside for any length of time.

"By the end of the 2020s, anyone who worked outside had to wear a full eco-hazard suit." The screen displayed footage of a construction site, with a squad of bricklayers wearing bright orange coveralls, and hard hats that incorporated UV visors and heavy-duty filter-masks.

"You won't believe this next shot," Annie said. "I had to go back to 2010 to find it. It shows how the world had changed in those two decades; how attitudes changed. It shows how building sites used to be—"

There were gasps all around when the image appeared: it showed a construction site where the workers wore only shorts, revealing bodies not only heavily muscled but deeply tanned.

"And if you think that's wild, how about this shot—" the teacher said.

This time there were exclamations of disbelief—even, I suspect, from the Numbers: the wallscreen displayed a beach full of people wearing trunks and bikinis, lying out in the sun.

"The Outside used to be viewed as healthy," Annie said by way of explanation. "There were phrases like 'The Great Outdoors,' and people went walking for the sake of it, to enjoy 'fresh air, the sun on their back, the wind in their hair'."

That was greeted with more expressions of derision and disbelief.

"But by the early decades of the 21st century the world was such a different, damaged place that the Outside was coming to be viewed as we regard it now: poisoned and poisonous.

"If things were bad in the west, imagine how awful it was in the developing world—"

"Surely pollution wasn't quite as bad there, because by definition development wasn't so intense," a young Number at the back of the hall said.

"The trouble is that the damage done to the environment had passed the point where its consequences were localized," Annie told him. "The very cycles of nature had been altered and contaminated—and they operate on a global scale.

"In addition, while development was less intense in the third world, it also happened to be even less-environmentally friendly. In the rush to secure the same living standards as the west there was no time or money to abide by even the inadequate token environmental safeguards adopted in more affluent countries. The pressure for development was overwhelming, fuelled by aspirations raised by multinationals and fed by offers of investment from those same companies; offers which the governments of poor countries could not afford to turn down. As markets became saturated and regulations were slowly tightened in the developed world—albeit too little and too late—the third world became increasingly attractive to multinationals. Take automobiles: the third world became a dumping ground for vehicles that failed to meet the steadily tightening emission standards in the west.

"To make matters worse, people in those poorer countries couldn't afford the prophylactics that became commonplace in the west—the expensive UV creams and filters, the treated water and processed foods.

"As a result of all this, the trends I referred to regarding life expectancy, fertility and mutations which were becoming apparent in the west were of a different order of magnitude in the poorer countries of the world."

There were gasps of shock and revulsion all around me as the screen was filled with the image of an ill-equipped hospital ward full of pathetic children with hideously deformed or missing limbs.

"Previously rare conditions such as anencephaly—when babies are born with parts of their brain missing—became increasingly commonplace.

"There was horror in the west at pictures like these: not just out of empathy at the suffering, but due to fear that a similar fate awaited the rest of the world.

"Unsurprisingly there was a backlash against the multinationals—"

A quick succession of images showed mass protests in London, Paris and New York.

"The increasing support for mainstream Green movements, which made their point by peaceful means such as mass marches and boycotting companies and products, was accompanied by a growth in what came to be known as Green Brigades—eco-terrorists who violently targeted cars and other signs of conspicuous consumption. Things previously regarded as status symbols came to be viewed as badges of shame; objects of desire became the focus of disgust—"

The picture now was of Park Avenue in Manhattan, showing blazing cars and boutiques with windows either broken or covered in graffiti.

"Unable to control the disorder, governments dug in and hoped it would die out.

"However, the Green movement went from strength to strength, until it was effectively setting the agenda. Mainstream political party manifestoes suddenly espoused measures which would have been electoral suicide a generation earlier: things like hefty eco taxes on cars and gasoline to tackle the consequences of pollution and provide investment in eco-friendly public transport.

"But as the environmental situation deteriorated—as it became apparent that even the most radical mainstream party manifestoes were inadequate for tackling such profound difficulties, that national boundaries and vested interests must inevitably lead to a fragmentary approach that couldn't hope to tackle problems of a global nature—so the feeling grew that existing political and economic systems were part of the problem and incapable of providing a solution.

"It was in this climate of fear and despair that the Ecosystem emerged—"

A loud bell interrupted Annie MacDougall, signaling the end of the period.

I was barely aware of the kids filing out around me. The history teacher had taken me back in time as vividly as a timesphere trip.

Once the last of the pupils had left, Doug's daughter brought me back to the present by saying, "Can I help you?"

CHAPTER 8

01000011010010000100000101010000010101000100010101010010

The History Teacher

"It's about your father," I said, starting to get up.

With her good hand, Annie indicated that Paula and I should stay seated. She came over to join us, and I studied her closely as she approached. The first thing I noticed was that her eyes were red and puffy, as if she'd recently sobbed her heart out. Far from having anything to do with her father's death, I was willing to bet she would have laid down her life for him.

As if defiantly trying to show us—well, Paula—that she was comfortable with who she was, Annie MacDougall stooped and used her mis-formed hand to turn a chair in the front row around so she could sit facing us. Things went horribly wrong; her fingers were too small to get a proper grip, and the chair slipped from her grasp.

Embarrassed, I looked away. To be more precise, I looked at Paula. I expected to see a sneer, or at least a smirk. But her expression was neutral, and I sensed she was fighting back pity rather than contempt.

Annie turned the chair around at the second attempt. As she sat down she stole a glance at Perfect Paula. My partner must have been doing the same thing at exactly the same moment, because Annie said to her, "It's okay to look. It's not okay to laugh, but it's okay to look. I'm used to people like you looking, but I never get used to the laughter."

"I'm sorry, I didn't mean to stare," Paula said quietly.

I nearly fell out my chair. It was the first time I'd heard Paula say she was sorry to anyone.

Come to think of it, it was the first time I'd heard any Number apologize for anything.

Annie MacDougall looked as taken aback as me. Now *she* apologized, saying, "I'm sorry. I didn't mean to make you feel uncomfortable."

Feeling left out, I found something to apologize for, too. "I'm sorry about your father," I said.

Annie turned her bloodshot brown eyes from Paula to me and nodded her thanks.

"I used to look into his shop now and again and we had some good talks," I told her. "I can't say I knew him well, but I liked what I did know. He always made me welcome. He always made everyone welcome, from what

I could see."

I watched Annie closely, looking for a sign that there was someone Doug MacDougall wouldn't have welcomed in The Plant Place. But she nodded in agreement, and all I saw in her expression was the infinite sadness of loss. "He was my best friend as well as my father," she said. "I can't believe he's gone."

I wasn't looking forward to putting my next question, but it had to be asked: "Can you think of any reason why he'd take his own life?"

Again I watched her closely, alert for any sign that she was lying or not telling the whole truth.

But the history teacher shook her head unequivocally.

I wanted to leave it at that, but it wouldn't take me any further forward. I had to probe a bit deeper. "Your father struck me as a cheerful guy with a positive attitude and a love of life. But, as I said, I didn't know him all that well. I'm wondering if there's anything I don't know about that was troubling him."

"If there was, then I don't know about it, either—and we were as close as a father and daughter can be. Or, at least, I thought we were," she said. "What's happened makes me wonder about that, and I can't tell you how awful a thing that is. I never doubted Dad in any way, which was one of the things that made him seem so amazing to me. Some of that's been taken away from me by what happened and the way it happened."

My heart went out to her, as it had when I first saw her deformity. I was guessing the anguish she was going through now was every bit as profound as that caused by her mis-shapen arm, Her next words did nothing to dispel the notion. "The father I knew and loved would never do something that would cause me so much pain. I still love him, but I feel like I didn't know him the way I thought I did. It's bad enough feeling that way about someone when they're alive and you have a chance to find out what it is you don't know about them. But when they're dead and you no longer have that chance. . . When your memory of them is all you have and it's made to seem imperfect and incomplete and it's something you can't think of without feeling doubt and hurt. . ."

She so obviously believed what she was saying that I'd no difficulty believing her when she said it.

I was more certain than ever that Doug MacDougall hadn't killed himself because I couldn't imagine him hurting anyone, let alone his daughter, in this way.

Changing tack slightly, I said, "Your father was as easy to get along with as anyone I've ever met, but do you know if he had any—"

She clutched at the words before the last of them was out of my mouth. "Do you think someone might have. . ."

"It's just a routine question." That wasn't quite true, and I felt bad about misleading her. If anyone deserved to know the truth about Doug MacDougall it was his daughter. It would be easier to tell her more of the truth if Perfect Paula wasn't there, so I turned to my partner and said, "Could you get Annie a drink of water, please?"

Paula looked bemused by the fact *I* was telling *her* what to do, albeit politely. But she nodded. I handed her my credit card, and said, "Charge it to this."

As soon as Paula left the classroom I said to Annie, "Look, the case is officially closed but I find it hard to believe there isn't more to it than meets the eye, so I'm trying to cover every base."

"I appreciate that more than you can realize. Do you really think he might have been. . ."

"I honestly don't know what to think. Except that things aren't quite what they seem." I saw a hundred questions forming in her mind. Since I probably didn't have answers to any of them, I pre-empted her by asking my own: "Can you think of anyone who'd have wanted to harm your father?"

"No. You know what he was like. He made friends, not enemies."

"Did he ever mention problems with the shop, a deal gone wrong, anything like that?"

She shook her head. "He was never going to be well-off, but he wasn't in it for the money. I think the sort of issues you're hinting at stem from greed, and my father wasn't a greedy person."

"Sorry to ask this, but what about his private life? Could there have been a spurned lover or a jealous husband with a score to settle?"

"Again, he was too taken up with his plants. After Mum died he wasn't interested in anyone else. It maybe sounds hard to believe, but that's the way it was."

"I can believe it," I said.

"When Dad wasn't in the shop he was prospecting for plants to stock it with," Annie told me. "I always thought he'd die of something related to the amount of time he spent Outside."

The door opened, and I changed to a more neutral subject: "If you don't mind me asking, how do you cope with those kids?"

"With great difficulty, but it brings out the best in me in a way an easier job wouldn't. My instinct is to shut myself away, but my spirit would end up as wasted and deformed as my arm if I did that. So I force myself to face down my fears—and I can feel good about myself for doing so, draw strength from my biggest weakness."

Paula set a glass of water down in front of the teacher.

"Thanks," Annie said. And then she looked at me and said, "I really appreciate this."

I knew she wasn't talking about the glass of water, and that was when I realized I couldn't let things lie. Until then my persistence had been down to a desire to honor Doug's memory and make a point to Perfect Paula—and the truth was academic to Doug because he was dead, while the thing with Paula was petty.

Now that I'd met Annie, finding out the truth about Doug MacDougall wasn't academic any more. There was a person's happiness at stake—a person who very much deserved to be happy—as well as points in a trivial game.

Which made it all the more galling that I'd asked all the questions I could think of and wasn't any further forward after hearing the answers.

It wasn't until I was on my way out that one last question occurred to me. I have to admit I felt like Lieutenant Columbo, one of my favorite Olden Days TV detectives. His catch phrase, delivered as he was about to exit stage left, was, 'There's just one more thing.' I resisted the temptation to say that and launched straight into my question: "Can you think of anything out of the ordinary involving your dad over the last few days? Anything that struck you as unusual or puzzling?"

She thought long and hard. I'm used to people being obstructive; I don't often see them trying desperately to help, like Annie MacDougall was. However, her efforts produced nothing more than a sigh and a shake of the head.

"Give me a call if you do think of anything," I told her.

She nodded.

I didn't expect to hear from her again. I certainly didn't expect to hear from her so soon; I was following Paula out the door when Annie did a sort of reverse Columbo on me, saying, "There is something, now that I think about it."

I stopped in my tracks.

"It's probably nothing."

Usually people are right when they say that, so I didn't get too excited. But occasionally they're wrong, so my pulse quickened a few beats and my voice was hoarse as I turned and said, "Yeah?"

"The day before Dad died he mentioned having read something 'remarkable.' I can't remember exactly how he put it, but he said it had changed how he thought about a whole lot of things; how he thought about life."

"Did he sound frightened?"

"The opposite: excited, in a good way."

"Do you know what it was he'd read?"

She shook her head. "Sorry. I get the feeling it must have been hard copy, though, because when I asked him about it he said he'd give me a read of it, like you'd say if you were talking about an Olden Days book or magazine rather than an ebook or something on the system database. In fact, now I think about it, why would he say that if he knew he was going to. . . If he'd intended—" she couldn't finish the question.

I couldn't think of an answer. I turned to Paula, and saw she couldn't think of one, either.

"Is that any help at all?" Annie asked hopefully.

Given how little we had to go on, anything was a help. Rather than put it like that, I nodded. "Remember, call me if you think of anything else," I said.

I paused after closing the door behind me, and watched

Annie MacDougall through the clear panel. She clutched the glass of water like it was all she had in the world to hold onto.

As I walked down the corridor I said to Paula, "Thanks."

"What for?" she asked, puzzled.

"Not sneering at her."

My perfect partner stopped, and said, "Do we really seem so awful to you?"

And all I could answer her with was silence.

CHAPTER 9

010000110100100001000001010100000101010001000101010100 10

The Green Man

I TRY TO LEAVE WORK BEHIND WHEN I GET BACK TO my apartment each night, but sometimes a case grabs hold of me and won't let go. Doug MacDougall's death was falling firmly into that category.

I started reading a travel article in a bid to relax and unwind, but my mind wasn't on it.

Soon I was sitting at my desktop computer screen, clicking through the digital images of Doug's apartment and trying to spot whatever it was he'd been reading the day before he died.

But there weren't any magazines lying around, and all the books were in the bookcase. I'd taken a close-up of the shelves, and that was the image I kept coming back to. The only lead I had was most probably in one of those books. Unfortunately I had no idea which book it was in, let alone what page it was on. Most of the spines were cracked and stained by water or faded by sun, making the titles difficult to read, so I rerouted the computer display to my wallscreen.

Staring at the giant image of books whose titles told of a world so different from my own, it wasn't long before I was thinking of Jen and her passion for what was left of that world, the natural world—and how her love of it and my love of her had been responsible for her death.

Because that was too painful to think about, I turned my thoughts back to the line-up of cracked and timeworn spines that lined Doug's bookcase and filled my wall. I was hoping one of the titles would leap out at me. But instead of inspiration all I felt was frustration and a gutting sadness at how much had been lost. I remembered reading in a book like the ones I was staring at that over 400 species of tree were recorded in a single hectare of rainforest back in the Old Days, and there were too many different kinds of flora and fauna to count; the best estimate was 10 million. And now all of that had been replaced by shifting desert sands or scrubland that barely supported any wildlife at all. I thought about how the change from one state to another had happened, about how people had believed nature was infinitely resilient and adaptable—and didn't realize they were wrong until it was too late. I thought about how one species after another suffered from one thing after another: from overexploitation and habitat loss, from the pollution that accompanied industrialization, and the climate change resulting from pollution.

The consequences had been deceptively innocuous at first: spring arrived a week or so earlier, and fall came a little later, and on the surface there was no harm done. But, if you scratched beneath the surface. . . Jen explained it to me by a single example: the longer summers gave more time for insects to breed, so more leaves of a particular kind were eaten, and the trees that relied on those leaves for life died off—and so one species was quietly lost here, another there.

And then, as the climatic tipping point Annie MacDougall had talked about was reached, the delicate balance of life all over the planet was disrupted with catastrophic consequences. Melting ice floes forced everything from polar bears to penguins into ever smaller areas, until eventually they'd nowhere left to go.

Southern temperate species were driven ever further south by warmer climates until there was no more land left for them to walk upon.

Alpine plants and the populations they fed and sheltered were forced higher up mountains until they ran out of rock to cling to.

Lush forests were turned to sere scrubland.

Coastal fringes were eroded and inundated.

Oceans became watery deserts as the currents that circulated nutrient-rich waters failed; coral reefs became bleached skeletons that crumbled in the superstorms.

All over the world, species were compelled to seek new habitats, and in each of them the delicate balance of predators and prey developed over thousands of years was destroyed in a decade or two, resulting in the extremes of extinction and plagues of pests.

And now more than half the plant and animal species were gone, and most of those that remained were on the way out. Habitats had been simplified, losing their richness and color; the wild was replaced by a wilderness almost wholly lacking in wonder. Only traces of it remained, hanging on precariously in the relics of old natural parks, nature reserves and places too extreme to have been profitably exploited during the Old Days. Such natural relics were tended with awesome devotion by volunteers whose vicarious guilt and shame, curiosity and sense of wonder led them to recklessly disregard the consequences to their own health in a bid to right the wrongs of past generations and leave something for those to come.

Awesomely devoted volunteers like Jen.

I felt a lump in my throat and a hollowness in the pit of my stomach, and I can't say how much of it was due to what happened to Jen and how much of it was down to what had happened to the world.

I forced my eyes to focus on the bookcase and my mind

to focus on the conversation I'd had with Annie MacDougall, and tried to connect one with the other. No matter how hard I concentrated, it wasn't happening. I don't quit easily, but there came a point when I felt like I could look at that photo forever and not find out anything more from it than the titles of the volumes in the bookcase.

After a sigh that was part weariness, part frustration, I switched off the wallscreen and took my evening shower. Like every other shower in the community it's set on a pulse program to save water. The first time you hit the start button you get twenty seconds of warm spray—enough to let you work up a lather with some shower gel. The next time you press the button you get twenty seconds to wash off the lather. The Ecosystem controls the water temperature according to your personal profile; Numbers like slightly cooler water, just like they prefer cooler rooms. It also goes by the time of day and the shift you work. If you're having a start-the-day shower, the rinsing phase ends with an invigorating cold pulse; but, if you're through for the day, the shower ends with a hot pulse to relax your muscles and make it easier to sleep. As my shower came to an end I thought about what it must have been like in the Old Days, before water and the energy to heat it were rationed. I imagined how good it would be to stand under those relaxing needles of hot water without worrying about them going off at any moment, letting them wash over every muscle in your body until all the kinks were gone.

Back in the real world, the relaxing needles of hot water disappeared before the kinks in my muscles.

By the time I'd toweled off I still wasn't any more relaxed in mind than I was in body. I knew if I turned out the light I'd lie awake, thinking over the MacDougall case and not getting anywhere. Experience told me the best thing to do was read until my eyelids went together, then I'd sleep as soon as I dimmed the lights. I squatted down in front of my bookcase, trying to make up my mind what to read. Like Doug's bookcase, mine is filled with volumes picked up on scavenging trips Outside—thanks to the shortage of paper, printed books have long been a thing of the past. The titles on my shelves are quite different from those I'd seen on Doug's, however. My bottom shelf houses pulp detective novels, while the middle one is full of photobooks by the likes of Robert Capa and Sebastiao Salgado. Their masterly images give credence to the old saying that a picture can be worth a thousand words. Every page is a window into the past, and I can look through some of those windows for hours.

I'd spent long enough playing at being a detective and looking at photos for one day, however, so it was the top shelf I turned to. It usually is, because that's where I keep my real treasures. None of the volumes on that shelf are properly bound, and almost without exception they're dog-eared and tattered, written in hand on water-stained or moldy, yellowed pages. The state of the paper and the legibility of the handwriting make them difficult to read, but more often than not my patience is rewarded by insights that bring the past to life in a way even a teacher as good as Annie MacDougall can't hope to do. There's so much ground to cover in a classroom or lecture hall that the past is inevitably portrayed in grand sweeps, but to me it's the everyday details that hold the key to understanding. Study the big picture, memorize the key dates, and you'll become knowledgeable; but read the everyday stories of ordinary people and you'll gain understanding. Books about the rise and fall of empires, the clash of civilizations and the lives of the men who led them usually leave me cold, but the accounts of ordinary people rarely fail to engage and surprise me. Pick up a book on ancient Egypt or the conquest of Mexico and you've got a rough idea what to expect. Pick up a diary of someone you've never heard of before, and I can guarantee somewhere in its pages will be things that shock you and things that put a smile on your face—and, the chances are, you'll find expressions of loneliness and love which stay with you long after you've forgotten the accounts of events which changed the course of history. More often than not with a diary you start feeling you know the writer and their friends. You want to know whether they passed their degree exams and what happened when they proposed to their fiancée; if the pet rabbit survived its bout of fly-strike, and whether Granddad got over his heart attack. You build up a picture of how they looked from what they wrote. I've often found myself returning to a house I took a diary from, looking for a photo of the person who wrote in its pages. Sometimes the diarist turns out to be uncannily like I imagined; sometimes they're hysterically different. Whatever, as I look at the photo I feel like I know the person in it. If it's a man I wonder if we could have become friends. If it's a woman I wonder if we might have been something more.

I reached for the last unread diary in my collection, not realizing it was to be one of the most affecting I'd ever come across. It was written in a notebook with a light brown cardboard cover that had RECYCLED PAPER printed on it. There was no name on the cover, just a matchstick figure drawn in green pencil.

The first thing I noticed when I opened the jotter was the tiny writing, telling me before I saw the date that I was looking at a diary from the last of the Old Days. Paper was so expensive by then that people crammed as many words as possible onto every page.

Sure enough, the date written in block capitals above the opening entry was *APRIL 11, 2016.* The entry beneath it read:

I'd expected the worst, but it still came as a shock. 'Carbon lung' is what the doctor called it. He said I have a year, maybe a lot less, maybe a little more if I'm lucky. He actually said that word: lucky.

He asked what I did for a living, and when I told him I'm a cycle courier, biking documents and parcels through the traffic jams, he just nodded as if to say 'I guessed you did something like that.'

It's so unfair. I'm only twenty-nine years old and it looks like I'll never get to be thirty. I'll never get to have a family, to experience the wonder of holding a baby and knowing I helped give it life. I'll never get to watch a son or daughter growing up, feel the thrill you must get from seeing things you recognize to have come from you and your partner, and the bigger thrill of seeing things that are wholly the child's own; of watching a unique personality take shape. Until now I never realized how magical any of that is, or how much I wanted to experience it for myself.

The next few words were smudged, and I wondered if a teardrop or two had blurred the ink. I think they said, *There are a whole lot of things I never realized until now.*

That took me to the end of the page. When I turned over to the next one, it said:

APRIL 12

I cried myself to sleep last night. I wouldn't have believed a grown man could do that. I must have used up all my self-pity, as well as all my tears, because when I woke up this morning my eyes were dry and I felt angry at God rather than sorry for myself. What's happening to me would be bad enough if I'd done something I deserve to be punished for, but it's the opposite. It's happened because I refused to be one of the selfish scumbags driving around polluting the planet. It's because I've chosen to take the 'healthy' option and walk and cycle all my life that this horrible, terrifying thing is happening to me. Where's the justice in that, God? If there is a god in heaven he can't be worth worshipping. Now, when I need to believe in God more than ever, I find it harder than ever to believe in Him. They say He works in mysterious ways. Well, I think I've solved the mystery. I think there is no god. I think man invented God and not the other way around; that we're products of chance and circumstance and we're kidding ourselves if we believe we're part of some grand design.

They talk about hard-earned truths; well, truths don't come any harder-earned than this one. I'm paying for it with my life.

APRIL 13

I'm meeting Sara today. It's the last thing I feel like doing, but it was arranged before I got the bad news. I was going to cancel, but I have to break things off with her sometime, and the sooner the better. For her and for me. The longer I spend with her, the more I'll grow to love her and the more unbearable this'll be.

I was thinking about it all last night, and the best thing seems to be to split up with her without disclosing the real reason why. Telling her would only ruin her life for the next year, or however long I have left, and I love her way too much to want to do that. Besides, I'm struggling badly enough as it is to cope with my own feelings. I don't think I could cope with hers as well. When she asks me why I want to break up, I'll say I don't love her enough for things to work out between us. It's going to be the hardest thing I've ever done in my life, but I have to believe it's a case of being cruel to be kind, that the short-term hurt will be for the best in the long run. Sara will be able to get on with her life, look for someone else, not be suspended in limbo with her life on hold until mine finally ebbs away.

APRIL 14

I should have known it wouldn't be that simple. When I told Sara I wanted to break up, and that I didn't love her enough for us to have a future together, she started crying. And then, before I knew it, I was crying, too. Even through her tears and mine—or maybe because of my tears—she must have been able to see I was lying, and that I loved her as much as one person can love another.

The writing blurred again at this point. However this time it wasn't due to tears having fallen on the page, but to tears forming in my eyes, because I knew the love he was speaking of and how much it hurt to lose it.

I had to wipe my eyes with the back of my hand before moving on.

My heart broke, and before I knew it I was telling Sara all the things I promised myself I wouldn't say—from what was happening to me, to what I felt for her. She wanted to stand by me, like I knew she would. She wanted to get married tomorrow, but I wouldn't agree. I love her far too much to have her life ruined as well as my own. I feel sick with myself for telling her, for being so weak and selfish. I feel. . .

The writing tailed off, but I knew how the diarist felt about the selfishness thing. I knew exactly how he felt.

I turned to the next page.

APRIL 15

No matter what way I look at things, all the future holds for me is heartbreak. So there's only one thing to do. All that's left to decide is how to do it. I lay awake all night thinking of a hundred different ways. The problem is, I'm scared of every one.

APRIL 17

I've settled on a mix of painkillers and gin. I don't have the guts to slit my wrists or jump out of a window or do anything else that's so obviously going to kill me. I mean, taking pills and a drink, those are things you do every day, so it shouldn't be impossible to make myself do them one more time: to take a whole packet of pills rather than a single tablet, a bottle of gin rather than a glass.

Now that's decided, all that's left is to write a note. I've been trying all afternoon and half the night but. . .

I wish I could be profound or touching, or at least witty and brave, really check-out in style. But I've never felt less clever or funny or brave in my life. I'm just hoping I can capture a tiny fraction of what I feel for Sara.

Or perhaps that would only make things worse for her.

Perhaps it would be better if I didn't leave a note at all.

APRIL 18

I'd intended making this my last day on Earth, but things didn't exactly go according to plan. I should be dead by now. But, instead of losing my life, I've lost a tooth and gained a reason to live. At least for one more day. I guess that's not a bad bargain unless you're fussy about your smile. I also guess it takes a bit of explaining.

We had one of those monsoon style cloudbursts that are becoming spookily commonplace. I waited for the rain to go off before heading out to the shops for painkillers and gin. How crazy is that: intending to kill myself, but not wanting to go out in the rain and get wet. Anyway, I was on my way back from the shops with everything I needed to get the job done when this jerk in an SUV went through a puddle and soaked me from head to foot. I felt a wave of water not just going over the top of my trainers but over the collar of my coat. Again, it shouldn't really have bothered me. I mean, it's not like I was going to have to wash or even dry the clothes, or worry about catching a chill from getting soaked. I might have let it pass if the muddy water hadn't ruined the pad I bought for writing my letter to Sara.

Whatever, all the anger building up inside me, that I hadn't been able to release because I'd nothing to vent it on, found a target in the SUV. Without stopping to think what I was doing I reached in my carrier bag, brought out the bottle of gin, and hurled it at the SUV. The back window didn't shatter but the bottle did, and the jerk of a driver slammed on the brakes and got rear-ended. He must have known what happened because, after flinging open his door, he didn't go for the driver who'd shunted him. He came after me.

He punched me in the face before I realized what he was going to do, then turned and ran back to his SUV and drove off and left me there with a bleeding nose and a loose tooth.

Okay, that's not exactly true. The bit about the bleeding nose and the loose tooth is kosher, but not the bit about him running away. He stood there for long enough to give me a chance for a square go, but I was too stunned (AKA scared). He was bigger and heavier than me, and I knew he'd beat me to a pulp in a fight. That shouldn't have bothered me, given the circumstances, but it did.

As I watched him drive off I was disgusted with myself for not having made a fight of it, and I was filled with rage at him and his SUV. I made up my mind there and then that I wasn't leaving this world until I'd exacted a measure of revenge. If I couldn't beat him up, I could at least do some damage to his SUV: I'd got a good look at his number plate as he drove off, and I could use it to find out where he lived.

By the time I got back home I'd replaced the broken bottle of gin with a can of spray paint, and the thoughts of suicide notes with notions of exacting sweet revenge on the black SUV. I was so pumped up I didn't bother changing out of my puddle-soaked clothes. I ran the license number through a search engine on my PC, and used the damp pad of paper I'd bought for my farewell note to write down the name that went with the license, and the address that went with the name.

I worked out a dozen ways to get there. I thought about what to wear to be as inconspicuous as possible, what weapons to take and what to carry them in. I felt like a general planning a campaign, like a soldier on the eve of battle. I had something to live for, even if it was just getting my own back in a petty feud.

I could hardly wait for night to fall. I found myself looking forward to the future, or at least the next little part of it, rather than dreading it.

I felt like a ninja as I made my way through the city, sticking to the shadows as I approached the street where SUV Man lived. When I got there his pride and joy was parked outside a garage that presumably housed his wife's planet-wrecker. I started getting ambi-

tious, wondering if the garage was locked and if I could get in and do some damage to whatever was parked in there, too. Then I laughed at how I was getting carried away. I can't remember the last time I'd laughed. I hadn't thought I would ever laugh again.

There was a pub within sight of his house. I grabbed a stool at a counter by the window and had myself some tall, cold beers, drinking them slowly, savoring the taste in a way I'd never done before. I noticed a whole lot of stuff I'd never noticed before, like the beautiful golden color of the beer. And, every so often, I looked up from my glass to the house across the street, watching the lights go out one by one until there was only an upstairs light left on. The barman called last orders, and I went for a walk through a nearby park and looked up at the stars, and noticed things about them I'd never noticed before, like how many there are.

The next time I approached the house the upstairs light was off. The drive was covered in tar rather than gravel, so I didn't have to worry about making any crunching sounds as I walked up it. I wanted to slash his tires but that would probably have set off an alarm so instead I took out my spray can, gave it a shake, and got to work. I started on the windscreen with your basic, unimaginative swirls, hurrying to do as much damage as possible before the car alarm went off and the bedroom light came on.

I relaxed a bit when there were no alarm bells or lights, and put more thought into what I was doing. By the time I got to his door panels I'd graduated to writing some words that made it plain exactly what his once shiny SUV was doing to the planet.

I stood back to admire my handiwork, then took off into the night, running and laughing like a carefree schoolboy. I hit half a dozen 'targets of opportunity' on the way, leaving each of them unfit to drive.

Somehow I know I'll sleep like a baby tonight, and when I wake up in the morning I'm going to feel like a new man.

I was ready for sleep myself, but couldn't put the diary down. I turned to the next page.

APRIL 19

I was right on both counts.

The stress of the last few days and the excitement of last night left me totally drained, and I was sound asleep within minutes of my head hitting the pillow. Before I slept, though, I heard something that set me thinking, that made me wonder if there isn't a God after all, and if there's maybe a reason for the stuff that's happened to me. I'd switched on the radio after switching off the light, and the BBC World Service news came on. I like it because they don't operate on the same sliding scale of values that some other stations do: you know, one Brit or Yank equals half a dozen continental Europeans equals several hundred Rwandans or Filipinos. Anyway, before I fell asleep I heard this thing about how climate change has affected some of the poorest countries in the world; about how the people who've contributed least to global warming are suffering the most. The ones who've so little to begin with are losing everything they have, including the chance to make a new start. I drifted off to sleep realizing this is about more than me. I realized it's not myself I should be killing, it's the people who've caused all this, who've poisoned me and the planet.

Well, I shouldn't be killing them, or then I'd be as bad as they are, but I should be doing things that'll make them think, or at least make it difficult for them to keep on living their selfish lives and screwing up the planet and other people in the process. I should be doing things like spraying paint on their cars so they can't drive them any more.

Suddenly I have a reason to live as long as I can, something to do that's worth doing. It's not difficult to believe that getting splashed by the puddle and punched in the face was fate, that there's some sort of grand design at work after all, and I have a part to play in it. Even if I can only take a handful of cars off the road for a week or so at a time, it all helps. It's indescribably fantastic to have something to think about that takes my mind off thinking about my own problems; to feel like I can do something that matters to the world with what's left of my life.

Anyway, I truly feel like a man on a mission. I've made up a list of every shop that might sell spray paint, and I'm going to buy a can or two in each one—I don't want to buy too many in any single shop in case I attract the wrong sort of attention. Don't get me wrong, I want *to attract attention, but to The Cause I've set out to further, not to myself.*

Then, once darkness falls, I'll get to work again.

I blinked away my sleep and flicked over to the next page, wrinkling my nostrils at the musty smell which was carried on the draught from the mildewed paper.

APRIL 20

A good night's work—14 confirmed kills and one partial (I saw headlights approaching in the distance and had to scarper before I'd fully 'decommissioned' car #15).

APRIL 21

There was good news and bad this morning. I was in a shop and the owner had the radio tuned to the local station. The news was on, and at the end of it there was a story about how the police are hunting 'the Green Man'. It seems as though I've been elevated to superhero status. I mean, the Green Man sounds like something out of a comic book or graphic novel, doesn't it. It's spooky to be hunted, but at the same time it's pretty damn cool to be a wanted man, not to mention a superhero. It's right what they say—truth really is stranger than fiction. If anyone had told me this was how my life was going to turn out, I'd never have believed them in a million years.

Anyway, what I heard on the radio got me thinking. It really concentrates your mind when you know the police are hunting you. So what I got to thinking was that I should either lay low or move somewhere else. And laying low really isn't an option, because I need the Green Man just as much as Planet Earth does. So it looks like I'll have to move on. It's probably for the best because it solves the problem regarding Sara—I have to forget about her and she has to forget about me because she has no future with me and I have no future, period. Funny, with all that's been happening I'd forgotten about that. I'll write her a note. I'm not sure exactly what I'll say, whether to tell her I'm the Green Man. Probably it's better that I don't. Maybe she'd be proud of me, but then again maybe she wouldn't understand. All I know about the note is that it's going to be a lot different from the self-pitying one I would have written a couple of days ago.

APRIL 22

I was trying to work out where I should move to, and suddenly it hit me: why limit myself to one place? Why not go on a tour, take my message across the whole damn country? I'll be sort of like David Janssen in that old black and white television show. The Fugitive, I think it was called. The one where he's wanted for a crime he's not really guilty of, and has to move from town to town to keep one step ahead of the law. He never stays in any one place for long enough to put down roots or get close enough to anybody for them to guess his true identity. I used to love that show. Now it looks like I'm going to have a chance to write, direct, and star in a whole series of my own. I have enough savings to last about a year, and, well, I won't need any more than that. Everything has worked out as though it's meant. I feel that more strongly with every passing day. Each time I decommission a car I feel like another hand is moving mine, that a greater force is at work through me. Call it God if you will, but I prefer to call it Gaia.

APRIL 24

Boy, did I get the surprise of my life this morning. I caught the sleeper train down to London and, when I got off, the first thing I saw was a headline on one of the kiosk billboards announcing that I (the Green Man) was there. I froze, like fugitives do in old movies when they see a wanted poster with their likeness on it. I couldn't figure out how they'd known I was coming. I mean, the paper had to have been printed before I'd even got on the train. Then I read the first paragraph of the story and realized what had happened: someone else must have heard about what I'd been doing and had taken on my mantle. At first I was angry that they were ripping me off. Then, when I put my personal feelings aside, I saw it was wonderful: I had my first disciple. Without intending it, I'd become a messiah, and my message was spreading.

APRIL 24

It looks like I've got more than one disciple. A lot more. Today's paper said a couple of hundred cars were 'decommissioned' (they said vandalized—how dare they) last night. I only took out 21, so I'm figuring there were about another nine or ten guys at work. Maybe twelve, like the twelve apostles.

APRIL 25

Holy schmoly!!! I made the TV news today. Or, should I say, we made the news. And the best thing was, they had a poxy vox or whatever it's called—you know, where they interview ordinary people and ask for their opinions—and the people who spoke out against me, or rather spoke out against us, sounded so selfish when they were doing it. Even some drivers conceded we had a point, and most of the people who didn't have cars talked about us like we were heroes doing a job that had to be done.

APRIL 26

Boy, the power of TV! A whole lot of people must have been inspired by what they saw last night, because there were Green Men at work in towns and cities all over the country in the hours after the news feature was aired. As a result we made the news again, and this time we were moved from being the funny story at the end of the show to being the second story. We would have been first if it hadn't been for a superstorm hitting New Orleans and finishing off the work that Katrina started a decade ago. They actually linked the storm to global warming caused by, among other things, car exhausts, and used that to segue into the story about the Green Men.

APRIL 27

I suppose it was inevitable. Any worthwhile cause will have its martyrs. One of my followers got caught 'green-handed' by the owner of an SUV last night and was beaten to a pulp and left to die in the street. I feel terrible, but in a way I also feel it's happened for a reason, like the things that happened to me. They interviewed the guy who found the body of our first KIA (killed in action) and he said, 'What that guy did to this Green Man, others like him are doing to the planet.' I couldn't have put it better myself.

APRIL 28

My disciple didn't die in vain. Far from it. Something amazing happened once word of the death—the murder—got out. Someone, somewhere, had the idea of reclaiming the streets, of using bicycles to form a rolling blockade. Word must have spread on the Internet, and this morning there were cyclists wearing green armbands and riding shoulder to shoulder on the streets of almost every city, causing traffic chaos. We had another KIA—a motorist apparently lost his patience and deliberately ran over one of the cyclists. The surrounding cyclists who saw what happened got off their bikes and dragged the motorist out of his car, and other people in cars got out to help the motorist. By the time the police arrived another five people were dead and dozens were seriously injured. Again, I do feel bad because I know none of this would be happening if I hadn't started spraying cars. But, then again, if cars hadn't poisoned me and the planet I wouldn't be out with my spray can. I just did what had to be done. I didn't realize what I was starting, though. Those scenes on the news today were like something from a movie about a world spinning out of control. But then I shouldn't be surprised, because that's exactly what is happening to the world.

If anyone's in doubt about that, they only have to look at the weather forecast for later in the week. 'The mother of all storms' is how the forecaster put it, and one expert they interviewed said it was the sort of storm you used to only get in the tropics, and even then only once every couple of decades. Now they're happening several times a year in the tropics, making whole cities uninhabitable, and it looks like they're starting to happen here. I suppose it isn't surprising given the fact we're getting the other kinds of weather they used to only get in the tropics—the heat and cloudbursts.

APRIL 29

There was a different kind of chaos on the streets today—people heading for high ground. All of London is at flood risk from tidal surges and the rain that's coming with the wind. They're expecting major structural damage and power cuts, and advising everybody to leave.

I think I'll catch a train back north. I've not been feeling so good lately, coughing up horrible black stuff, waking up with my boxers and T-shirt soaked in sweat that I'm sure is due to more than the sweltering nights. I just want to go back home.

I turned over the next page but there was no more writing on it. I tried to imagine the chaos and panic that must have filled the next days of the Green Man's life. I wondered how much longer he'd lived, and how he'd died. I couldn't decide if he'd been unbearably self-righteous or heroically altruistic, a visionary or plain nuts.

I just hoped he'd made it home.

CHAPTER 10

01000011010010000100000101010000010101000100010101010010

Outside

THERE WAS A MUSTY SMELL IN MY NOSTRILS WHEN I woke up the next morning. I'd fallen asleep with the diary in my hands, and it was lying on the bed beside me. The events it described came flooding back so vividly it was as though I'd lived through them. No doubt I'd dreamed about Green Men and traffic jams, street fights and hurricanes.

I got up and put the diary in my bookcase. It was a tight fit. Not wanting to damage the timeworn jotter I didn't force it all the way in. If I had, the chances are I'd never have solved the mystery of that other bookcase, the one in Doug MacDougall's room. It was the shadow that did it, the one cast by the jotter sticking out a centimeter or two. I'd seen a shadow like that before, stared at it for hours the previous night without recognizing its significance. I hurried over to my computer and flashed up the photo of Doug's bookcase on my wallscreen. Sure enough, there it was: a vertical dark band in the middle of the top shelf. I looked at the spine of the book immediately to its right, the one casting a shadow. It had obviously been difficult to put back in, suggesting it was the last one to be taken out.

It was called *Lichens and Mosses of the World.*

It was difficult to imagine a less promising title for a book that held the key to a mystery, but at the same time I felt sure this was the last thing Doug MacDougall had read. I was equally certain that somewhere between its covers was the passage that changed his outlook on life—and that there was a good chance it explained his death. It might have been a coincidence that Doug died before he could tell his daughter about his 'amazing discovery,' but I'm not a big believer in coincidence. I've lost count of how many cases I've cracked by making a connection between things that appear to be linked only by chance.

If there was such a connection in this instance, I wouldn't find it without getting my mitts on a copy of *Lichens and Mosses of the World.*

I started with the Ecosystem, searching by author because his name, Jay Bright, was shorter than the book's title. Sure enough, *Lichens and Mosses* was in the ISBN index, but nobody had bothered digitizing it. I wasn't too surprised. You can earn pleasure points by adding to The Sum Total of Human Knowledge, but the number of points you get is related to the profundity of the original content and the value you've added by your own powers of analysis. *Lichens and Mosses of the World* didn't have any *obvious* potential for providing rich pickings on either count. Still, Doug MacDougall had apparently found something startling in it and, just as I couldn't rest until I discovered what had happened to Doug, so I couldn't settle until I found out exactly what had shaken his world.

Since Doug's apartment had already been cleared out I couldn't simply help myself to his copy of *Lichens and Mosses of the World.* I had to find another copy.

I had to go to the old city.

"You've never been to the old city?" I asked incredulously.

Perfect Paula shook her head.

I'd told her my theory about the book and what I intended doing about it and, before I knew it, I was trying to persuade her to come with me to the old city. Suddenly it seemed very important that she came; at least as important as getting a copy of the book. I wanted to find out if Perfect Paula had a sense of wonder to awaken. I wanted to find out if there was a truly human being deep inside her. The strength of my desire to see if she'd loosen up when outside the community, if the change in surroundings would change her, took me by surprise.

"I'm as baffled that you make trips to the old city as you are that I don't," Paula told me. "Why damage your health when there's no need? We have everything we need right here in the community."

"Aren't you the slightest bit curious to see what it's like?" I asked.

"I can do that with a timesphere."

"It's not the same. It's not the same at all."

"What's different?"

I didn't know where to begin. It was like trying to describe color to a person who can't see, or music to someone who can't hear. Paula looked at me curiously. I waited for her to sneer as I struggled to articulate. When she didn't, I realized she hadn't just asked the question because she thought I'd have difficulty answering it, which is what Numbers often do. She genuinely wanted an answer. I tried my best to give her one: "It's a different world, and you can be part of it in a way you can't in a timesphere. You can reach out and touch things; think about what they were used for, and by whom.

"You can open doors and step into other people's lives, learn something about how they lived from the things they gathered around them. Some houses leave you cold and unmoved, or just plain depressed, but others captivate you. The past comes alive around you, and having the chance to explore it is amazing in a way that nothing in the community is, not even the timespheres. You want to open every door and drawer or just walk slowly from room to room. And, as you do, you start to feel a presence not your own."

"Don't tell me you believe in ghosts, Travis," she said, and now there was a hint of a sneer on her face and in her voice.

"No, but some places definitely have an atmosphere, and when you go there it doesn't take much imagination to hear the echo of old footsteps and voices," I said. "There's a story in every house. There's a mystery with clues in every room, in every cupboard and drawer and box."

As clearly as I saw signs of old lives in those derelict houses, I saw confusion in Paula's eyes. I guessed she was torn between mocking contempt, envy, and curiosity; perhaps she was wondering if she'd feel any of the things I'd talked about on visiting such a place.

"Why not come with me and find out," I said.

"What?" she asked.

"Why not come with me and find out if you can feel any of those things, too."

The assurance I was used to seeing in her eyes had disappeared altogether, and I knew she was taken aback that I'd read her mind so completely.

Then it was her turn to surprise me. I'd expected her to come up with a whole host of perfectly logical reasons for not venturing to the old city with me, but she didn't say a single word, just nodded.

We did a search on the Olden Days Database—largely

drawn from the Internet which was at the heart of life sixty years ago—and found two libraries within walking distance that had listed *Lichens and Mosses of the World* in their catalogues. One was in the old city of Dundee. I guessed that was where Doug MacDougall got his copy. The other library was on the far side of the river, in what had been the middle-class suburb of Newport. I thought that was our best bet.

Okay, I also wanted to go there because it was a bit further away, giving me more time with Paula. Then there was the fact it was made up of gorgeous old stone villas; if anywhere could enchant Paula, it was there.

After stocking up with four filtermasks apiece—the most you're allowed in any one day—we breathed into the first of them and set off on our little adventure.

I noticed a change in Paula as we made our way down to the old city. Her stride shortened and she began looking around, not straight ahead like Numbers usually do. I'd forgotten how startling the change from community to old city is the first time you make it, because I've walked from one to the other so many times. There's no boundary wall or fence, no moat or ditch, but the demarcation is just as abrupt. The narrow, well-maintained streets give way to wide, potholed roads strewn with masonry, broken furniture, and burnt-out cars. The regular, tiny-windowed, ten-story havens and the low gray factories are replaced by a bewildering assortment of buildings of all shapes and sizes scattered about here, there and everywhere. There are towering thirty-story apartment blocks with their windows blown out by hurricanes, and the tattered remains of flapping curtains forlornly adding flashcs of color. . .

The remains of factory chimneys shorn off halfway up by superstorms, looking like the lightning-struck stumps of petrified trees. . .

And the spires of churches where people once gathered to worship a God who would eventually abandon them. Or maybe they abandoned Him to worship the new god, the Ecosystem.

There are old tenement blocks with water-stained and crumbling walls; with plants sprouting from chimney pots, and rusty drain pipes dangling from the roofs and hanging off the gables. The windows are boarded up or gape darkly, with discolored net curtains like smoke-darkened flags of surrender hung out by defeated inhabitants who'd long since given up the ghost. The doors hang off their hinges, or have been beaten down by the desperate hands and feet of the hungry and thirsty; their faded and tarnished plaques spelling out the names of people who don't live there any more, above letterboxes that no longer swing open with anything except the wind.

There are brick walls covered in graffiti that was meaningless when it was written, let alone now.

Signs advertise products that haven't been made for decades, or name streets hardly anyone has walked for sixty years; traffic lights and lamp-posts no longer light up.

I hardly noticed any of these striking sights, because I was watching Paula as she took them in. She didn't say anything. I had the feeling that, for once, she was at a loss for words. She spoke plenty but in a different language, one made up of barely audible gasps of shock and surprise, uncharacteristic hesitations and disbelieving shakes of the head.

I spoke before she did, saying, "It's like the old city has learned everything there is to know about how to look the worse for wear, and doesn't try to hide its knowledge: every way stone can crumble and wrought-iron can rust; plaster can peel, paint can fade, and wood can warp and splinter; every way a road can be cratered and potholed, a pavement pitted and broken."

Paula nodded, unable to take her eyes off the dereliction around her, and said, "Yes, that's exactly what it's like, but I couldn't have put it like that."

"You don't get a true impression from watching movies or hearing teachers talk about it, do you?"

She shook her head. "You get a picture, but it's incomplete in some way I can't describe."

"It's the stuff you can't describe that gives it atmosphere."

A gust of wind blew back a curtain as we walked by, and Paula's eyes opened wide in fright. I should have laughed at her, because *they* regard displays of emotion as a sign of weakness, and *we* love nothing better than witnessing such a nervous reaction in them. But for some reason I didn't laugh or even smile at her alarm. Instead, I said, "It's okay, it's only the wind."

Paula looked as if there was something she wanted to say. It was a few moments before she said it: "What about Outsiders?"

There was a widespread belief that gangs of deformed, desperate crazies or lone lunatics roamed the old cities, searching for food and ready to ruin your day in a variety of unimaginably unpleasant ways if you were unlucky enough to run into them. They were supposed to be discredited renegades from the community, and the misshapen offspring of people who hadn't made the move to the havens in the first place. Some people had preferred to stay in the old cities—elderly folk who didn't want to leave their homes, animal lovers who couldn't bear to leave their pets, and opportunists who saw the chance to move into the biggest and best of the abandoned houses, to enjoy material wealth they'd only dreamed about before. Most of them found their way to the community in the end, though—when water stopped flowing from the taps and there was no more power at the flick of a switch; when there was hardly any more food and drink left to loot, and competition for what remained became so fierce the last semblance of law and order broke down; when the toxic haze became truly choking and the heat stifling, relieved only by storms that blew down buildings and rain that flooded any streets which hadn't already been inundated by rising rivers and encroaching oceans and seas. Those who remained Outside led short and miserable lives, if the diaries I'd found from the last of the Old Days are anything to go by. If there had been a second generation of Outsiders I hadn't seen any sign of it. As for discredited renegades from the community, they nearly always came back and gave themselves up, driven by thirst and hunger and the realization they were sentencing themselves to death if they stayed Outside.

"The Outsiders are what used to be called an urban myth," I said, as we made our way down toward the river.

"A what?"

I was surprised she didn't know. I'm used to Numbers knowing everything. But then they don't deal in myth and legend, only facts and figures. "An urban myth," I said. "They're stories that used to circulate in the Old Days, usually telling of terrible things happening to people. They were related second-hand because the victim was always a friend of a friend. A classic is the one about a woman licking an envelope—it's from the days when people sent paper letters by post rather than e-mail—"

"I gathered that, Travis."

They can't help themselves from picking you up if you state the obvious, so I didn't take it personally, and carried on my merry way with the shocking little tale. "She cuts her tongue as she licks the gummed flap of the envelope, and doesn't think any more of it. But over the next few days her tongue swells up to three times its normal size."

Actually, the version I'd heard had her tongue swelling to twice its normal size, but you have to embellish these things before passing them on. That's the whole point.

I carried on: "She goes to the doctor, and he thinks it's just an infection and gives her some broad-spectrum antibiotics. They don't help. Her tongue keeps swelling, and that night she wakes up and can hardly get a breath. She goes through to her bathroom and looks in a mirror and. . ." I paused for effect.

"And what, Travis?"

"And she looks on in horror as. . ." Just as they can't help themselves from putting us down if we state the obvious, we can't help provoking displays of emotion from them.

"Travis!" Paula said impatiently.

"Her tongue splits open and a bug crawls out," I said, concluding the cheery little anecdote.

"That is gross."

"The idea is, there were tiny roach eggs in the envelope gum, and one of them got in her tongue through the cut and—"

"I gathered that, too, Travis. And of course a roach egg sac is too big not to be noticed by someone licking an envelope, and holds a lot more than one egg, so it can't be true."

I might have guessed she'd know that. She obviously wasn't sure of the truth about Outsiders, though. It wasn't something you could be sure about unless you'd actually spent time Outside. So I gave her the benefit of my experience: "The only people I ever see in the old city are citizens like myself, wanting to spend an hour two in search of the past, or just to get out of the confines of the community."

The center of the old city was spread out below us. The streets were flooded, and the upper levels of shopping centers and office blocks rose from the muddy water like man-made islands. Where once cars, buses and lorries had queued nose-to-tail, the traffic now comprised a few citizens paddling along in rowboats and inflatable dinghies on treasure-hunting or sightseeing trips.

A couple of miles away, on the other side of the river, lay Newport. It was built in the 1800s along the sloping south bank of the river. Its main road ran parallel to the water. All the houses below the road had gradually been swamped by the rising river. The houses on the hillside above the road had escaped the inundation, and from this distance they looked untouched. You couldn't see the storm damage, the missing slates and crumbling chimneys, the broken windows and rotting doors. If you shut out the dereliction on either side of you, and the flooded city center directly ahead, you could almost believe there were people living in those grand villas across the water.

While the upper village looked much as it had in photos I'd seen taken from this vantage point sixty years earlier, the land around them was very different. To the left, where the river flowed into the North Sea, the dunes and coastal pine forest of Tentsmuir had vanished without a trace, and all that remained of the village of Tayport was the top of a church spire and a lighthouse. The rolling fields of winter barley and golden wheat and the lush pastures and copses that once separated Tayport from Newport were also gone. What remained above water was nothing like the green and pleasant land I'd seen in photos of the mid 20th century. The lower reaches were salt-poisoned from the sea, and the slopes above them were covered in heather and scrubby gorse and thorn. As for the trees, most had long since been cut down for firewood by the last of the Outsiders, or toppled by the hurricane-force winds of the superstorms. All that remained were jagged stumps giving a godforsaken look to the horizon.

"It must've been so different from the community," Paula said, looking at what was left of Newport. I didn't know if she was thinking aloud rather than talking to me, but I responded anyway, saying, "You'll have a better idea of just how different once we get there."

While Paula kept staring across the river I turned my attention to the scene closer at hand, searching for a boat or dinghy. You find them tethered to lamp-posts and the top of bus stops and traffic lights all along the water's edge. I waded out to the nearest one, getting soaked to my knees and trying not to think about how dirty the water was. Paula was still staring across the river by the time I undid the rope and hauled the dinghy up the street to where she stood. I held the boat steady while she got in, then joined her and paddled us across to the road bridge.

The south bank of the River Tay had been joined to the north by a late 19th century rail bridge and a 1960s road bridge. The rail bridge came crashing down during a superstorm in 2022 but the road bridge remained, albeit minus lamp-posts and with the look of a causeway because the river had risen so high. The access road was flooded halfway up, so when the bottom of the boat scraped against its asphalt we weren't too far short of the bridge proper.

Paula got out and watched as I tethered the boat to the railings at the side of the road.

"Won't someone take it?" she asked.

"They won't have got this far unless they have a boat of their own."

She looked annoyed at herself for not having thought of that. "What about someone coming from the other side?" she said in an effort to redeem herself.

"Anyone on the other side will have come from this side."

She looked really annoyed with herself now. The logic that would let her answer those questions was usually intuitive; the fact she'd asked them told me how shaken she'd been by her first sight of the old city.

Again, something made me resist the temptation to mock her, and I tried to ease her embarrassment by saying, "To be on the safe side, I'll hide the paddle somewhere. It's a good habit to get into—never leave the paddle in a boat you want to come back to. Even if you're a good swimmer, you don't want to be spending too much time in this sort of water."

Realizing I'd stated the obvious, I waited for Paula to put me down. She started to say something but stopped herself, just as I'd stopped myself from mocking her. Some sort of understanding passed between us, unlike anything that had happened before. It was the kind of moment marked in old Meg Ryan rom-coms by simultaneous smiles, followed by an embarrassed silence, and then both people speaking at once and each stopping to let the other continue before breaking up into laughter. But this wasn't a movie, and we weren't Tom Hanks and Meg Ryan. We were a Name and a Number. So there was no smiling or laughter, just the awkward silence. It was broken by Paula being practical: "We better get a move on. I'm starting to taste my filtermask."

I could taste mine, too—a bitterness on my tongue. Before long there would be an acrid burning at the back of my throat. It would make me cough, and the mask would fall off. The membrane is designed to dry up when it's impregnated by toxins to the point that wearing it does more harm than good. When this happens you either have to slap on a new one or, better still, get back to your haven. They're not called havens for nothing.

There was something haunted and haunting about the

bridge's empty tollbooths and, despite the stifling heat, I shivered when I stepped into the nearest one to hide the paddle.

We walked the first half of the bridge in silence. It took about fifteen minutes. I spent most of them thinking about the brief moment of understanding I'd shared with Paula, and the rest of them wondering if Paula was thinking about it, too. It might have been my imagination, but I thought the silence was awkward in the way it is when two people are thinking of a way to break it, as opposed to when they don't like each other.

And now we did have one of those moments when two people speak together. I started to ask if her filtermask was okay, just as she said, "Every footstep—"

We stopped and laughed, and for once we were laughing with each other, not at each other.

When we'd finished laughing I said, "What were you about to say?"

"Just that every footstep makes me feel like I'm stepping into the past."

"You sound excited."

"You sound surprised."

With my usual tact and habit of speaking before thinking, I said, "I didn't think you were interested in the past."

I could have bitten my tongue off as soon as the words were out, because I realized they'd destroyed whatever had been building between us. Sure enough, there was a familiar coldness in her expression and voice when she said, "Do you mean 'you' as in 'me' or as in 'us'?"

I had to think twice about that because of the phrasing—logical, but inelegant—and suddenly it was like we were speaking different languages and back to being as far apart as two people can be.

I tried to change the subject, saying, "We're more than halfway, now."

She gave me the sort of withering look she'd refrained from after my last statement of the obvious, and the silence that followed *was* the awkward kind you get when two people are angry at each other. Or when one is angry at the other, and the other is angry with himself.

Before long Paula began clicking the fingers of her right hand. It's one of the things Numbers do when they get bored and fidgety. They need to focus on something and, because they're not good at dreaming or imagining or wondering, they focus on clicking their fingers with perfect regularity. It's also something they do when they want to annoy Names. I don't know why it bothers us, but it does.

So I started whistling. I'm not sure why it annoys Numbers, but it does. Come to think of it, it annoys me. Especially when it's coming through a filtermask, because the thin membrane gives a hissing sibilance.

Paula stiffened at my whistling, and I got the feeling she'd been clicking her fingers out of boredom rather than a desire to annoy me. Whatever her motivation before, now she definitely did want to annoy me. I knew that because she began clicking the fingers of her other hand as well. Loudly.

I responded in typically mature fashion, accompanying my whistling with some percussion, courtesy of the palms of my hands and the railings of the bridge.

Paula turned and glowered at me.

I smiled sweetly and said, "I do requests."

"Here's one: go jump off the bridge."

"Whoever said Numbers don't have a sense of humor?"

"I wasn't joking."

"Has anyone ever told you how pretty you are when you're mad?"

I'd intended to be sarcastic, but once the words were spoken I realized I meant them.

I think Paula did, too, because her fingers froze in mid-click, and another one of those slightly bewildered, wholly bewildering looks passed between us.

There was a bit of all the earlier kinds of awkward silences in the one that followed, all jumbled together in a mix that made it more confusing than ever.

Luckily we were nearly at the end of the bridge. It made landfall halfway up the hillside, so there was no need for a boat. Once we stepped off, turned right and made our way down a flight of steps we were on the main street of the village. To our right the water lapped over the top of cottages once idyllically situated at the river's edge. On our left, derelict villas rose three or four deep up the hillside, their gardens choked with gorse, thornbush and cacti.

Each breath started burning my throat. I coughed, and raised a hand just in time to catch the filtermask as it fell off. After pockcting the darkened, desiccated membrane to hand in for recycling, I put on a new one. Paula did likewise, then we set off along the street. Once my fresh filtermask softened enough to let me talk, I said, "The library's only a couple of hundred meters along the road."

Paula didn't give any indication she'd heard.

"Sulky bitch," I mumbled.

She turned to me in disbelief and said, "What was that?"

"I said, the library's only a couple of hundred meters along the road."

She gave me a look that almost had me reaching for my knockdown to protect myself.

I gave her another of my innocent, winning, boyish smiles. Well, it wasn't innocent or boyish, so I suppose it wasn't winning either. Which explained why Paula's look got more withering.

Since the smile didn't work, I tried something else. "Pick a house," I said.

"What?"

"We've time for a quick look around a house, as well as the library. So, pick a house."

I expected her to argue and be all focused and businesslike, so it was a surprise when she said, "Okay." She looked past me and her gaze settled on a house about a hundred meters away. “That one,” she said. And then she surprised me again, this time by saying, “It’s straight out of a Jane Austen story.”

I must have looked at Paula for longer than I realized, because she turned from the house to me and said, “What?” the way you do when you’re suddenly aware someone’s studying you.

“Nothing,” I said, and headed toward the villa, doubting if anything in it could surprise me more than Paula had.

CHAPTER 11

0100001101001000010000010101000001010100010001010101010010

March of the Penguins

"It's enormous," Paula said as she looked around the living room of the old villa. "How could people be so wasteful of space?"

"Look at the beautiful cornicing," I said, admiring the intricately carved moldings around the join between walls and ceiling. I shot a quick glance at Paula to see what she made of it. She was grimacing. "Don't you like it?" I asked.

"I can't look at it without thinking how unnecessary it is." She looked around the room, pulling another face as she took in the fireplace with its rosebud-pattern tiles, and the line-up of porcelain figurines on the mantelpiece. "I find all the clutter so distracting and unsettling," she told me. "It really jars on my nerves."

"Can't you appreciate the craftsmanship? Can't you appreciate these things for their beauty?"

"Beauty comes from functionality and simplicity, Travis," she said. It was like she was giving me a lecture, and talking about an absolute rather than something in the eye of the beholder.

As we moved through the house I spent more time studying Paula than my surroundings. I had the feeling she was looking around with detached, scientific curiosity. The notion was confirmed when we got to the kitchen. Whereas she'd barely given the beautiful ornaments and paintings of the living room a second glance, she picked up every culinary gadget she came across, no doubt more interested in determining what they'd been used for than thinking about the people who'd once used them.

After working her way through the gadgets, Paula headed for the next room. She hesitated in the doorway, and I peered past her to find out what she was looking at. All I saw was a room with a big table and half a dozen bow-legged chairs.

Then I realized what had drawn my partner up: the heavily patterned wallpaper.

"You can't imagine living here, then?" I said. I'd meant it as in, 'It's not the sort of place you'd like to live in?'

But there was such an air of bewilderment about Paula when she sighed and shook her head I had the impression she'd taken my question literally. Her next words, and the sadness in her voice, confirmed it: "I can't hear any of those voices you talked about, Travis. I can't even hear the echo of old footsteps. I can't relate to the people who once lived here. It's not only that they're total strangers. . . It's not just like I've stepped back in time. . . It's like I'm on another planet."

Listening to her, watching her, I wanted to put my arm around her.

As we moved through the rest of the house I searched desperately for something that might fire her imagination. Instead, I found only things that intrigued me, like how there were big electrical fans in every room, and moth-eaten mosquito nets draped over the beds.

And then, lying on an antique desk in one of the bedrooms, I found a diary. I tried not to get too excited as I picked it up. As often as not when you come across a diary the pages are blank or the entries get shorter by the day and stop altogether after the first couple of weeks. But a quick riffle through this one revealed page after page of flowing script. I picked an entry at random; it's a thrilling way to form a first impression, to let a person from the past introduce their personality and their world. The page was headed *FEBRUARY 21, 2025*, which tied in with the mosquito nets and electrical fans. Things really were heating up by then.

Before I could read the entry below the date, Paula's voice stopped me: "We better get a move on, Travis." She sounded bored, as well as concerned about running out of filtermasks.

Reluctantly I closed the diary and put it in the hip pocket of my dark blue coveralls.

I was about to join Paula in the hallway when I noticed a collection of movie discs in a cabinet below the bedroom video screen. I love old films, so I couldn't resist a quick glance to see if there were any worth adding to my collection. None of the first few titles stood out. But then I came to one that stopped my heart beating. The breath caught in my throat, and the room started spinning.

"Travis!" Impatience replaced the boredom and anxiety in Paula's voice, but I didn't care.

I swallowed back the lump that had formed in my throat, and bent down to reach out for the movie. My legs were so unsteady I had to kneel on the floor. I didn't realize a tear had rolled down my cheek until it splashed on the cover of the DVD. And I didn't realize Paula had been standing in the doorway watching me. Not until she said, "Travis?" in a voice full of bewilderment and concern.

"Travis?" she said again. "What is it?"

I'd never heard such puzzlement in her voice before. But then she'd never seen me like this before.

Paula knelt down beside me and looked at the cover of the DVD. The words on it said *March of the Penguins*, and the picture below the words showed an emperor penguin looking down at its newly hatched chick.

"What's wrong?" Paula asked.

"You wouldn't understand," I said, and put the film back. Embarrassed that Paula had seen me this way, I got up and hurried past her. I walked quickly out of the room and then out of the house and along the street toward the library.

I heard Paula calling out behind me: "Travis, I think there's a storm on the way! We should turn back!"

I knew she was right. The sky had darkened and lowered while we'd been in the house, and something in the air made the hair on the back of my neck stand on end. But I didn't even look around to see if Paula was following me, let alone turn and head back for the bridge. I kept going toward the library, wanting to get away from Paula and the penguins. . . Wanting to forget my past, and at the same time to remember it. A few fat raindrops splashed around me, and instinctively I pulled up the hood of my coverall. The rain's not as acidic as it used to be, but it's still toxic enough to cause some major irritation if it comes in contact with your skin. I saw the library up ahead—housed in an old school that became surplus to requirements when the fertility rate went into freefall—and made a run for it as the heavens opened.

I had a head start on Paula, but she was right on my heels by the time I reached the library. No sooner had the door closed behind me than it swung open again as she hurried out of the rain, which was bouncing off the pavement.

We pulled down our hoods and shook ourselves dry. Then we stood there looking at each other, with the rain hammering down on the roof and splashing into puddles around us where slates had been torn away by the countless superstorms of the last half century.

Paula spoke first. "What was all that about?" she asked.

"You wouldn't understand," I told her.

"Don't be so patronizing," she said with a hurt and anger that took me by surprise. I'd never seen her show so much emotion. And then her voice cracked as if something was breaking inside her, and she said, "How do you know what I'm capable of understanding?" In little more than a whisper she added, "How could you possibly know, when I don't even know myself?"

And now I did put my arm around her.

She was supposed to rest her head on my shoulder and sob quietly while I stroked her hair and reassured her with words and my sheer physical presence that everything was going to be okay. But, instead, she threw my arm off angrily. A flash of lightning lit up the world outside, as if the elements were perfectly in tune with her emotions—although, if they had been, I suspect the lightning bolt would have struck yours truly and left a pile of smoking ash in my place.

"You treat us like we're robots, like we have no feelings," Paula said.

"That's how you act."

"Has it never occurred to you at least some of that, for

at least some of us, is *just* an act?"

It hadn't occurred to me. Not once in all my dealings with Numbers. But then, I was starting to realize Paula wasn't like other Numbers. It dawned on me the differences must have something to do with her emotional flaw, and her next words bore that out: "Has it never occurred to you that we're not all alike, however much we look it? That some of us feel things the others don't, maybe things like you sometimes feel?"

Speechless, all I could do was shake my head.

Paula turned and walked away, disappearing behind the nearest stack of shelves.

When I rounded the corner she wasn't scanning the books, she was leaning against them, face resting on her forearms, shoulders shaking ever so slightly. Just as a storm was breaking outside the library, so a storm was breaking inside my partner. A quiet storm that had been building for a lot longer than the one outside. My heart went out to her even though I didn't understand what was going on inside her. I put my arm around her. She still didn't put her head on my shoulders and her arms around me. She didn't even turn to look at me. But she didn't pull away. I held her until her shoulders were no longer shaking. And then I whispered, "Let me tell you about the penguins."

I led her over to the table and sat down opposite her. While the rain thundered down above us and the lightning flashed, I began to tell her why the sight of the adult penguin gazing down at its chick had sent a tear rolling down my face. "It was Jen's favorite film," I said.

She ignored that, obviously wanting to show she was still mad at me. But curiosity soon got the better of her. Looking more like a little girl than the ice maiden I was used to, she wiped her killer cheekbones dry with the back of her hands and said, "Who was Jen?"

"My wife," I said. "God, how I miss her," I added, the words coming out before I knew I was going to say them. "She loved animals, spent a year working in a nature reserve."

"Why would someone risk their health like that?"

"It's the only chance to experience what the world was once like, albeit a far less wonderful version of it," I told her. "Anyway, she started getting so breathless that she had to give it up. She got a job caring for the animals in the genetic breeding program, but—" I thought I'd stopped myself in time.

However, Paula correctly guessed what I'd left unsaid: "The genetically engineered specimens were a pale imitation of 'real' animals. They didn't have the same spirit and unpredictability. They didn't have the same passion, and Jen couldn't love them the way she'd loved the wild animals," she said bitterly.

"Paula. . ."

"It doesn't matter," she said. But her voice and the look in her eyes told me it did matter. It mattered a whole lot more to her than I would have believed before we crossed the bridge.

Trying to change tack, I said, "Jen felt horrible at seeing the animals confined, although she knew it was in their best interests given the state of the planet. And she felt ashamed and guilty at the knowledge that their plight and the planet's was caused by the selfishness and greed of our forefathers."

"So where do the penguins come in?" Paula asked. "Is it to do with the fact they were among the animals worst hit by climate change?"

"They did come to symbolize the plight of the animal kingdom, but to Paula and me—" I stopped when I saw the look on her face.

"You said, to 'Paula' and me."

"I'm sorry, I meant Jen and me." If I'd had any doubt over how I felt about the woman sitting across from me, that Freudian slip told me everything I needed to know.

"What did penguins mean to Jen and you?" Paula asked, as if what I was saying was more than a way of passing time while a storm broke.

"I met Jen on a treasure-hunting trip, in a house like the one you and I were in a few minutes ago. I was looking for cameras—"

Paula rolled her eyes and said, "Travis, you can't even take pictures with them."

"I know, it's just. . ." But I couldn't explain it.

A few days earlier—a few hours earlier—Paula would

have let me flounder and sneered while I did so. But now she said, "What was Jen looking for?"

"Wildlife books. We all have our holy grail, an object we long to come across on those treasure-hunting trips, something that means far more to us than it should. For Jen it was the book *March of the Penguins.* She found it in that house, and that's where I found her. The moment I set eyes on her I. . ." My voice died away as I recalled the first time I'd seen Jen. My heart stopped just from the memory of that moment, from the memory of her.

This time Paula didn't prompt me. She gave me as much time as I needed to come back out of the past and rejoin her in the library. I suspect it was longer than I realized. "I walked back to the community with Jen and we found laughter came easily, and words, too," I told Paula when I was ready to go on. "The only word that didn't come easily was 'goodbye.' We made it easier to say by arranging to say hello again the next day. And at the end of that next day, it was even harder to say goodbye. I always hated saying goodbye to her, and when I saw her again each evening it was like seeing her for the first time. Every time she smiled at me it stopped my heart," I said. And then I remembered who I was talking to, and said, "That must sound laughable."

But Paula wasn't laughing. She was looking at me like she'd never really seen me before, like she hadn't really known me until now.

So I kept on talking. "*March of the Penguins* was her favorite movie, and it was what we watched on our first date. She used up two days' food rations in the Community Store to buy us some treats, and we had a movie night in her apartment."

"That sounds so romantic," Paula said, and the longing in her voice was a revelation. It was then I began to suspect what her emotional flaw was: a belief in the most illogical thing of all—love.

"Ever seen it?" I asked.

Paula looked confused, as if she didn't follow. I'd hardly ever seen that look on the face of a Number. The few times I had, I'd given them a taste of their own medicine by sneering at them and trying to make them feel stupid. It never occurred to me to do that to Paula now. Instead, I said, "*March of the Penguins*—it's the most incredible movie. Have you ever seen it?"

Paula shook her head.

"It's about what the emperor penguins went through to bring their young into the world. It's truly humbling. I know they were hard-wired by evolution; they were acting purely out of instinct, and there's a danger of anthropomorphizing their motives. But there's this one scene that shows a father penguin who's gone without food for weeks to incubate an egg. He's balancing the egg on his feet and is hardly able to move because if it rolls onto the ground it freezes in seconds. Anyway, the egg finally hatches, and when the father looks down and sees this tiny face emerging—when he sees his chick for the first time—no one will convince me he isn't feeling something every bit as profound and moving as what we call love."

Paula should have sniggered or sneered. She should have been sarcastic, or at least asked me to get to the point. But she surprised me again, saying, "It's moving just listening to you talk about it. I can see why the film means so much to you."

"No, you can't," I said.

Paula looked as though I'd slapped her, and I realized that although we were getting to know each other in ways which hadn't seemed possible before, there was still a profound difference between us and misunderstanding was never far away. "There's a bit more to it than that," I said quickly.

She looked relieved her capacity to feel wasn't being called into question.

"Jen had spent so long Outside that her immune system was seriously weakened. I could see it in her breathlessness, the way she got tired quickly, caught all the viruses that were doing the rounds of the haven and took an alarmingly long time to recover from them. I didn't know how seriously weakened she was, though. Not until she told me that having a child was even harder for her than it was for other women, because in the unlikely event I was fertile enough to do my bit, her damaged immune system meant she'd grow weaker each day the child inside her grew stronger.

"I told her not to worry about children; I wouldn't feel I'd missed out on anything if I was sharing life with her. . ." My voice choked and I found it hard to go on.

Using maternal instinct, or feminine intuition, or something else I'd never dreamed she possessed, Paula was able to say the words for me: "But Jen was feeling the same thing as the penguins."

I nodded.

I looked out of the window, not knowing how much of the misting was on the glass and how much was in my eyes. "She didn't make it past her second trimester," I said. "I should never have let her try. I feel like I'm to blame for—"

My words were interrupted by the scraping of a chair. The next thing I knew Paula was sitting next to me and her arm was around me and my head was on her shoulder.

That wasn't the way it was supposed to happen.

That wasn't the way it was supposed to happen at all.

CHAPTER 12

01000011010010000100000101010000010101000100010101010010

Phantom Pregnancy

I SEARCHED PAULA'S EYES FOR ANY SIGN OF MOCKERY as we moved apart, but found none. I'd never opened up to anyone like that. I hadn't thought I ever would. Especially not to a Number. Especially not to Paula. What she did next surprised me as much as what I'd done; she gave my hand a gentle, reassuring squeeze. In a strange way, it was harder to deal with than mockery.

Then Paula pushed her chair back and walked over to the window. The rain was hammering off the glass hard enough to break it if it hadn't been broken already. Paula watched the rain coming down, and I watched Paula.

"If it doesn't let up soon we'll have to make a run for it," she said.

I prayed for the rain to go off, because trying to keep up with Paula on a six-kilometer run would be almost as embarrassing for me as the way I'd just opened up to her. Fit as I am, I'm no match for a Number over that distance. I moved my chair back, meaning to join her at the window to see if there was any sign the storm was passing, but something jagged the back of my thigh and jogged my memory.

The diary.

I took it out, opened the cover, and fell headlong into another world. It was a world on the brink of collapse, a society on the point of imploding.

The first page read:

DECEMBER 26, 2024

I've never had the slightest urge to keep a diary, but Mike looked so happy when he gave me this I know I should at least make an effort to fill its pages. Besides, there's so much going on that's worth writing down. Not in my life, but in the world around me.

Take the other day, for example; there was a bit on the news about how it's the first time no one in Britain has placed a bet on there being a White Christmas.

As for Christmas itself, it was as melancholy a day for Mike as it was for me. He tries to hide it, but I know he feels it as much as I do. There are little give-aways, like his face when he hears the neighbors' kids screaming with delight as they open their presents. It's like a knife in the heart for Mike when he hears those sounds, and for me when I look at him as he listens to them. Our house is filled with love, but it's not filled with laughter and fun. This Christmas I think we both came to accept it never will be, that all the books of scientific advice for how to improve your chances of conception, all the following of old wives' tales and all the money spent on IVF has been for nothing. Mike was quieter than usual, and I'm sure that was why.

All day I had the feeling there was something he wanted to say. Sure enough, after a Christmas dinner of forced smiles and hollow laughter and more than a few drinks, he said he'd understand if I wanted to go to a sperm bank. There's as big a run on that kind of bank as there was on the other kind during the Wall Street crash ten years back—it seems more men than not have a critically low sperm count these days, so it's a classic case of demand increasing as supply declines, and price escalating as a result. It would mean remortgaging the house, but that isn't why I don't want to do it; I don't just want a baby, I want his baby. I didn't tell him that. I didn't have to. I just thanked him and shook my head, and he knew. And then, on the rug in front of the fireplace, we. . .

Well, that's not for a diary, even one that probably no one will ever read. Let's just say it was pretty special because there was a massive storm outside while we were. . . Anyway, the wind was so strong I thought it was going to tear off the new storm shutters Mike fitted after the last time the glass blew in. At one point there was a flash of lightning and a crack of thunder directly overhead and the whole house shook. The timing couldn't have been more perfect, because it happened right as we. . .

Well, we laughed and laughed. And then suddenly we weren't laughing any more and I knew that, for all the talks we have when we console each other with the notion our lack of luck is for the best because of the way the world is going, we both hoped with all our hearts the thunder and lightning might be some sort of sign—

I was about to turn to the next page when I was aware Paula had joined me at the table. Like me, she was caught up in those elegantly written words on the yellowed paper. Numbers read the printed word much more quickly than Names do, but they struggle with handwriting, so I asked, "I'm not going too fast for you, am I?"

She shook her head distractedly, reading the last few lines. A tear formed in the corner of her eye and rolled down her cheek. I brushed it away gently with the back of a finger, and when she looked at me I smiled.

She seemed bewildered by my expression, so I explained it to her: "You're beginning to imagine, Paula, and to wonder."

And then she smiled, like a little girl, and did something I'd never seen a Number do. She blushed.

I think we both felt we were getting closer in more than a physical sense, and knew that whatever was happening between us was a fragile thing that might shatter if we tried to express it in words, or if we even looked at each other. So, instead, we looked at the yellowed pages of the diary and let someone else's words bring us together; a stranger who'd probably died before we were born.

DECEMBER 27

We ended up spending most of the day in bed. I'd like to say it was a purely romantic thing, but there was more to it than that—another power cut because of the storm. It was still windy outside, and too dark inside to read without straining your eyes, so there wasn't much to do except. . . Well, you know.

At first it was all very cozy—spending the day in bed, eating by candlelight. But it's the sort of thing that grows old quite quickly, and you can't help wishing you could flick a switch and the lights and videoscreen and computer would come on and you'd get your life back. It's all a bit spooky. I mean, you only used to get storms like this once every five or ten years, but now it seems there's never more than a few weeks between them.

We agreed to limit ourselves to one candle because they're getting so hard to come by. I'm writing by its flickering flame, watching the wax melt. There's not much left, so I better stop now.

Paula coughed beside me, and at the same time a catch at the back of my throat told me my own filtermask was spent. I spat it out in my hand and put on another one while Paula did the same. She got up to check on the weather. My filter had softened enough to let me speak by the time she came back. "Any sign of it clearing?" I asked.

She shook her head. She didn't look all that sorry, even though we were in danger of using up our filtermasks before we got back to the community.

The next few entries in the diary dealt with mundane

things—friends coming over to dinner, a New Year party—so I flicked through the pages until something caught my attention. It was under the date *JANUARY 15:*

Mike came home late again and in a truly foul mood. He'd forgotten his phone, so I'd no way of contacting him to find out what had happened. I have to confess I was torn between being worried and wondering if he's seeing someone else.

When he finally arrived I felt ashamed of myself for thinking that, because there was no faking his temper and frustration. It turned out he'd been running short of petrol and, knowing what the queues are like, he'd been putting off going for more. But by tonight he couldn't put it off any longer. He waited for over an hour in the queue and then, when he was within three cars of the pump, the station ran out.

I've got to admit he was in such a bad mood he was getting on my nerves, going on about how the US should have known after what happened in the wake of the Second Gulf War that starting a third one wasn't the way to end to all the petrol price rises and shortages. He's got a point, but I suppose nobody could have guessed just how catastrophic the backlash from the war would be. They're calling it the 'Hydrocarbon Holocaust,' and some scientists are saying it's at least partly to blame for the way the weather's going nuts. One expert said it was the straw that broke the camel's back, which I suppose was appropriate given the Middle Eastern connection.

I flicked through some more pages, stopping at *FEBRUARY 7*:

It's official: going outside is bad for your health. At last a government minister admitted that the mix of car exhaust fumes and the fallout from all the environmental terrorism in the Middle East has made the air dangerous to breathe. He said there was no cause to panic, because it only slightly increases your chance of illness. But the moment he said there was no need to panic, I knew we were in trouble. Lots of other people must feel like me, because after the government minister they interviewed a professor who predicted there would be a run on facemasks and those new domestic air-conditioning units that are supposed to purify the air as well as regulate its temperature.

This is a horribly selfish thing to say given the global nature of the problems, but I'm worried about my job in the camping shop. I mean, who wants to buy tents and hiking gear after hearing stuff like that?

FEBRUARY 11

Dear Diary, I'M PREGNANT!!!! I'll write more tomorrow, once it's sunk in. For now, I still can't believe it. I'm shaking, I'm laughing, I'm crying. I keep on picking up the phone to call Mike, and then putting it down again because I want to actually see his face when I give him the news. I never believed in God or magic or fate or anything until now, but I keep thinking it was Christmas night, and that the lightning had something to do with it.

FEBRUARY 12

I had it all planned: I was going to keep calm, let Mike get in and take off his jacket and shoes, then give him a welcome-home hug as usual and whisper the good news in his ear. But the instant he opened the door he knew something was going on (I suspect the fact I was standing at the far end of the hall, like I'd been waiting there for the last hour for him to appear, had something to do with it). He took one look at me and said, "What's wrong?" and there was so much concern on his face and so much excitement inside me that I just shouted at the top of my voice: "I'M PREGNANT!"

I've never seen ANYONE, let alone Mike, look so stunned.

And I've never seen anyone look so happy as he did in the moments that followed. I didn't have to walk down the hall to hug him because he ran down the hall to hug me. He hugged me so hard it hurt. And then he drew back in alarm. I knew it was the start of him wrapping me up in tissue paper and that it'll soon get wearing, but I don't mind. I don't mind at all.

There was a wistful sigh of the kind I'm used to hearing, but for once it didn't come from me. It came from Paula. I was more sure than ever that her emotional flaw was related to love in some way, and began to suspect it came bundled with a maternal instinct. Watching her, I got the impression she was seeing more than words on the pages of a diary. She was seeing a man and a woman, maybe even imagining what it was like to be the woman. It was only then I understood how big a cross her emotional flaw must be to bear. She'd feel apart from her fellow Numbers, aware she was profoundly different from them in some way—and yet she'd also feel apart from people like me, bewildered by our lack of logic, by our ability to dream and to feel a sense of wonder. I understood why she'd built a shell around herself and tried to be the archetypal ice maiden. And I understood why it would be almost impossible to keep the act up all the time, why she could maybe manage in public, but not in private as well. The need to love and be loved isn't superficial, is it? It defines your soul, which might be why Numbers appear so soulless.

Then again, I might have been reading too much into a single sigh.

I turned some more pages. The next couple of dozen entries described the hopes, fears and indulgences of any expectant mother at the start of her pregnancy. I turned those pages quickly, because so many of the words on them echoed things Jen had said. Each time I broke off from the pages to steal a look at Paula I saw things in her eyes that looked like what I felt in my heart when the pregnant woman's words chimed with Jen's.

The next entry I stopped at was for *MARCH 7:*

I was right about my job. The boss said he has to let me go. I can't say I'm surprised. Between the winter storms and summer heat, air that's not good to breathe and water that's not safe to drink, who wants to go camping any more? Since the outdoors is increasingly being seen as something to be endured rather than enjoyed, he's going to go in for a new line of products altogether: face masks and protective rainwear, things like that. He needs to cut his overheads to a minimum and, since I was last in, I can't bitch about being first out.

The timing sucks, though. I suppose you need all your money at the best of times when you're expecting, and these are far from the best of times. Prices are going through the roof. Take food; they say there's less of it because of the bad weather, and it costs more to transport because of the fuel crisis. Mike said not to worry about money, but I can see he's *worried.*

The following entries were reviews of movies and books, a petty argument and a passionate kiss and make up. And then:

MARCH 9

It was the Scottish Parliament elections yesterday, and Mike and I stayed up late to watch the results come in. It was quite chilling. The biggest gainers were the Greens, which was good, but Scotland First was close behind, standing on a platform of pulling out of Europe and closing off the border with England. Mike hit the nail on the head when he said what was so loathsome about them: they appeal to our fears and bring out the worst in us, rather than inspiring us to be our best—and I've a feeling that in the years to come people will have to be at their best. I worry about things like that in a way I never used to. I worry about what sort of world the life growing inside me is going to be living in.

MARCH 27

Something horrible happened at the supermarket today. I slept longer than I meant to—it's getting uncomfortably hot already, although it isn't even April yet, and I lay awake until dawn and then slept until way past noon. Anyway, by the time I got to the supermarket the shelves were almost cleared. My bump is plain for all to see, but still somebody pushed me out of the way to get to the bread counter because there were only a few loaves left. I watched those loaves disappear in front of my eyes. One person took the last three, and the person who'd pushed me aside started arguing with them, saying it wasn't right that someone should take three loaves. Voices were raised and it came to blows, and by the time the security guards arrived to split them up they were fighting like animals, screaming and scratching and tearing at each other. The worst of it was, they were respectably dressed middle-aged women. What's happening to people? Is this what the future holds? Will we all have to get like that in order to survive?

APRIL 2

It's time for my three-month check-up. I'm keeping everything crossed, not just my fingers. I've not told Mike about the check-up, because he'll worry. As for myself, I'm not the worrying type. But this is different. Usually I find it easy to be optimistic, but this is too important, and I don't want to tempt fate.

"I'm getting a bad feeling for her," I said, without knowing quite why.

Paula nodded, as if she understood exactly what I meant.

I turned to the next page. *APRIL 3* was blank, and so was *APRIL 4*.

I turned to *APRIL 5*. The handwriting was noticeably less neat. It said:

I've been too upset to write anything for the last couple of days. After the doctor gave me the news, I phoned Mike at work. When he answered I wasn't able to speak. I burst into floods of tears. I think he must have guessed what was wrong before I got myself together enough to be able to tell him. He's trying to be strong for both of us, but I know that inside he's as broken up as me.

I can't believe God could be so cruel.

"She lost the baby," Paula guessed, her voice little more than a whisper.

The next few pages were blank. Then, under *APRIL 8*, there was more writing:

We're going to see the doctor together. He said the sooner the better. I wouldn't have believed any decision could be so hard. Mike and I sat and talked about it until the early hours. We talked about the sort of life such a badly deformed child would have, and if we'd been talking about someone else's child it would be obvious that it wouldn't have much of a life at all. But when it's your child you ask yourself: Would it be better than no life at all? We talked around some things that are hard to say, hard even to write in a diary no one will ever read. And in the end we were more confused than we'd been in the beginning. We fell asleep on the sofa in each other's arms, which should have been romantic, but instead just left us stiff and weary come morning.

APRIL 9

Despite all the talking, in the end we asked the doctor what we should do. I don't mean we asked him to advise us; I mean we asked him to decide for us. We wanted him to play God, but he refused. Mike turned to me and said he'd go along with whatever I wanted.

I'd like to think he was trying to be considerate, but I can't help feeling he was doing to me what the two of us had tried to do to the doctor—and I know I'll never feel quite the same about him again because of it.

Jesus, as if I didn't lose enough today.

More empty pages.

APRIL 16

I thought I was feeling about as low as I could get, then today. . . I'd had these horribly itchy spots for about a week. I'd assumed they were mosquito bites, but then this morning when I got up I went to scratch one of them on my back and felt something like a scab. It fell off onto my finger, and when I brought my hand back in front of me there was this disgusting thing that must be a bed bug. I feel sick just thinking about it. I know it's not my fault—with the water shortages there's no way to change the sheets more than once a fortnight, and in this heat you want to change them every day. Still, it makes me feel like a slatternly housewife, and indescribably loathsome. I'm too ashamed to tell Mike. We used to tell each other everything. Now we hardly speak at all, except to argue.

I tried consoling myself with the thought that this is no world to be bringing a child into. But then I considered all the other mothers with children, and that thought was no consolation at all.

I flicked through the rest of the diary but the pages were empty.

We just sat there, as if under a spell. I broke it by coughing as the bitterness of a tainted filter hit the back of my throat.

"We better get going," I said.

It was no longer raining. We should have left whenever the downpour eased off—we were cutting it fine with our filters—but neither of us had noticed the storm passing.

"Aren't you forgetting something?" Paula asked as I headed for the door.

I looked at her, puzzled.

"What we came for, Ben."

It was the first time she'd used my given name. I was taken aback, so Paula had to provide the answer to her rhetorical question: "*Lichens and Mosses of the World.*"

She laughed at my forgetfulness, but there was nothing unkind about it.

We found the book quickly, and set off for the bridge.

Our filters were too tainted to wear by the time we got there, so we stopped to change them. As I was spitting the old one into my hand, I heard Paula say, "Damn!"

She'd dropped her fresh filtermask in a puddle. The filthy water must have been as toxic as it looked because the tissue disintegrated in front of our eyes, as if steeped in a bath of pure acid.

Taking out my last filtermask, I put it in the palm of my hand—and then, before Paula realized what I was about to do, I put my hand over her mouth and held it there long enough for the protective membrane to soften and become as much a part of my partner's face as her skin.

"Ben," she said, when I took my hand away.

"It's okay," I told her.

"But. . ."

"It's my fault you're out here in the first place," I said.

But we both knew there was more than that behind what I'd just done.

CHAPTER 13

01000011010010000100000101010000010101000100010101010010

THE ECOSYSTEM

WHEN PAULA AND I GOT BACK TO THE COMMUNITY we said a long goodbye of the kind that has few words but plenty meaningful looks—though I wasn't sure exactly what the looks meant, and I'm willing to bet she wasn't, either.

Saying goodbye to Paula meant all I took to bed was *Lichens and Mosses of the World.* The first thing I noticed when I opened the book was a musty smell that made me think conditions between its pages were ideal for the propagation of its subject matter.

I read every word on the first page but didn't get any clues, and didn't even get interested in lichens and mosses.

The prospect of reading another couple of hundred pages wasn't a particularly pleasant one, so I flicked through them and looked at the photos, hoping something besides a musty smell would leap out at me. It wouldn't have been quite so bad if the book was about plants that at least had leaves and flowers, but *lichens and mosses*? One picture looked pretty much like the next, and the captions underneath were mostly in Latin and meant even less to me than the photos.

The text itself might as well have been in Latin, I realized as I ploughed through the turgid prose. I had to read every second paragraph at least twice because my thoughts kept drifting off on a tangent. Occasionally the tangents took me to Doug MacDougall's flat and his daughter's classroom, but more often they took me to the Newport library.

After dozing off half a dozen times, waking with a start when the book fell out of my hands and clobbered me, I finally fell into a proper sleep on page 132.

I woke up at five in the morning after a dream like something from *Day of the Triffids*, with me as Howard Keel, and a heroine who kept changing. One moment she had Paula's face and Annie MacDougall's body, and the next moment it was the other way around. I don't know which version was most disconcerting. Then I remembered Jen had turned up in my dream, too. At least her head did. The rest of her was a penguin, and she was waddling over the bridge.

I was glad to get back to the book, which shows how messed up my dream was. Forcing myself to go back a dozen pages, because I'd been so sleepy when I read them I could have missed something of importance, I went from page 120 right through to the finish. For the sake of thoroughness, I even scanned the index.

When I put the book down at 6.30 a.m. I was no further forward than when I'd picked it up eight hours earlier. I knew a little more about lichens and mosses than I'd ever expected to, but I still knew a whole lot less about what lay behind the death of Doug MacDougall than I wanted to. I shouldn't have been disappointed, because there was no certainty that what he'd read had anything to do with why he was killed. Even if it did, there was no guarantee he'd read it in *Lichens and Mosses of the World.*

But alongside my disappointment was a frustration which spoke volumes, and what it said was that deep down, in the place where intuition and experience give birth to hunches that are right more often than not, I still believed I was holding the key to a murder mystery in my hands, rather than a boring book on plants.

The thought of re-reading that book in an attempt to spot something I'd been too weary to notice first time around wasn't as appealing as the thought of getting Paula to pore over its pages and see if she spotted anything that had eluded me. Even more appealing than either of those thoughts was the thought of Paula. Since it was too early to get up for work, I lay there thinking about her and going over the events of the previous day. They would have seemed like figments of my overworked imagination if it hadn't been for the tattered book lying on the bed beside me, tangible evidence I'd actually visited the library on the other side of the river. I replayed every expression I'd seen in Paula's eyes, every word that betrayed an emotion I'd never believed she possessed. . .

And I wondered what it would be like when we met up in the station house an hour from now. Part of me couldn't wait to see her again; part of me was scared of what would happen when I did. I envisaged three likely scenarios: she'd pretend the previous day never happened, and we'd go back to the way we'd been before; she'd overcompensate for having opened up to me, and act even colder than usual; or we'd pick up where we left off the previous evening, when we'd exchanged smiles in the airlock of Haven Nine. The smiles had given way to a heart-stopping moment when each of us briefly considered kissing the other. Then we'd laughed at our embarrassment, and after the laughter died away she'd said, "Thanks, Ben."

"What for?" I'd asked.

"For giving me your last filter. . . And for a day like no other."

Then came our long goodbye, the one that was short on words but big on meaningful looks.

And now it was a new day. I was hoping it would be like yesterday, but feared it might be more like all the other days.

The moment I walked into the station house, I knew my fears had been a whole lot closer to the mark than my hopes. I gave Paula a smile like the one I'd given her the night before, and in return got nothing more than a curt nod of acknowledgement. Maybe she was worried about compromising our professional relationship, or maybe she was scared of getting hurt on a more personal level. Wanting to reassure her on both counts, I said, "Paula, about yesterday—"

She cut me off in mid-sentence—the way Numbers infuriatingly do when they're not interested in what you have to say—by asking, "Any progress?" She pointed to the copy of *Lichens and Mosses of the World* I carried under my arm.

I shook my head. Fixing her with my most deeply meaningful look, I said, "I suppose it was a long shot, and I feel a bit silly for thinking anything might have come of it." I was talking about more than the book, and I'm sure she knew it. I waited for some sign: a softening of her expression, if not a reassuring word or two. But she went back to studying her screen as if she hadn't heard.

"Do you want to let things drop?" I asked. Again I was talking about more than the MacDougall case.

Paula hesitated. I like to think the pause reflected some inner conflict between head and heart, but maybe that was wishful thinking.

"That might be for the best," she said. "I don't think it

was going anywhere."

Now I knew *she* was talking about more than the MacDougall case—and that she lacked conviction, because she didn't look me in the eye when she spoke. It was as if she was afraid I'd see something in her expression that belied her words.

"I think it'd be a shame not to find out and always to be left wondering," I said. "I think that'd be worse than trying and failing."

Still not looking at me, Paula said, "Why don't you do some door-to-door inquiries, and check out MacDougall's shop?"

And now I could tell she *was* just talking about the case, and she'd chosen her words with the intention of getting me out of the station house because it was too awkward sharing it with me after what had happened yesterday.

Somewhere between the station house and The Plant Place I came up with a third possible explanation for Paula's brush-off. It might not have anything to do with fear of compromising our professional relationship or getting hurt on a personal level; now the storm had broken and she was back in the clinically controlled environs of the community, maybe cold logic had taken over and led her to conclude Names were indeed too flawed to be worth getting close to, just like conventional Numbered wisdom said. Maybe now that the shock of seeing the remains of the old world first-hand had worn off, the fact that it was people like me who'd ruined it had hit home.

Or maybe the very thing that initially drew her to me—the depth of my feelings for Jen—had in the end convinced her that love was another name for desperate, pathetic need, and it was doomed in the same way as the old world. Maybe for those reasons, and others, the contempt she felt as a Number was so strong it was bound to overpower the emotional flaw that had let her relate to me for a little while as a Name—and led her to conclude that love was something to deny herself at all costs.

The choking tightness in my chest and emptiness in the pit of my stomach at the prospect of losing Paula almost as soon as I'd found her suggested she had a point. . .

And then I thought about all the great times I'd had with Jen, and was ashamed of myself for doubting love was real and mattered and meant something; that it was worth more than everything else in the world put together. It wasn't the ability to love that doomed a person, I realized—it was losing that ability.

And suddenly I knew I wasn't ready to give up on Paula, any more than I was ready to forget about Jen.

Or to give up on solving the riddle of Doug MacDougall. Suddenly I wanted more than ever to show Paula my instincts and hunches and all the other things that prevented me from seeing the world in black and white and interpreting what I saw with cold logic were traits to be admired, not viewed with a mix of pity and contempt. I wanted to show her logic alone wasn't enough, that there were questions it couldn't answer, mysteries it couldn't unlock.

Okay, I admit it: I also wanted to show her what a clever boy I was. I wanted to impress the pants off her, and the best way of doing it was by solving a puzzle that had defied her logic, because that's the one language Numbers understand above all others.

Showing Paula that simple logic could lead you to the wrong conclusions about a death might encourage her to make a leap of faith and accept that it could lead you to the wrong conclusions about life, and about love.

The shopkeepers on either side of The Plant Place weren't any help. They did their best, which told me their affection for Doug was genuine, but they were obviously as baffled as me by his death.

I got back to the station house an hour before lunchtime. I could tell it had been a slow morning because Paula had managed to get halfway through *Lichens and Mosses of the World*.

"Spot anything that would have changed the way Doug MacDougall viewed the world?" I asked. I hadn't meant it as a point-scoring challenge, but Paula took it as one and snottily answered me with, "Find out anything that would explain who killed him, and why?"

I shook my head and said, "Mind if I take the book over to Annie MacDougall? I'd like to see if it means any more to her than it does to us."

Paula handed me the yellowed old volume without saying a word. I'd meant to wait until my lunch break to take it to Annie, but the atmosphere in the station house was so awkward I decided to head down to the classroom now; I'd rather spend the next half hour listening to Annie MacDougall's lecture than Perfect Paula's deafening silence.

I paused outside the door of Annie's classroom, stopped in my tracks by the arresting image on the wallscreen behind her. It was newsreel footage from the last of the Old Days, and showed a crowd throwing petrol bombs at a church. A minister came running out to stop them, but they hurled abuse at him.

And then someone in the crowd threw a petrol bomb at him.

Annie's students were so taken up with the horrific footage I doubt if any of them noticed me entering the classroom. I know Annie didn't because I was watching her, and she was watching the wallscreen. She was completely caught up in the events of another time and place, and the challenge of transporting her pupils back there and helping them understand what they were seeing.

Annie froze the wallscreen picture as I sat down at the nearest empty desk. The still image was one I recognized from a dozen photographic books I'd picked up in the ruins. It was an iconic picture, summing up the Last Days the way the photo of a napalm-burned Little Girl Running summed up the human cost of the Vietnam War. The photographer had clicked his shutter just as one of the burning bottles shattered on the step the minister was standing on. The man of god was looking down in disbelief and horror as the erupting flame set light to the hem of his cassock.

So powerful was the image that it helped Annie sum up a whole lot of profoundly important trends in a few words: "To begin with, people turned to prayer in the face of the worsening global crisis. Church attendance increased for the first time in decades, and a host of bizarre religious sects and cults took root and flourished.

"But, as a succession of environmental and then economic tipping points were reached and things got worse, not better, there was a widespread and profound loss of faith in religions and in God.

"It was matched by a loss of trust in conventional political systems. Unable to control the disorder on the streets, or the things that caused it, governments either dug in and hoped it would die out or reacted with draconian clampdowns."

Half a dozen pictures in quick succession showed running battles in the streets of cities around the world. The color of skin and uniform differed from picture to picture, but the subject matter was remarkably similar. Lines of police and soldiers in riot gear formed protective cordons around parliament buildings or charged through streets, wielding batons and scattering crowds of protesters before them, trampling placards and banners and people underfoot.

"While mainstream political parties saw their power base crumble away, the Green movement went from strength to strength until it was effectively setting the agenda. Conventional political parties began espousing measures which, a generation earlier, would have been electoral suicide.

"However it was far too little, and much too late. The problems people had feared but thought would be for other generations to face were suddenly upon them, and the consequences were more apocalyptic than they could have imagined: from superstorms and food shortages to intolerable pollution that caused chronic disease, declining fertility and an increase in the frequency and severity of birth defects.

"As it hit home that these dreadful things weren't aberrations but rather the new norm, so it became apparent even the most radical mainstream party manifestoes were inadequate for tackling such profound difficulties; that national boundaries and vested interests would inevitably lead to a fragmented approach which couldn't solve problems of a global nature. The feeling grew that existing economic and political systems were part of the problem and incapable of providing a solution."

Now there were pictures of government buildings in flames: the Capitol in Washington, the Palace of Westminster in London, Holyrood in Edinburgh.

"Scientists and environmentalists who'd previously been derided as cranks and doom merchants became respected voices and gave birth to a new branch of science called ecologics, using computers to analyze the problems facing people and the planet—and to suggest solutions.

"Such an approach had been attempted in the past, but without success because even the most powerful computers lacked sufficient processing power to factor-in the multitude of complex, interacting variables which had to be considered. What made ecologics different was the development of software that linked terminals together in the biggest revolution since the Internet.

"All around the world—in homes as well as offices, in schools and universities—users were asked to make the new software their operating system. By doing so, not only did they increase the processing speed of their own terminal, they massively increased the overall computing power available to the scientific community. A similar approach had been tried once before, in the Search for Extra Terrestrial Intelligence, but the take-up was limited to interest groups—"

"People who believed in UFOs and little green men," a Number chimed in with undisguised derision.

"That's one way of putting it," Annie said. "Anyway,

now the uptake was on a truly global scale: a powerful indicator of the growing realization of impending catastrophe, and the widespread recognition that only by working together could it be averted; a reflection of people's disgust at vested interests and international squabbles.

"As the increasingly dire ecological predictions started coming true, pressure mounted on governments around the world to pursue ecological solutions; solutions which all the individuals hooked up to the operating system felt they'd played a part in formulating.

"This pressure led to the formulation of a UN Special Commission on Ecologics."

A view of the Hall of Lost Footsteps in the United Nations building in Geneva flashed across the wallscreen.

"A resolution was unanimously passed, formally recognizing both the extent of the crisis facing the peoples of the world and the role ecologics could play in averting or at least mitigating it."

The next shot was of solemn-faced diplomats gathered in a General Assembly, each with a hand raised in assent.

"A new charter was drawn up, formalizing the imperatives that would guide what came to be known as the Ecosystem as it drew up the directives which would, in turn, guide us." Annie turned from the screen to the class, and asked, "Can anyone tell me what the First Imperative was?"

The small boy I remembered from the previous day as Frankie raised his hand.

One of the Paretos started to answer, but Annie talked over him and said pointedly, "Yes, Frankie, would *you* like to tell the class."

He nodded, and said, "The First Imperative is that The Common Good shall outweigh the interests of individuals, of . . ."

His voice tailed away. The silence was filled by snickering that told me where the Paretos were sitting.

If I'd been any closer to Frankie I'd have whispered the last few words of the answer to him. I could tell Annie wanted to give him every chance to remember.

The Pareto twins doubtless got bored at exactly the same moment as each other because, before Frankie could find the words or the teacher could help him, two identical voices completed the First Imperative in perfect harmony: "of companies and nations."

Annie nodded. "That's right." The Paretos must have been sneering unbearably, because she added, "I hope you realize that remembering the words is meaningless unless you understand the spirit they were spoken in."

I smiled. She was a match for them—but only just, and they were barely thirteen or fourteen years old. That thought wiped the smile off my face.

Annie, who'd paused to add weight to her words, carried on, "So, national governments came to be viewed as part of the problem, not the solution, and were gradually sidelined—"

"Didn't they jealously guard their sovereignty?" a

Number asked with obvious disdain for the people of the Old Days.

"Strangely enough, no," Annie told him. "Everything suggests they were actually glad to be relieved of responsibility for a situation that was spiraling out of control. Besides, whereas governments had previously been under pressure from their citizens to stand up for national interests in international forums, now the opposite was true."

"So national governments were content to be reduced to the role of civil services administering Ecosystem directives," the Number said. I had to turn around and confirm with my own eyes that the speaker was only about fourteen years old, because the language and logic were so far removed from what I'd been capable of at a similar age.

I turned back to Annie in time to see her nodding. "Yes," she said. "Nationalism had been completely discredited, replaced by a sense of the brotherhood of man. Borders were seen to be irrelevant in the face of global forces that didn't recognize them; and the challenges of the future were so great that past differences were consigned to history as it dawned on people everywhere that co-operation was not only desirable but a matter of life and death.

"Even so, it's quite remarkable that ecologics came to be trusted so implicitly. Can anyone offer explanations to account for this?"

I couldn't resist a look around. The Numbers were separated from the Names almost as clearly by their expressions as their features: Frankie and friends were at a loss, while the Paretos and other Numbers had their usual knowing look. One after another they reeled off a list of reasons:

The Ecosystem can't be physically controlled by any one interest group or individual as it has no single physical location.

Its processing power is so great it can instantly spot any attempt to subvert it.

It can act for the long-term common good in a way individuals are incapable of.

Annie nodded. "Its first action was to instigate what became known as The Reckoning—a global audit using remote-sensing to assess the state of the planet in terms of flora, fauna, and mineral resources, and determine the extent of environmental degradation. Not only was this a practical necessity, it was a symbolic calling to account." She clicked the tiny control stick in her hand, and the wall behind her became a view of the Earth from an orbiting satellite. Tearing my eyes away from the breathtakingly beautiful image of a blue planet wreathed in swirling clouds, I studied the young faces around me. The Numbers might as well have been staring at a blank wall, but the Names were so awestruck that to look into their eyes was as wonderful as looking at the picture of the planet.

Annie continued. "The Ecosystem then calculated the maximum rate of resource exploitation—and thus the population—which could be sustained; and how best to sustain that population, balancing quality of life against the need to minimize our—"

"Their," one of the Paretos corrected her with ill-concealed exasperation, sounding like a parent who was weary of chastising a forgetful child.

Annie didn't acknowledge the interruption, but didn't quite carry on regardless because she said, "against the need to minimize the global footprint. It also drew up a strategy to safeguard the remaining flora and fauna, and to implement remedial action to mitigate the impact of past pollution where possible.

"This represented a fundamental shift in the approach to politics and economics: an attempt to adapt population numbers, lifestyles and living standards to suit the planet's diminished carrying capacity, rather than adapting the planet to suit man's increasing appetites.

"While all this sounded fine in theory, the first test of ecologics in practice was how it would manage the transition from old world to new.

"Riot-torn, flood and storm-damaged cities—" the wall behind her became a devastated cityscape—"had to be replaced with new towns. This was done using money and manpower freed up by a peace dividend brought about by the unprecedented global accord; no country was in a position to defend itself let alone attack another. Nationalism, like consumerism, became a dirty word in light of the undeniable need to pull together.

"A trickle of aid allowed some ecological communities to be developed in the Third World, but it amounted to little more than token gestures because the developed world needed all its resources to save itself." The devastated western cityscape was as nothing compared to the sprawling shanty town which now occupied the wall behind Annie MacDougall. It had been filmed from the air, and stretched as far as the eye could see. In a choked voice, Annie said, "Life expectancy plummeted in such places, and each generation was less numerous than the last. The places and people basically withered and died.

"In the developed world key buildings were moved to safer sites, with our community being a prime example." The wallscreen showed the distinctive horizon of my home community, Dundee, with half-built havens ranked up a hillside.

"The sites were chosen according to their proximity to resources and existing population centers. Lee slopes were favored, because they were high enough to avoid flooding and yet sheltered from the full ferocity of the superstorms.

"The overall form of the communities, and of the buildings which make them up, is dictated by functionality and the desire to minimize their footprint, so one community is remarkably similar to another. Fully-serviced apartment blocks—havens—were built around the core of key buildings. Initially the havens were for people who'd lost their homes in floods and storms, but gradually they expanded outward to accommodate everyone."

"Didn't some people refuse to leave their homes?" a Name asked.

"Yes, for various reasons, some people did stay in the old cities."

"So the transition acted as a selection process, weeding out the most irrational members of society," a Number said.

"I'd never thought of things in those terms," Annie said, taken aback by the callousness underlying the youngster's interpretation of the events she was describing.

Once Annie gathered herself, she continued, "The controlled environment of the communities proved ideal for nurturing a new society and implementing its rules, principally by means of credit cards which record what you contribute to society and what you take out.

"Meanwhile preserves, staffed by altruistic nature-loving volunteers, were created in those parts of the Outside with the highest concentrations of endangered species." The wall behind Annie was transformed into a scene from a rainforest. A young woman in green coveralls was reaching up towards the lower branches of a tree, and a monkey was reaching down to take the food she held. The shot looked slightly out of focus, but it might just have been my eyes blurring with a tear or two as I thought about Jen.

"Breeding centers using genetic engineering were necessary for the continuation of many species due to the sterility induced by pollution—"

The lush green jungle was replaced by a stark, logica

gray clinic in which a lab technician held a pipette above a test tube.

"And it soon became obvious that a similar program was needed for people; the genetic damage caused by pollution was being carried on down the generations, resulting in falling fertility and increasing fetal abnormalities."

The Paretos sniggered in perfect unison, and when I turned around I saw they were looking at a Number who'd drawn up his arm, pressing the back of his wrist to the front of his shoulder and turning his fingers into claws in cruel mimicry of Annie MacDougall's deformity.

I turned back to Annie and was relieved to see she was looking at the wallscreen image of the lab. I guessed she knew it was better not to look at the class at that point in her lecture.

"There were fears this genetic engineering would be used to control population quality as well as quantity," she said. "However these concerns were eased when the Ecosystem generated the Human Nature Directive—"

"The Nobody's Perfect Bill," Frankie piped up.

Annie nodded. "Yes, Frankie, the Nobody's Perfect Bill, which stipulates that all Numbers are to be given randomly generated cosmetic and emotional flaws."

Now it was the Names who sniggered, and this time Annie was able to look out over the rows of desks and the pupils who sat in them. I did likewise, and saw that almost without exception the Numbers exhibited various degrees of discomfiture. The exceptions were the Paretos, who looked smugger than ever.

Annie didn't let the fidgeting Numbers stew in their juices for quite as long as I would have done before continuing with the lecture. "Once the immediate crisis was averted, the Ecosystem recognized that, in order to prevent past ethnic, religious and nationalistic divisions from reappearing, it had to provide challenges that would unite mankind for the future. So it initiated the MaP project, also known as The Search. Does anyone know what MaP stands for?"

Frankie raised his hand enthusiastically. Before Annie could point to him, or anyone else, one of the Paretos said, "Meaning and Purpose."

Fighting back her obvious irritation, Annie said, "That's right. It's a bid to understand the universe and man's place in it, in a way that no one mind—however brilliant—" she added pointedly, "could hope to do."

"In one way or another, you'll all play a part in The Search over the coming years. For some of you it will be a hobby. For others it will be your life's work. I'm sure all of you have heard of MaP and are curious about how it will affect you, and how you will affect it. Well, this is where you find out."

Rather you than me, Annie MacDougall, I thought. The Search was a vast subject, and I wouldn't know where to start if I had to explain it.

Annie took it in her stride. "There are three aspects to the project: a study of the aspirations and achievements of people of the past; an analysis of the dreams and desires of current citizens; and an attempt to further our knowledge of science in order to build a better future.

"This latter aspect will appeal to those of you who are more scientifically minded—"

"You mean Numbers," a Pareto said.

"I try to avoid genetic stereotypes," Annie told him.

"Why, if they accurately reflect reality?" the same student asked.

Good luck fielding that one, I thought.

"Because prejudice is ugly, and an open mind is beautiful," Annie said.

That deserved a round of applause. But, of course, she didn't get one.

"Anyway, this scientific strand of The Search basically consists of attempts to formulate what used to rather charmingly be referred to as a Theory of Everything—a means of explaining the entire universe, from sub-atomic interactions to the formation of galaxies; a way of accommodating the theories of relativity, gravity, and strong and weak magnetic forces without contradiction.

"As for the other strands of The Search, those dealing with the past and present, they involve an analysis of individual expressions of thought and feeling.

"The basic premise is that individuals are incapable

of comprehending the big picture, the sum total of human knowledge. One lifetime isn't long enough to learn all there is to know, and no single intellect is large enough to make sense of the musings of all others. Only the Ecosystem has the computational power to discern common threads and pick out any underlying purpose and progression. In effect, only the Ecosystem has a realistic chance of determining where people are going and why they're trying to get there."

"Of finding the meaning of life," a student said, the awe in her voice telling me she was a Name.

Annie nodded. "So much for the general concept behind MaP. What you're all probably wondering is how The Search affects you. Well, for those who develop a profound interest in science or the humanities, MaP offers the prospect of a lifetime of research, and a reward that can be measured in terms of knowledge gained as well as credit earned.

"For the rest of you, who will go on to be teachers or doctors, technicians or LogiPol officers—" a glance in my direction let me know my presence hadn't gone undetected—"or any one of the thousand other trades and professions that allow communities to function, The Search represents a hobby, a pastime, and a chance to earn extra pleasure points, while at the same time educating yourself and adding to The Sum Total of Human Knowledge."

"Can we pick any subject to study?" a student asked.

"Yes," Annie answered. "Say you're interested in history, as I am, you can pick a single life—either someone famous, or an ordinary person who has left some lasting expression of their thoughts and feelings. Or you can pick an era, the length of which will vary according to the period you choose. The record from prehistoric times is so scant that if you select a study period from back then, the era might be a thousand years long; whereas if you choose the 20th or 21st century the timescale is more likely to be measured in seconds."

"You mean the study of a single second can be the work of a lifetime?" a Name asked, again sounding slightly awed.

Annie nodded. "Yes—and you'll only have scratched the surface of that second. Whether you study a particular person or a period, the approach is the same. You learn as much as you can about your chosen subject, sort through the insignificant stuff—"

"How do you determine what's significant?" another Name asked.

"Good question. It'll be answered at university, where you won't so much study particular subjects, but rather how to study: how to sort the grains of truth and knowledge from the inconsequential chaff; and how to present your conclusions to the Ecosystem for synthesis and analysis—"

The bell rang to mark the end of the study period.

The Numbers filed out one by one and the Names followed, taking longer and chatting in little groups.

Then I was alone with Annie MacDougall.

CHAPTER 14

01000011010010000010000010101000001010100010001010101010010

THE BOOK THAT NEVER WAS

PREOCCUPIED WITH CRACKING THE CASE IN ORDER to impress the pants off Paula, I'd forgotten what it meant to Annie MacDougall. I was truly ashamed of myself when I saw how expectantly Doug's daughter looked at me. "Have you found anything out?" she asked eagerly.

"I think I know what book your dad was reading," I told her, holding up *Lichens and Mosses of the World.* "What I don't know is why it would change his views on life. I was hoping if you looked it over, you might pick up on something I missed. You're much better qualified to see it through your dad's eyes than I am."

I held out the book but she didn't take it. "It's okay," she said. "I have Dad's copy at home—I cleared out his bookcase. I've been working my way through the contents, trying to find what he'd been so struck by, but I didn't know where to start. I haven't got to that book yet, but I'll give it a go tonight."

I felt more than a little foolish when I thought of my little expedition to Newport library; it hadn't occurred to me that Doug's next of kin might have the book.

"Can I swap your father's copy for mine?" I asked. I'd read *the* book from cover to cover without finding any answers, but I hadn't read *Doug's* book. None of the words or pictures had jumped out at me, but maybe there was something in Doug's copy that wasn't in mine: dog-earing that marked out the last section he'd read, a well-thumbed page indicating a passage he kept coming back to, or even some notes scribbled in a margin.

Annie looked puzzled by my request. But, after I explained, she nodded and said, "We can go up to my apartment and pick it up now."

When we got there Annie used her deformed hand to steady the pile of books stacked in the corner of her living room, and her good hand to extricate the volume that matched mine. "No marker or dog-eared pages," she said, examining the book as she came over to join me on the sofa.

"That would be too much to hope for," I said.

The only unprinted marks on the first few pages were those left by time and dampness. However Annie, who was sitting to my right, stopped with the next page half turned. I gently finished turning it for her so I could see what had grabbed her attention. I spotted it right away: a sentence in the second paragraph was underlined with a pencil mark that looked like it had been drawn days rather than decades ago.

We both leaned over the table to read the sentence, but it just described the association between fungal hyphae, whatever that was, and cells that facilitated photosynthesis. I couldn't imagine it was anything to get too excited about, even if lichens were the sort of thing you found exciting. "Turn the page," I said, filled with a horrible premonition of what I was about to see.

Sure enough: more underlined sentences.

Annie flicked through a couple of dozen pages, and there were sentences underlined on almost every one. Her excitement replaced by disappointment, she said, "The underscoring hardly narrows it down at all—there's way too much of it. Dad was probably picking out key points for his thesis."

"He always did a thesis when he read a book?"

She nodded. "And he scanned the book in to the database. He needed all the credit he could get to buy water for his plants."

Something occurred to me, and I said, "Can I see the book, please?"

"Help yourself."

I took the slender volume from her and opened it at

the centrefold. There were underscores on virtually every page. I raised a hand to my jaw and rubbed my goatee, like I often do when I'm trying to work something out.

"What is it?" Annie asked.

"Your dad had obviously read at least half the book, and yet there was no record of any chapters on the Ecosystem database. I don't know about you, but I find it tedious sitting at my computer, turning page after page and holding it up to the screen to scan it in, so I never wait until I've finished reading the whole book; I scan each chapter in after I've read it. Everyone I know does pretty much the same thing. If your dad did likewise, I'd expect to find at least a couple of chapters in the database."

"I'm afraid I was never around when Dad was doing stuff like that, so I don't know how he went about it."

I made a mental note to check how Doug had input his previous books. There would be a record of whether each was entered in one continuous period, or in the normal fashion of one or two chapters at a time. If Doug had worked the same way as everyone else, the opening chapters of *Lichens and Mosses of the World* would have been added to the Ecosystem database—and their absence from it might mean someone had deleted them. I had absolutely no idea who would want to do such thing, and even less idea why they'd want to do it. It was hard to believe the moldy old botanical book contained something that anyone found remotely threatening. . . But it wasn't impossible to believe, the way it would have been if the first few chapters of the book had been on the database, and if Doug MacDougall had been standing behind the counter of The Plant Place rather than pushing up the daisies, as they used to say. All of this was making me keener than ever to discover the last thing he'd read.

Then I had an idea of how I might find it. I flicked through the pages again, this time beginning at the back. There were no pencil marks on the last six or eight pages. Picking up on my mounting excitement, Annie said, "What are you looking for?"

"I'm just hoping your dad hadn't finished reading the book."

"Why?"

"Because if he hadn't, there's a good chance the last underline will show us the final thing he read."

"Whatever it was he was so excited about, in other words."

I nodded.

Annie drew closer to me. I used the pad of my left thumb to hold the bulk of the pages back, and the tip of my right thumb to pull them loose one at a time. My excitement grew with every page that didn't have a pencil mark on it, and I sensed Annie's did, too.

Finally, about two-thirds of the way through the book, I came to a couple of underlined sentences—the last passage Doug MacDougall had marked out. The words were below a photograph of a rock covered in some sort of bright yellow growth which, given the title of the book, was presumably a lichen or moss. If I had any doubt these were the words which made such an impact on Doug, it was dispelled by the three exclamation marks penciled at the end of the underscored passage.

Annie must have been a little short-sighted because she asked, "What does it say?"

I read out the passage: "Immaculata solaris, pictured above, has no common name because it is not commonly known, living only in the most extreme of alpine environments. Studies show it to be remarkable due to more than its vivid color and hardiness, for it is not part of any food chain—it does not feed on anything but sunlight, and nothing feeds on it."

"That's it?" Annie said, her bafflement matching my own.

I answered with a nod after looking at the next page; there was a photo of something else, and no more underscoring.

I turned back to the photo of *immaculata solaris*, and re-read the words beneath it. If they had any great significance, I couldn't see what it was.

"Does that mean any more to you than it does to me?" Annie asked.

I shook my head and said, "I'm sorry."

"Where do we go from here?"

I couldn't bring myself to tell her I was at a dead end,

that this was my only lead and I couldn't follow it any further. So I said, "I'm not sure, Annie."

She glanced at her i-band and said, "I better get back—I've got a class in five minutes." She stood up and I did likewise. "Do you want to take Dad's copy of the book with you?" she asked.

I didn't see the point, but returning it to her would be an admission I was giving up. Annie MacDougall deserved better than that, as did her father. So I took the book back to the station house with me.

Paula looked at her i-band pointedly. My lunch hour had probably lasted 61 minutes. "You're late, Travis," she said.

That was it: all my frustration at the lead having petered out, and my bewilderment at the change in Paula's behavior between yesterday and today, boiled over. "How come I'm back to being 'Travis'?" I asked. "What happened to 'Ben'?"

"It's not appropriate."

"So why was it appropriate for a little while yesterday? What's changed?"

She didn't answer.

"Are you going to pretend nothing happened in the library, that there wasn't some sort of chemistry between us?"

Her silence and inability to look me in the eye told me

this was exactly what she intended doing.

"Damnit, Paula, how can you be so cold about it?"

"Because I'm a Number," she said, bitterly, "and my head tells me love is an illusion, a weakness."

"So how come there was no scorn or mockery in the way you looked at me yesterday when I was talking about Jen, or when you saw the way I'm starting to feel about you?"

"Because my heart tells me something very different from my head, and for a little while I listened to my heart," she said. "Have you any idea how confusing it is to desperately want something, and yet at the same time believe that what you want isn't worth having?"

"Paula, have you ever been in love?" I asked.

She shook her head.

"Then how can you believe it isn't worth having if you've never experienced it? I don't understand that."

"That's the whole point. You can't understand, because you're not a Number. You don't think the same way we do. You're not genetically hard-wired like we are. You have an open mind."

"But you came close to believing in love yesterday. I know you did."

"Maybe being away from the community helped me forget who I am, what I am."

"Maybe it let you be yourself. Maybe for the first time in your life you were starting to find out who you really are."

"It's probably just that my surroundings were so unfamiliar they preoccupied my head and left my heart free to do its own thing. . . And during the storm, when I saw how much you cared about Jen, when I realized you were starting to care about me. . . I don't know. All I know is I felt like a different person for a little while yesterday. I felt like I imagine a Name must feel."

"And now?"

"Now I feel foolish when I remember yesterday."

And to think that until 24 hours ago I'd looked on Paula as being a Class-A ice maiden, a woman who was so together she wouldn't come apart in any circumstances. Especially not a set of circumstances like this. "Look," I said, "don't you think it's at least worth giving things a—"

"These things never work out between Names and Numbers. We both know they always end badly."

"But you're not like other Numbers."

"And I'm not like a Name. I'm neither one thing nor the other, but I'm probably more like a Number than a Name, Travis. . . Ben. I don't even know what to call you. I just know there's no chance of things working out.

"You don't know that. You can't know that."

"What I know is that listening to my heart, the way Names seem to, leaves me horribly confused. Listening to my head and trying to forget about my heart, like I'd always done until yesterday, makes life a whole lot simpler."

"It might make life simpler, but I'm willing to bet it also makes it a lesser thing in some way. In every way. A pleasure's more than doubled if it's shared, Paula, and a burden is more than halved. Jen taught me that.

"Then I hope you find another Jen."

"That's not how it works."

"How does it work?"

"I don't know, I just know it does work; not always, but when it does it makes life come alive. I saw your life come alive yesterday, and it was a truly amazing thing to watch. And I felt my own life come alive, in a way I believed it never would again."

For a moment I thought she was going to reach out for me, hold me, maybe kiss me. In that moment her eyes truly were windows into her soul, and I saw a longing as intense as my own.

But the moment passed, and her eyes became cold and so did her voice when she said, "I don't want to talk about this again, Travis. Not ever." She swiftly changed the subject, pointing to the book I carried and saying, "Didn't MacDougall's daughter want to read it?"

I was so preoccupied by what we'd been talking about moments earlier that I couldn't work out what she meant now.

"You've brought the book back with you; did Annie MacDougall not want to—" she was interrupted by a call.

If the call had come a couple of minutes later—if I'd had a chance to explain to Paula about the book, to read out the last passage Doug MacDougall underlined—it would have changed everything. But the call came in before I could answer her question, and seconds later we were hurrying up in the lift to level seven, where a row had turned violent. It was between a Name and a Number, of course. It made Paula's point more eloquently than any words, but she didn't give me an 'I told you so' look.

For once she looked like she'd rather have been wrong than right.

When we got back to the station house Paula did what I think of as the 'paperwork,' even though paper is way too precious to be used for administrative tasks and everything's processed electronically. I suppose I've just seen one Olden Days cop show too many.

While Paula spoke to her screen, I used mine to check back on Doug MacDougall's contributions to The Search. I knew I wasn't likely to turn up any new leads, just add to the validity of the lead that had dried up, but I'd nothing better to do. And besides, I take a pride in never giving up until I have to. I think the fact we can't match Numbers in terms of logic drives us to outdo them in other areas, like sheer dogged determination. Most of the time all it leads to is weariness and frustration for us, and a mocking sneer from them. But occasionally it pays off and *we* get to sneer at *them*.

It turned out Doug MacDougall had scanned in over fifty books, all of them about plants—and not one was input in a single continuous session. The most likely explanation for the absence of any digitized chapters from *Lichens and Mosses of the World* seemed to be that, for some reason, Doug had decided not to scan it in. But that didn't ring true. The pencil marks indicated he was writing a thesis about it, and he wouldn't submit a thesis without scanning the book in to give it context. Another explanation was that he'd decided to digitize the book in one long session. But that didn't ring true, either, because he'd never worked that way before, not once in over fifty contributions to The Search, and people tend to be creatures of habit.

The only other thing I could think of was that for some reason there had been a delay in processing his latest entries. I did another search on *Lichens and Mosses of the World* to see if the database had been updated since I last checked.

It had, but not in the way I'd expected.

There was no record of the book's existence at all. Not even in the ISBN catalogue.

Either I'd uncovered some sort of conspiracy, or I was making something out of nothing. Trying to stay calm, I weighed up the evidence. The first time I'd searched for the book, when I was just looking to get a copy of it to read, I'd queried by the author's name because it was shorter than the title. Perhaps there was some fault in the cross-referencing, so the book only came up if you keyed in the author, not the title. It seemed unlikely, but more likely than the other explanation: that someone had removed all reference to the book's existence—and ended Doug MacDougall's life—because of a yellow moss that wasn't even part of any food chain.

So I queried my screen using the author's name.

Nothing.

Not only had no book by that title ever been entered into the database, no such book had ever been published.

So how come there was a copy of it sitting on my desk?

I tried a different tack, concentrating on the plant itself. If *Lichens and Mosses of the World* contained the key to whatever was going on, which seemed increasingly likely, then the book itself was merely a container, and the actual key was the golden yellow substance in the photo. I riffled through the pages and stopped at the one with the picture of *immaculata solaris*. I read the underlined words again: Immaculata solaris, *pictured above, has no common name because it is not commonly known, living only in the most extreme of alpine environments. Studies show it to be remarkable for more than its vivid color and hardiness, for it does not feed on anything but sunlight, and nothing feeds on it.!!!*

The important thing had to be the fact that *immaculata solaris* was unique—and the properties that made it so. Over and over again I read the same fifteen or twenty words: *it is not part of any food chain—it doesn't feed on anything but sunlight, and nothing feeds on it.*

When I knew the words by heart and there was no point reading them any more I turned my attention to the accompanying photograph. But all I saw was a splash of pretty color on a dull gray rock.

Wondering if the words and picture would mean any more to Paula than they did to me—and hoping the attempt to work out their significance would draw us together, as the search for the book itself had—I looked over the top of my screen at her and said, "Does this mean anything to you?"

The voice that answered me came from my hear-ring, not my partner: a 'Rusher' was running amok in the gym.

We hurried out of the station house.

While we waited for the elevator Paula said, "What were you going to ask, Travis?"

If she'd called me 'Ben' I would have told her. But I was so irked by the cold 'Travis' that, to annoy her, I just said, "Never mind." It was pathetic and childish, I know. My only excuse is that I'd no idea how significant those underlined words truly were.

I'd no idea that Doug MacDougall hadn't been exaggerating when he said they changed everything.

CHAPTER 15

0100001101001000010000010101000001010100010001010101010010

When the Wind Had Many Names

I did some more staring at Page 127 of *Lichens and Mosses of the World* when I got home, but before long my thoughts drifted to Paula. I considered calling her to ask for help. Okay, what I really mean is I wanted to call her, and the mystery moss was just an excuse. But she'd see right through me. She'd hear the longing in my voice and, if we met up, she'd see it in my eyes, confirming her belief that love was just another word for desperate, pathetic need.

Maybe she had a point. After all, I missed Jen desperately, and I had to admit there was something pathetic about how much I longed for Paula to open up to me again the way she had while we sheltered from the storm.

Just as I was at a dead end with Doug MacDougall's

murder, so I felt caught in a hopeless Catch 22 with Paula: it would take a lot of love to short-circuit the 'hard-wiring' that made her inherently predisposed to interpret passion as need—and yet the more she saw I loved her, the needier I'd appear.

One intractable problem would have been bad enough; two at once was too much. My head was starting to hurt, so I put Doug's book away and reached for one that would help me forget about his death, and about Paula.

The book I grabbed was *More Than Seven Wonders* by Calum Tait. I let the words and pictures of the long dead travel writer take me away from my own world—with its soul-destroying blacks and whites and shades of gray, its confines and sterility—to a time when the world was a bigger, brighter place and all of it was worth seeing. Although I've read the introduction a hundred times, as often as not when I pick up the book I read those first two pages again, because the words which fill them strike a symphony of chords with me:

If the only traveling you do is along the path of least resistance it can seem like there are only seven wonders in the world. When each day is spent going through the motions, going to the same places and seeing the same faces, life is a lesser thing in some way, in every way; security becomes stagnation and a house becomes a prison.

So what other paths are there to follow? Well, how about these: the Silk Road, the Salt Route, the Frankincense Trail; the Way of a Thousand Kasbahs, the Royal Road of the Incas, the Pacific Crest Trail.

What about traveling back in time, following in famous footsteps and seeing fabled sights in far-off lands. . .

Or going wherever people are making the most of the present: filling a diary with the dates when people in different parts of the world gather to celebrate the good things in life, then turning the pages and going to the places to find out what form the festivals take; not just being a spectator but adding your life to the celebrations—dancing each night away until the music stops or until you drop, not caring where the dance takes you or whether all that it makes you is tired in the end. . .

Or just picking the name of a wind that sounds enchanting and exotic: the khamsin or sirocco, the chinook, the mistral, the bora—finding out where it blows and going where it goes; if it's a warm wind walking into it, if it's a cool breeze keeping it behind you, never knowing where the next day will find you or worrying about that any more than the wind does.

I felt a choke in my throat at the thought that even those old, romantic sounding winds were gone now, their names all but forgotten, replaced by an oppressive, toxic breeze and periodic superstorms that would flatten you rather than carry you to the four corners of the world. How could the people who went before me destroy something as ephemeral as the wind, something that was everywhere and nowhere and epitomized freedom and restlessness? What chance was there for anything else if even the breath of Mother Nature and her wordless, timeless whispering had failed to survive? How could people whose ancestors had the capacity to come up with such musical sounding names as khamsin and sirocco have lost so much of their soul? How had they gained so much knowledge and yet lost so much wisdom?

Those were as baffling as the other questions I'd faced that day, so I turned back to the book.

Learning a little more with each of these days about different lifestyles, what people have in common and what makes them unique. . . Listening to the rhythm of the language they speak, the music they sing to, the music they dance to, the background sounds that accompany their lives—and when you leave each place taking with you some things worth more than any material possessions that money can buy: an understanding of the people you've met and the world they live in, and a deeper understanding of yourself.

I wondered how Calum Tait had felt—a man who obviously hadn't sold his heart and soul, who hadn't bought into the bargain that material things were worth destroying the world for. I wondered if he'd had any idea how quickly the world he was describing would be destroyed; if he'd had any notion that he'd be among the last generations who would be able to see it. And I wondered if he'd experienced any guilt at the fact that, in seeing the world, he'd helped deny to others the very things he so profoundly appreciated himself; the planes he'd criss-crossed the skies in did their bit to add to the lethal pollution.

After a wistful sigh I turned to the first chapter. The photo accompanying it was of a white monument in the shape of a stylized ship's prow with a line of seafarers on it, each looking to the far horizon. The monument was in Lisbon, and the chapter, called *Voyages of Discovery*, was about the spirit that had moved those men as powerfully as the wind that filled the sails of their ships.

Imagine waking up one morning and hearing that a new continent had been discovered. Think of all the wonders such vastness might contain: plateaus and plains; rivers, waterfalls and great mountain chains; mighty civilizations, fallen empires, myths and legends that endured. In their wildest dreams could Columbus and those who followed in his wake have foreseen mountains the shape of Sugar Loaf or a river the length of the Amazon; the stepped pyramid of Kukulcan, the tale of feathered serpent Quetzalcoatl, the legend of El Dorado?

Imagine what it would be like to come across such things for the first time. Imagine what it would be like to discover a continent. You just about can imagine it with a monument like Lisbon's one to The Discoverers beside you, with so much history behind you, and an open horizon ahead of you. There's something about distant horizons—they do to the imagination what love does to the heart.

I felt that choking sensation in my throat again, accompanied this time by a tightness in my chest, because that one sentence seemed to sum up everything that was missing from my life.

Standing there, I wondered how the horizon must have looked five hundred years ago to someone who had vision as well as simply sight; someone who guessed that the waves of uncrossed oceans broke on distant shores.

Such men helped draw the map of the world depicted in mosaic below the monument to the Discoverers, its shape so different from the crude, hand-copied maps they'd set out with; the maps they'd spread out on sea chests and weighted down with astrolabe and dividers, compass and lodestone, to study in cramped cabins under the light of oil lamps that swung with the swell of the sea.

I thought about how different the maps they brought back looked from those they set out with, and the drama that lay in drawing the differences. I thought about Bartolomeu Dias sailing south of the equator, half-expecting to encounter a ring of fire encircling the middle of the world, and beyond it a torrid zone uninhabitable because of the heat—and finding in their place the Gold Coast, Table Mountain and the Cape of Good Hope. . .

Vasco da Gama, sailing east after south and pioneering the passage to India. . .

Ferdinand Magellan, sailing around the world without turning to tack back the way he'd come—the first time in history a crew traveled so far in one direction they ended up back where they'd started. . .

And of course Christopher Columbus: maybe it was religious fervor or thoughts of gold or glory that spurred him on, but I like to think he was as interested in the smell of exotic spices as the price they'd fetch if he brought them home. I like to believe he treasured newfound knowledge above wealth. . . That he wondered what other people's languages sounded like; what clothes they wore and what habits of the other kind they adopted; the shape of their houses and how they built them; the music they made, the steps of their dances, and the stories they told; what gods they feared and worshipped; what games they played, and what they did to fill the last hour of light at the end of each day. I'd like to believe he thought more about those things than about the weapons of war those people carried and how willing they'd be to use them; how they measured wealth and how willing they'd be to share it.

Maybe Columbus didn't wonder about those other things, but it doesn't really matter to me; it's fun just to stand in a place where you can see the sky meet the sea, feel the heartbeat of history inside yourself, dream a greater man's dreams.

Those voyages of discovery made more waves than any ocean. The people who embarked on them didn't just write a couple of pages in the history of the world; they wrote a whole new book. When you stand in a place like the Monument to the Discoverers, that book opens up in front of you. The pages turn themselves and soon you're caught up in tales that awaken a sense of adventure in even the quietest heart.

The first footprints might have faded from the farthest shores, the last of the three-masted ships has long since sailed, the oceans are charted now and the countries all have names; but, standing in the shadow of the monument and looking out to the horizon, it's easy to imagine there are still voyages of discovery waiting to be made.

And the great thing is, as long as you can dream and imagine and wonder, then there are.

The terrible thing was that Calum had been wrong about that: I could dream and imagine and wonder, but there were no more voyages of discovery waiting to be made.

I let out another of my wistful sighs. Like Jen's memory,

Calum Tait's book was bittersweet, and for the same reasons: sweetness from the thought of wonderful things; bitterness from the knowledge that those things are gone forever.

I was prepared to put up with the bitter for the sweet, however, so I flicked through the pages of the book, looking for my favorite passages. One described what Calum saw when he looked from the top of a natural, sphinx-like outcrop beside Table Mountain in Cape Town, seeing with his imagination as well as his eyes:

From the Lion's Head you can gaze into the heart of Africa: see veldt and savannah and tropical rainforest; Great Rift Valley and High Atlas Mountains; rainbow rising over Victoria Falls and snows crowning Kilimanjaro.

Coasts of Slaves and Barbary, Gold and Ivory; blowing sands of Kalahari, Namib and Sahara; flowing waters of Limpopo, Zambezi and Congo, Niger and Nile.

Migrating zebra, charging rhino and stampeding elephant; sprinting cheetah, leopard up a tree and lion at a kill; sidewinding trail of snake in sand dune and silhouette of giraffe at sunset.

Places with names like Zanzibar and Dar es Salaam; Timbuktu and Tamanrassat, Bujumbura and Ougadougou.

Africa is the fabled land that lies beyond the far horizon. Africa is an adventurer's dream.

And just as I'd wondered how it felt to discover a continent, so I wondered how one could be lost. I wondered how such richness and diversity could be turned to dust and carried away by a wind that no longer had a different name in each place it passed, that no longer had a name at all.

The turn of a page took me to:

Cape Town's Two Oceans Aquarium, where I saw a pair of seahorses drifting with their tails curled together. I don't know if that's how seahorses embrace, but they were like a courting couple, enchantment embodied. It's hard to believe they share the ocean with nuclear submarines; they're too serene to belong to the same planet as beings who've devised weapons of mass destruction.

And it was hard for me to believe such things once existed in oceans that were now all but empty.

I was in mid-sigh when my hear-ring crackled into life: "Ben?"

It was a woman's voice. At first I thought it was Paula, and my heart raced at the fact she'd called my by my first name again; at the notion she might be feeling some of the same things for me that I was for her, and feeling them too strongly to deny.

"I just wanted to say congratulations."

My heart sank, because I recognized the voice as Annie MacDougall's. I was so disappointed it was a few seconds before it dawned on me: I'd no idea what she was congratulating me for.

"You have heard about it, haven't you?"

"Heard about what?" I said.

CHAPTER 16

01000011010010000100000101010000010101000100010101010010

LITTLE SHOP OF HORRORS

"YOUR NAME CAME UP IN TONIGHT'S LOTTERY DRAW."

All of a sudden things were looking up, big time. I went through the list of lottery prizes in my mind. They range from a timesphere season ticket to a trip on a jetliner. Usually the jetliners only carry cargo, but every month one of the smaller models takes on passengers. If you can't afford to buy a seat—and they're priced so high few people can—your only hope of making a trip is to win the lottery. I'd once read an article about the logic behind such trips. The Ecosystem apparently calculated they represent one of the most cost-effective ways for it to redeem pleasure points. Only a couple of seats were for sale on each trip, and they were priced high enough to cover all the costs.

Meanwhile the lottery sales for the other seats added up to a vast amount of points, which were effectively being redeemed at no cost to the Ecosystem—all it was providing in return for them was hopes and dreams, only a few of which it had to fulfill. As a bonus, the lottery represented a way of adding a small, harmless element of unpredictability to an otherwise predictable world, giving people something to look forward to every week—the hope of a dream coming true.

"Please tell me I didn't just win a timesphere ticket," I said.

"No, you hit it big time," Annie told me. "Top prize—two seats on the next jetliner."

Annie had been through a bad time and needed cheering up, and I felt guilty at my failure to work out what had happened to her dad, so I said, "Would you like to come along?"

She laughed. "I wasn't hinting. It's amazingly kind of you to ask, but I couldn't take so much from someone I barely know. Besides, it's a transatlantic crossing to Niagara Falls, no less—you should take someone you love."

I didn't say anything to Annie MacDougall. I was too busy thanking a god I hadn't believed in until a few moments ago. If any place on the planet could put Paula in the mood for love, it had to be the most romantic waterfall in the world.

I went to bed dreaming about standing beside Paula with the spray from Niagara blowing in our faces and a rainbow rising above the Horseshoe Falls. It was as good a dream as I've ever had.

Until I put my arm around Paula, and her hand was where her elbow should have been. Just like Annie MacDougall's.

It was a relief when my hear-ring crackled into life at that point.

My relief didn't last long; the call-out was an urgent one, to someone on the point of flatlining in apartment 479.

I tumbled out of bed, pulled on my coverall and raced for the elevator. I fired some questions into my i-band as the lift doors closed behind me. By the time they opened two floors later I knew that the occupant of 479 was a man called Tim McCann who was the same age as myself. He lived alone and was on the point of dying alone—there was no record of anyone else entering his apartment. We were told at LogiPol College to assume nothing, but sometimes you can't help yourself—and, as I hurried along the corridor, I assumed I was about to encounter another overdose victim.

Paula was at the far end of the corridor, and she wasn't assuming anything at all; she slotted her ID card into the reader with one hand, and drew her knockdown with the other. I broke into a run, but Paula charged into the flat before I got there.

The scene was pretty much what I'd expected: a man on a bed, one arm dangling to the floor. The hand at the end of the arm was almost touching a syringe on the carpet.

Paula took on the task of first-response medicare, while I slipped on a pair of skintex gloves and did the detective bit. The set-up was so similar to what had happened with Doug MacDougall I couldn't help think there was more to things than met the eye in flat 479, just as there had been in flat 331. With that in mind I bagged the syringe for forensic testing and gave the apartment a once-over.

Tim McCann's passion in life was obvious; the walls were lined with an assortment of Olden Days bookcases containing tattered and mildewed paperbacks. A quick glance gave me an insight into his tastes: Hemingway, Steinbeck, Chandler, James M. Cain and a whole lot of sci-fi.

I went over to his desk and checked his computer. It showed no record of any activity in the previous few hours. The drawer beneath it held an Olden Days diary and a pencil. I put them in my plastic bag along with the syringe.

By that time the medics had arrived and there was nothing more to do except watch them cart Tim McCann away.

I longed to tell Paula the good news about my lottery win and invite her to Niagara Falls, but resisted the temptation because I couldn't think of a less romantic set of circumstances for extending the invitation.

So we went our separate ways and I tried to get back to sleep.

When we met up again it was in the station house a couple of hours later. I called Community General to ask about Tim McCann. He wasn't dead and he wasn't going to die. Well, everybody's going to die. I just mean he wasn't going to die anytime soon. Theoretically, I should have been able to ask him what had happened, and why. There wasn't much point in asking him anything, though, because it would take about a thousand days for an answer. He'd overdosed on Slo-Mo.

Since I couldn't ask Tim McCann anything, I asked Paula something: "How would you like to go with me to Niagara Falls?"

I explained about my lottery win.

I was sure she wanted to go—who wouldn't, because it was a once-in-a-lifetime chance to see one of the most amazing places on the planet—but she said, "I don't think that would be a good idea."

"Why not?"

"I promised myself I'd never go Outside with you again."

"I thought you had a good time. I've never seen you so happy."

"That's the whole point."

The old rom-coms I'm so fond of were often based on the differences between the sexes, and the way men can never understand women. I had a lot more than that to contend with here; I think the genetic divide is far deeper than the gender gap. I gave up trying to fathom things out for myself and asked her straight out: "How can you not want to do something that will make you happy?"

"The time I spent with you Outside made me want to

be something that, when I got back to the community, I realized I couldn't be."

"I don't—"

"We've been over this, Travis. I might be ablc to feel love in a way other Numbers can't, but I can't believe in it any more than the rest of *them*. . . of *us*. Just thinking about it has got me confused about who I am, what I am."

"This is Niagara Falls I'm talking about, Paula. Make up a list of the top ten most—" I nearly said 'romantic,' but stopped myself in time—"beautiful places on the planet, and this has to be on it."

I could tell she was weakening. "You'll never get another chance to see it. If you don't take it, you'll always wonder what it would have been like."

"I can see what it's like from a timesphere."

"Do you really think that's the same thing? Do you honestly think you won't regret it for the rest of your life if you say no."

"I'll get over it. Easier than I'm likely to get over the regret if I say yes."

"Look, it's not as if we'll be alone, like we were in the library. And we'll be so taken up with the falls we'll hardly be aware of each other."

"Thanks," she said sarcastically.

"Take it as a compliment—I want you to come so much I'm prepared to lie to you."

She smiled; the first crack in her armor.

Inspired, I said, "I'll tell you what, I'll do a deal with you. I've got a copy of the old Marilyn Monroe film *Niagara*. I'll bring it in this afternoon and you can watch it tonight—and if it doesn't leave you wanting to see the falls for yourself, I'll say no more about it. Okay?"

"Only if you agree to say no more about it before I've watched the film, as well as after."

"Deal," I said.

"Good. Maybe I can get on with doing the report on McCann, then."

While she did the paperwork on Tim McCann, I checked up on his background. It turned out he made a living from writing eBooks. Mainly neo-noir, if the titles were anything to go by. He'd churned out one every eight months, regular as clockwork, for the last ten years. I recognized some of the titles, which were borderline trashy. I think I've read a couple, but they couldn't have been too memorable. It was four months since his last story came out. He should have been halfway through the latest one, but there was no sign of anything on his computer.

I thought about what that might mean.

I thought about the way there was no sign of *Lichens and Mosses of the World* on the Ecosystem database.

There was probably a perfectly reasonable explanation. In fact, two came to mind at about the same time. To check out the first one I went into the evidence bag and brought out McCann's diary, thinking maybe it was blank when he found it and he'd been using it to write out his latest story long-hand.

But when I opened the diary the writing was in pen, not the pencil I'd found in his desk. The ink was faded and the words described a day in the life of someone from the Old Days. I put the diary in the thigh pocket of my coveralls. Bedtime reading for tonight.

The other explanation for the lack of a new work in progress seemed to be the most logical one: writer's block. Either Tim McCann had run out of ideas or couldn't think how to express them. That would explain why he'd turned to drugs.

Everything made sense. I metaphorically patted myself on the back.

It turned out I was a bit premature in doing so, but I didn't realize that until later.

An hour later, to be precise. With nothing else to do, and mindful of the advice about 'assuming nothing'—not to mention the whole Doug MacDougall situation—I'd taken the syringe and pencil along to the forensics lab to get them tested.

"You're not going to believe this," the lab technician said.

Unable to improve on that statement as a way of introducing the forensic results to Paula, I repeated it word for word when I got back to the station house.

"Don't tell me, there aren't any prints on this syringe

either," she said.

"No, there's a perfect set of prints."

"But they're not McCann's."

"Wrong again."

"So what's the problem?"

"The prints on the pencil are from his left hand."

"And the ones on the syringe are from his right," Paula guessed.

She was correct about that, and also with the rest of what she said: "And you're thinking someone else injected McCann, then pressed McCann's fingers on the syringe to get prints on it, not realizing he was left-handed."

I nodded. "It's not impossible that Tim McCann injected the syringe with his right hand, but it's unlikely. Add the fact he'd never used drugs of any kind before, and the case doesn't look quite so open and shut as it did when we first walked into his apartment, does it?"

Paula sighed.

"You sound like you need a break," I said helpfully. "A day off. A change of scenery."

"Travis, we had a deal."

"And I intend holding you to it," I told her. Glancing at my i-band I saw it was almost lunchtime, so I headed for my flat to dig out my copy of *Niagara*.

That night—while, if all was going according to plan, Paula was watching the movie and being blown away by a backdrop so stunning it upstaged even Marilyn Monroe—I settled back to read the Olden Days diary I'd found in Tim McCann's apartment. The first few pages painted a vivid picture of the diarist, and it wasn't an attractive one. He was a taxi driver put out of business by the rising cost of petrol, and he basically wanted to rant about the influx of southerners who'd come up to Scotland in the wake of the London Floods. He didn't have much else to say once he'd made his point about how much harder it was to get work because they were taking all the jobs. Another three paragraphs, to be precise; his diary ended halfway down Page 6.

I didn't bother reading those last three paragraphs, because what was on Page 7 looked much more interesting. The printed day and date had been scored out. In block capitals, written in pencil, were the words, *THE PET SHOP*.

The handwriting under those words was completely different from the diary entries. It was smaller, more disciplined, and ran across the printed date dividers. And it was in fresh pencil, rather than faded ink. I quickly saw that the content was as different as the appearance.

It was a novel. Tim McCann's latest work, no doubt. Within a few pages he'd drawn me into a world of the future, just as the travel articles of Calum Tait drew me into the past. While the world Calum described was one I lamented the loss of with my heart and soul, tomorrow's world was one I quickly came to fear.

Cities were completely enclosed in domes. The fertility of people living in these sanitized biospheres was beginning to recover, but the outside world was still a toxic, sterile place. As a result, resources were even more limited than at present, creating a problem the governing computer solved in a logical but chilling way. It was assumed everyone would live for eighty years, so a couple were expected to use 160 years of consumables. If they had a child, the total resources allocated to the three of them stayed at 160 years. In short, any parents who wanted their child to live a full life had to agree to end their own existence prematurely. This created heartbreaking acts of self-sacrifice, not only involving parents never living long enough to see their children grow up, but a husband ending his own life to give his wife longer to live, or vice-versa.

There were no such dilemmas for Numbers in this world. They felt no urge to have children of their own, and were content to do the logical thing and let genetic engineering maintain the balance between population and resources.

As if the scenes Tim McCann described at The Passing Place—where parents went to be put down—weren't bad enough, there was another harrowing twist. The idea was that you could transfer your credits to a dependent and declare yourself inValid but, rather than going to The Passing Place, you could go to what was known as a Pet Shop. You were literally putting yourself in the shop window, and anyone with enough credit to spare could buy you and take you home and feed you, in return for your undying gratitude and obedience. Such shops met the need for pets in a world without animals, and status symbols in a world with few material possessions.

McCann's novel told of children entering one such shop with morsels to feed 'pets' they couldn't afford to take home; and of a pet rescue circle comprising Names who'd banded together to buy a 'pet' which they'd take turns sharing their food rations with. The scene where they had to choose which person to save from The Passing Place was a truly distressing one.

The final passage Tim McCann had written was equally disturbing, but in a very different way. It started with a group of Numbers entering the shop and saying they wanted to buy some pets to act as their dancing tutors. It was quite plausible, since most Numbers have a limited repertoire of dance moves and execute them in a mechanical fashion. Anyway, they'd asked the inValids to go through everything from hip-hop to waltzes with imaginary partners.

Then, at the end of the pathetic little talent contest, the Numbers gave a collective sneer which made it clear they'd never had the slightest intention of taking an in-

Valid home.

I was glad Tim McCann hadn't written any more. I couldn't imagine it was the sort of story that had a happy ending.

I switched out the light, trying to forget about *The Pet Shop*, and turned my thoughts to Paula.

In an ideal world I would have dreamed about Niagara Falls and Paula or Marilyn Monroe. Come to think of it, in an ideal world I would dream about Niagara Falls, Paula, *and* Marilyn Monroe. If I had to choose two out of the three, I'd have forgotten about the falls.

What I actually got was one and a half out of three: Niagara without the falls, but with Paula.

Oh, I also got Jen—and a guilty conscience for not having included her in my initial three wishes.

Unfortunately, I got something else as well. The Pet Shop.

How predictable was that?

The Pet Shop was located slap bang in the touristy heart of the town of Niagara Falls. And of course I was in one of the display cabinets, and Jen was in another one. Her hands were pressed to the glass and she was whispering something to me that could have been 'I love you' or 'Help me.'

Behind her, in another cabinet, someone was waving to me. Their face was hidden because Jen was in the way. All I could see was the waving hand. It was Annie MacDougall's hand, shriveled up and growing almost right out of her shoulder.

A bell tinkled behind me. It was a small brass bell, over the door of the shop, and it announced the arrival of a Pareto.

He walked past me and stopped in front of the cabinet containing Jen. Annie MacDougall knocked on the glass with her withered hand to get his attention, but all she got was a sneer. The Pareto turned back to Jen and said something I couldn't make out. Then Jen was taking her clothes off and turning around slowly so the Pareto could inspect her. He nodded his approval to the shopkeeper, who I noticed for the first time.

It was Doug MacDougall.

In front of my eyes, Doug and the Pareto haggled over what Jen was worth, and finally Doug said, "I'll throw in the other one for nothing, a 'buy one, get one free'."

My heart skipped a beat, thinking Doug was talking about me and I'd be joining Jen.

But after Doug unlocked Jen's cabinet he moved over to the glass case containing Annie.

I had both hands pressed to the glass of my case as Jen was led out of the shop. As she passed by she put one hand up to press against mine.

And then she was gone, and I knew I would never see her again.

As Annie MacDougall passed she tried to press her hand against the glass next to my palm, like Jen had done.

But she couldn't reach, and in the end she just waved me goodbye with her withered, armless hand.

Annie left the little shop of horrors just as Perfect Paula came in.

My LogiPol partner got me to strip, which was a role reversal from my other kind of dreams—the daydreams, where you actually have some say in what's going on. Anyway, stripping for Paula was fine by me, although it would have been a whole lot better if she'd reciprocated and I hadn't been in a glass case.

What happened next wasn't so good, however—she looked me over from head to foot, and a mocking sneer appeared on her face. I didn't have to be a psychotherapist to figure out her sneer had something to do with the inadequacy Names feel in the presence of Numbers.

As if that wasn't bad enough, after looking me over and mocking me Perfect Paula turned to Doug MacDougall, shook her head and left without a backward glance.

Doug came over and said, "Sorry, Ben. Better luck tomorrow."

After switching off the lights Doug walked to the door, turning over a cardboard sign so the word CLOSED faced the outside world. He hesitated with his fingers on the door handle, as if he'd forgotten something, and came back to the counter. He brought out a bowl and shoved it through a slot near the foot of my display cabinet.

"Goodnight, sleep tight and don't let the bed bugs

bite," he said, and headed for the door. The brass bell tinkled, but I didn't see Doug MacDougall leave The Pet Shop because I was looking down at the bowl.

It was full of golden yellow moss.

CHAPTER 17

01000011010010000100000101010000010101000100010101010010

The Trip of a Lifetime

"You owe me an apology," I told Paula at the station house the next morning.

"Sorry."

"That's not what you were supposed to say."

"Okay, Travis, what was I supposed to say?"

"You were supposed to say, 'what do I owe you an apology for'?"

Paula sighed, then said, "What do I owe you an apology for?"

"Making me take all my clothes off, sneering, then walking out the shop without buying me."

"Sorry," she said. "Happy now?"

"Don't be a spoilsport. You were supposed to ask what

on earth I'm talking about."

"I don't think I want to know."

I told her anyway.

"You're making me glad I can't dream," she said. But we both knew that wasn't true.

"Last night was enough to make me wish I couldn't dream, either," I told her.

"I watched the movie," she said. Her abrupt change of subject caught me by surprise. It shouldn't, because it's a Number trait I should be used to by now. Whereas we say something like 'by the way' to warn whoever we're talking to that we're about to change tack, Numbers don't observe such linguistic niceties. I suppose it's because their brains work faster than ours and they don't need any warning of a change of subject to make sense of what follows. Sometimes I think they do it on purpose to throw us and make us look stupid—like I must have looked as I tried to follow Paula's conversational shift.

Then it dawned on me. She was talking about *Niagara*. Trying to sound casual, but not quite pulling it off, I said, "And?"

"It looks like an amazing place."

"You'll come then?"

"I'd like to, but it probably wouldn't—"

I didn't let her get any further. I hate the word 'probably.' *They* use it all the time, and it makes me think they're constantly weighing up all the possibilities to reach the most logical conclusion without the slightest emotional input in the decision-making process. If I had to pick one word that summed up the difference between *us* and *them*, it would be 'probably.' Notice I didn't say it would probably be 'probably.' "Paula," I said, "forget what would 'probably' be for the best, and for once in your life do something spontaneous without analyzing the likely consequences. Listen to your heart and tell your head to shut up."

"It's not that simple."

"Why not?"

"You can't change who you are, what you are."

"Can't you see that's exactly what you're trying to do? Part of you wants to go with me to Niagara Falls. I know that for sure, just as I know you can't ever be happy or fulfilled if you continually deny part of what you are."

"What's wrong with that sentence is it went on eleven words too long."

I counted back my words but ran out of memory before I ran out of fingers. The very fact Paula had been able to effortlessly count the words in real time should have made me want to give up on her. But, for all the differences between us, something drew me to her so powerfully that giving up wasn't an option. "Paula, you talk about not being able to change who you are, what you are—I think the problem is you're not sure of who and what you are. The community, where everything is geared to logic, doesn't let you express the part of yourself that's all about emotion."

Paula still didn't look ready to say 'yes' to the Niagara trip, but she wasn't saying 'no,' so I said, "Look, I'm shallow enough to admit I'm hoping whatever it was that happened between us in Newport library will happen again at Niagara Falls. I'm hoping it'll happen more powerfully, too powerfully for you to deny. But, more than that, I'm hoping that going to Niagara will let you find yourself. I'm hoping its wild beauty will set your spirit free." That hadn't occurred to me until I said it—my motives had been of a more selfish and sordid nature—but I didn't feel disingenuous once the words were spoken because I meant every one of them.

"Won't I be more conflicted than ever when I get back?" Paula said.

"You'll have a better idea of who you are."

"Maybe the whole problem is that I'm afraid to find out."

"How can you be comfortable with yourself if you don't really know who and what you are?" I said. "You make it sound like you're scared there's some sort of monster lurking inside you, when in fact it's the opposite."

"You mean the monster's on the outside."

"No, I mean there's something even more beautiful inside than outside. I mean you're only half the person you can be. Occasionally I've glimpsed the other half: in the fleeting moments of doubt and uncertainty that sometimes cloud your eyes; in the flashes of longing or sadness that are gone almost before I can recognize them for what they were—gone so quickly I used to wonder if I'd imagined them, until we were in the library and I saw them for long enough to know for sure what they were. I saw the real you for the first time in the library, Paula, and there's so much more to you than the person I see every day in this place—" I gestured to the spartan logica gray surroundings.

"I don't know what to say," Paula told me.

"You don't need to say anything, just be at the jetport at quarter to six tomorrow morning."

The jetport is built into the lower slopes of the hill, near the long, low factories the freightliners supply with raw materials. I meant to arrive there nice and early, but decided at the last moment to shave off my designer stubble.

There were seven people in the small passenger terminal by the time I finally got there.

Including Paula. She was standing in the middle of the terminal, looking lost and alone.

Two Paretos sat in the seats that lined the left-hand wall. They were dressed in gray coveralls with gold wings. Not big wings as in angels, but little ones of the kind that are embroidered on flight uniforms. They were toying with logic puzzles, not making any attempt at conversation with each other, let alone anyone else.

The other four people stood at the small, toughened glass windows at the far end of the terminal. The variety of their hairstyles, height and build told me they were Names. Their body language confirmed it: the smaller man, whose hair was bleached blond, had his arm around the shoulders of the woman beside him. The other man, who was taller and had dark hair, held his partner's hand.

Paula was watching the four Names. The man with bleached hair said something, and the others laughed. I wondered if Paula would have laughed if she'd been part of the group. I wondered which group she felt closer to, the pair of Paretos or the four Names. Maybe she wasn't sure about that herself. I hoped she'd have a better idea by the time the day was out.

"Paula," I said, as I walked toward her. She was startled by my approach, as if she'd been miles away.

Then it was my turn to be startled. For once, Perfect Paula was wearing a hint of makeup: no lipstick—she probably figured it would get grotesquely smeared on her filtermasks—but a touch of eyeliner.

Taking in the fact I was clean-shaven, Paula said, "You look ten years younger, Travis. You should have shaved your beard off years ago."

"That would have made me look about twelve," I said.

I didn't get the laugh I'd hoped for, but at least I got a smile.

The sexless Voice of Reason came through the loudspeakers: "Niagara flight crew, report to craft. Passengers be advised, take-off is in fifteen minutes."

"Excited?" I asked Paula.

She nodded, and there was a sparkle in her eyes I'd never seen before.

"We should introduce ourselves," I said, glancing at our fellow day-trippers.

Paula hesitated, like this was something she'd been dreading, then nodded.

The four Names heard us coming and turned from the windows, no doubt curious about who they'd be sharing their big day with. I barely merited a glance—all eyes focused on Paula. The laughter stopped and the smiles died away. There was no overt hostility in their expressions, just a draining away of the warmth.

With my usual tact and diplomacy I broke the ice by saying, "Okay, which two schmucks paid ten thousand points for their seats?"

Paula rolled her lovely silvery-blue eyes. "The two of us aren't friends or anything," she said apologetically to the new buddies I'd just made. "We just work together."

That got her a smile from Mr. Bleached Blond—a small, carefree-looking guy in his twenties; and a "Have you ever thought about looking for another job?" from the dark-haired older man—a serious type who looked like Michael Rennie in *The Day the Earth Stood Still*. He followed his little witticism by turning from Paula to me and saying, "Incidentally, *we* all won our tickets on the lottery, so we thought *you* were the schmucks." The tone of his voice and coldness of his eyes made me think he had some Numbered blood. It would be unusual, but not unheard of; for some reason unions spanning the genetic divide almost never result in conception. I suspect Paula detected Numerical traits in him, too, because I sensed some of the tension going out of her. Relaxed isn't a word I'd use in connection with my partner, but at least she was looking a little less uptight.

Just as I like comparing people to Olden Days actors, so I have a habit of judging their personalities by their appearance. My LogiPol training told me not to do it, but experience has shown my instincts are usually right. I had the young bleached-blond guy, who turned out to be a Community General surgeon called Jonny Adams—pegged as someone you'd have to work hard to dislike. He'd enjoy a good practical joke and wouldn't take anything short of a triple-bypass too seriously—and even then, only if his patient died on the table. Come to think of it, I could picture him shrugging his shoulders after a botched operation, saying, "Oh well, you win some, you lose some," then restoring the morale of his theatre assistants by pinging a bloodied rubber glove at them across the lifeless corpse.

His wife was small and slight, with dark brown, bob-cut hair and the look of someone who was never short of an opinion or hesitant about expressing it. She introduced herself as "Dr Heather Adams—a researcher at Community General," while giving me a handshake that was a lot firmer than her husband's. I'd no trouble figuring out who wore the trousers in that relationship. Jonny appeared blissfully content, though. I've heard that some men enjoy being bossed around by their partners.

As for Michael Rennie, he turned out to be a professor by the name of Frank Faraday, and was an astrophysics lecturer in the learning zone. Somehow I hadn't pictured him being a scriptwriter for a comedy show, although I have to admit his crack to Paula about looking for another job wasn't bad. At least, not bad for someone who had very little sense of humor and took himself way too seriously. His wife was a sweet blonde who obviously adored him. They were as apparently mismatched as Arthur Miller and Marilyn Monroe. But since no one had told them they were incompatible they hadn't realized it, and seemed to get along fine. She introduced herself as Margot, and said she was a homemaker.

Michael Rennie asked what *we* did, but fortunately the loudspeakers crackled into life again, signaling an announcement was imminent and saving me from disclosing my vocation. I'm not ashamed of what I do, it's just that people—well, Names—tend to get edgy when they discover you're with LogiPol, even if they've done nothing wrong and you're not doing anything to make them think you suspect they have. And these four would be edgy enough around Paula as it was. At least until they saw she wasn't like other Numbers. The crackle of the loudspeakers also saved me from inventing a title for myself so I wouldn't feel out of my depth, what with a couple of doctors on one side of me and a professor on the other. I think 'Commander Travis' has quite a nice ring to it, but I'm not sure anyone except Margot would have bought it.

"Passengers for Niagara Falls, be advised that boarding takes place in ten minutes," the Voice of Reason informed us. "On insertion of your ID card in the reader to the left of the airlock doors you will each be allocated eight filters from the adjacent dispenser. There is no need to use them during the flight as the passenger cabin is a sealed unit. Flight time is two hours and twenty three minutes, and you will have four hours at Niagara."

"I hope they give us a barrel to go over the falls in," I said.

Paula gave me an 'I can't take you anywhere look.'

I gave her my best boyish smile.

Her heart melted and she smiled back.

Well, okay, that's not exactly true. What she actually did was roll her eyes again. I leaned forward and whispered, "If you keep doing that, one of these days your eyes'll go all the way around, and then where'll you be?"

Her heart might not have melted, but at least she smiled. Actually, she was fighting back a laugh. I didn't think my crack about her eyes rolling backward was all *that* funny. Then I realized she was looking over my shoulder at Frank Faraday. I half turned and saw the professor had hauled a pipe out of the pocket of his coveralls. There was no tobacco in it, of course—smoking was outlawed from day one in the communities. At first there were lots of conduct violations and penalty points levied on people who'd scavenged cigarettes and tins of tobacco from the old cities, but the problem sorted itself out when there was no more tobacco left to scavenge. However there was no law against shoving an antique pipe in your mouth. Which was a pity, because I found it intensely irritating watching the professor chew on his. I wondered if he found it an aid to concentration, or if it was pure affectation. Or maybe it was something deeper, a subconscious way of denying the Numbered blood I was sure ran through his veins. Then again, he might just like to have something other than some teeth and a tongue in his mouth.

I could imagine him taking it out in class—the pipe, that is, not his tongue—and tapping the empty bowl in the palm of his hand while he pondered something profound, or conducting an imaginary orchestra with it in the privacy of his apartment.

I was going to ask if he wanted a light, but Paula dragged me away before I had a chance. She can't have known what I was about to say, but she knew I was about to say something and no doubt guessed it would be better if Professor Faraday was out of earshot when I said it.

"Behave, Travis!" she scolded as she led me over to the seats vacated by the Paretos.

"I'm just excited," I told her. "I've always wanted to see somewhere like this."

After a few moments Paula said, "Is it the sort of thing you're thinking about when you look without seeing?"

"I'm sorry?"

"When you daydream, I've always wondered what sort of things you dream about."

"I dream about lots of things."

"Tell me about some of them, Travis."

"Only if you call me Ben—for today, at least."

"I could bring you up on charges for blackmailing a superior officer."

I offered her my hands and said, "Go on, cuff me."

"Why do I get the feeling I'd be acting out some sort of fantasy for you if I did?"

"Looks like you already know what I dream about."

She laughed. But when the laughter died away her expression was more thoughtful than if she'd only been thinking about my handcuff fantasy. "What do you really daydream about, Ben?" she asked.

So I told her: "Blue skies and far horizons; breaking waves and tall grass blowing in the wind.

"Places with names that sound like they come from lines of poetry: Shanghai, Samarkand and Marrakech; Timbuktu and Kathmandu. Traveling to them on steam trains, sailing ships and propeller-driven planes; by gypsy wagon or caravan of camels.

"Seeing the sights that lined the Silk Route, Salt Road and Frankincense Trail; the Way of a Thousand Kasbahs, the Royal Road of the Incas. . . Following in the wake of Columbus, the footsteps of Marco Polo, Livingstone and Stanley, Lewis and Clarke. I dream of seeing the world the way it was when Calum Tait saw it."

"I've heard of the others but not of him," Paula said.

"He was a travel writer near the end of the Old Days. I analyze his articles—that's my contribution to The Search for Meaning—then I use the pleasure points I earn to go on timesphere trips to the times and places he wrote about. Somehow those trips never capture my imagination the way his words do, though. In the timesphere I can see the big things he wrote about: the castles and cathedrals, palaces and bridges, mountains and beaches—"

"What's missing then?"

"The little delights he said make life come alive."

"Such as?"

"Unexpected things that are different in each place, that he'd never read about in guidebooks. Things like a butterfly with brilliant blue wings as big as his hand in a rainforest in Brazil; two dragonflies doing a mid-air dance around a 1000-year-old scholar tree near the Forbidden City in Beijing; seahorses drifting with their tails entwined like lovers in the Two Oceans Aquarium in Cape Town. . .

"Things like seeing perfectly sober people stop to listen to buskers in Barcelona and start to dance right there in the street. . .

"Sitting on the slopes of the acropolis in Athens at sunset and listening to people who'd been washed up by the tides of travel all around him; hearing every language under the sun and not understanding a single word, but knowing what was being said by watching the people as they spoke—the lovers with their arms around each other, the loneliness of solitary travelers looking on. . .

"Seeing the body of a saint being carried through the streets of Seville and feeling a kind of religious awe, even though he wasn't sure if he believed in God, let alone religion. . .

"Visiting the Kennedy Space Center and hearing a young boy ask an astronaut what size spaceships were, and the astronaut answering that spaceships come in all shapes and sizes but the most important one is planet Earth, and we're all part of the crew. . .

"Watching a bride and groom being toasted with vodka in St Petersburg, hearing chants of 'Gorko! Gorko!' and learning that the word means bitter, and Russians used to shout it after a wedding because they believed life could be bitter like vodka, but the kiss of a bride made it sweet."

Paula went very quiet, then said, "I love the sound of those names and places and things, but I can't connect with them or relate to them like you so obviously do. It's as if I lack an imagination for these things to capture, a race memory for them to awaken. They belong to a world so different from the community that I can't conceive of it—it takes more imagination than I have. If I read those articles it would be like they were written in a foreign language. They wouldn't fill me with wonder, they'd leave me cold. And listening to you talk about them makes me feel less than human in some way."

"Believe me, you didn't seem less than human in the library, Paula."

She gave me something like a smile, then said, "Speaking of libraries, I brought along a book to read on the flight. I didn't want to annoy you by playing with a logic puzzle."

"You can tell that annoys me?"

She answered me with a laugh, unslung her shoulder bag and brought out a tattered old book. *Lichens and Mosses of the World.*

"How far did you get before I took it from you to give Annie MacDougall a read?" I asked.

"Halfway through the third sentence of the second paragraph on Page 97."

She could doubtless tell me word for word what the sentence said.

"I've been meaning to ask what was on your mind before the call came in about the druggie the other day, when you handed the book to me and said: 'Does this mean anything to you?'"

"I'll show you," I said. I reached for the tattered old volume and flicked through the pages until I came to the photo of the golden moss. "It looks like this is the last page Doug MacDougall read," I told her as I handed back the book. "I'd been going to ask if you could think why those underlined words would change how he viewed life and the world."

Like all Numbers, Paula loves a cerebral challenge. She turned her attention to the book and I got the feeling she'd forgotten I was there. The color drained from her face as she read the paragraph in question. She swallowed and read it again, and I knew it meant a whole lot more to her than it did to me.

"What is it?" I asked.

For once she was lost for words.

I took the book from her and re-read the underscored sentences, trying to see what I'd missed first time around and Paula had spotted right away.

Immaculata solaris, *pictured above, has no common name because it is not commonly known, living only in the most extreme of alpine environments. Studies show it to be remarkable for more than its vivid color and hardiness, for it is not part of any food chain—it does not feed on anything but sunlight, and nothing feeds on it.*!!!

I could have looked at the paragraph forever and not seen anything more than a collection of innocuous words. "Paula—"

"I can see why he was killed," she said, staring at the photo of the moss. "But not how. Unless, it must have been. . ."

"Paula, what's going on?"

She looked from the book to me, and said, "Don't you see: 'it is not part of any food chain—it doesn't feed on anything but sunlight, and nothing feeds on it'."

"So?" I said, exasperated at not being able to grasp the significance of the brief passage. "I can't think of anything less meaningful. I can't think of any less likely motive for murder."

"It changes everything," she said, as if thinking aloud rather than speaking to me. "At least, from the Ecosystem's point of view."

"WHY?"

I'd spoken so loudly the other two couples looked over. I wasn't caring about them or Niagara Falls any more. All I cared about was discovering what had got Doug MacDougall killed and cast some sort of spell over Paula. Something in my voice must have broken that spell, because Paula looked at me and said, "Don't you see? If the moss isn't part of any food chain it's not part of any bigger picture, of any grand design. It's tangible proof life can exist for its own sake, just to enjoy the light and warmth of the sun."

"And?"

"Consider the implications for the Ecosystem."

"You've lost me."

"Think about it: The Search for Meaning and Purpose is an integral part of the Ecosystem. At first people were drawn together by the crisis that destroyed the Old World. Now that we've adjusted to a new way of life, and are no longer faced by crisis, we need another common cause to unite us. That's what The Search for Meaning is." She looked at the photo of *immaculata solaris*. "This moss undermines the very foundations of The Search."

Now I saw what she was getting at, but still it was hard to connect the little patch of color in the faded photograph with a threat to life as we'd come to know it.

Paula helped me out. "It raises the possibility that there is no meaning, that our only purpose is to enjoy the light and warmth of the sun and blossom in beautiful colors before fading away."

"So why has all this only come to light now, after the Ecosystem's been going for over fifty years? Hundreds of people will have read the book in that time." Remembering how dull it was, I revised my estimate: "Well, tens."

"Not many Names would make the connection. Most Numbers would, but it's not the sort of book a Number would read. MacDougall must have been the first person to reach the profound conclusion about *immaculata solaris*—but, unfortunately, he didn't realize its wider implications."

"So he'd have put together a thesis, expecting a vast reward in pleasure points—"

"But the Ecosystem identified the threat this new

knowledge posed, and wiped out the thesis—and the man who'd written it," Paula said.

"A computer couldn't kill Doug MacDougall."

"No, but it could have issued a directive ordering his death."

"I've a good idea who would carry out such a directive without question."

"A Pareto," Paula said.

I nodded.

"A Pareto could move like a ghost, because the Ecosystem would literally open doors for it, and wipe all trace of its movements from the database," Paula said.

I was glad I was sitting down because I felt dizzy as I tried to take it all in.

Paula was a couple of steps ahead of me, and those steps had taken her to an even more frightening place. "Tra—" She corrected herself and continued in a dread-filled voice, "Ben, have you used the Ecosystem to make any inquiries about *immaculata solaris*?"

I nodded. A cold sweat broke out on my forehead and palms as I realized what she was getting at. If Doug was killed for what he knew, and the Ecosystem had reason to believe we were on the brink of finding out what Doug knew. . .

Suddenly my lottery win looked more like the upswing of an executioner's axe than a stroke of good fortune.

Paula's next words echoed my last thoughts: "Do you think it's just a coincidence your number came up?"

"I'm not a big believer in coincidence."

"Neither am I. Especially when my life's at stake."

I looked at the other two couples. They were deep in animated conversation, oblivious to the possibility they might be marked for death because of something I'd done. "What about them?" I said. "Isn't life sacrosanct to the Ecosystem? Isn't that one of its guiding principles?"

"Yes, but its over-riding imperative is to further the greater good. It would take whatever action is needed to ensure the good of the many, regardless of the cost to a few."

"Still, wouldn't it have found a way to get rid of the two of us without sacrificing innocent lives, like it managed to do with Doug MacDougall?"

Paula looked at the two couples standing at the window and said, "Nobody bought their tickets for this flight, did they?"

"Apparently not."

"Maybe their lottery win didn't have any more to do with good fortune than yours, Ben. I think we should go and speak to them, find out a bit more about what they do."

I nodded. Worried I'd be distracted by that ludicrous pipe I said to Paula, "You better take Michael Rennie and—"

"What?"

"Sorry, the professor and his wife."

Bemused, she nodded.

We got up and went our separate ways.

Reasoning it was a safe bet Jonny Adams didn't pose any

sort of threat to the Ecosystem, I concentrated my charm on his good wife, the researcher at Community General. There wasn't much time, but one of the things they teach you in LogiPol is how to get people to tell you things you want to know without them realizing what either of you are doing.

It turned out her special interest was a bacterium called *deinococcus radiodurans*, which can apparently survive thousands of times as much radiation as a human. It was the sort of subject that would glaze my eyes under normal circumstances. But the present circumstances weren't exactly normal, and I didn't have to feign interest when I asked her to tell me more.

Alarm bells went off when she told me she'd recently discovered the enzyme which allowed *dinosaurus radiowhatever* to repair its damaged chromosomes.

My eyes did start glazing over when she started going into details, and I used the old 'cocking my head to one side and pretending I'd just had a call on my hear-ring' routine to excuse myself.

I didn't know if Paula'd had a chance to find anything out, but there wasn't any more time to spare because the boarding call would be coming over the loudspeaker at any minute. So, after extricating myself from the clutches of Mrs. Dr. Adams and her bacteria, I extricated Paula from the clutches of the professor. This time it wasn't difficult to avoid making any cracks about his pipe because I had something else on my mind. I got it off my mind as soon as we were out of earshot of the Faradays and the Adams Family. "Heather Adams has made some sort of breakthrough in discovering an enzyme that lets chromosomes damaged by radiation repair themselves," I told Paula. "I'm thinking that's got to have implications for repairing DNA damaged by pollution."

"And restoring the fertility of plants and animals. . . And people," Paula said.

I nodded. "Her number coming up when she's made such a profound discovery has to be more than a coincidence. The trouble is, I can see how Doug's discovery might be seen as a threat by the Ecosystem, but not how Heather Adams' breakthrough can be viewed as anything other than good news."

"I think I can," Paula said. "And then there's Faraday."

"What's he done to earn the wrath of the Ecosystem?"

"Proved the existence of God."

"What!"

Before she could explain, the loudspeakers crackled into life: "Passengers for Niagara Falls, please enter the airlock."

"Ben, we can't get on this flight," Paula said.

I didn't take any convincing. Something told me the jetliner wasn't going to get as far as Niagara Falls. It would either crash and burn, or put down in the middle of nowhere and take off minus its passengers.

"We can't let *them* get on, either," I said as Jonny and

Heather Adams and the Faradays approached.

"I'm not sure there's any point trying to stop them," Paula told me, thinking with pure logic. "If all six of us refuse to board, it'll be obvious we know what's going on. We'll have condemned ourselves to death as surely as if we got on the flight."

She was right, but as the two men and their wives walked past us into the airlock I couldn't look them in the eye. I started to go after them, not sure what to say but sure I had to say something. Paula pulled me back. "There's nothing we can do to save them, Ben. I'm not even sure there's anything we can do to save ourselves."

The inner doors of the airlock remained open.

Waiting for us.

"Passengers Travis and Paula enter the airlock," the Voice of Reason said.

Heather and Jonny and the Faradays turned around to see what the holdup was.

What they saw was not a pretty sight: Paula had shoved two fingers down her throat moments earlier and now she was doubled over, delivering what I believe used to be euphemistically referred to as a street pizza.

The smiles of the four people in the airlock froze, and then turned to expressions covering pretty much the whole spectrum of disgust. I expected good old Dr. Jonny to help, but Margot was the only one who made a move.

Paula looked up as the professor's wife approached and

said, “It’s okay, it’s something I ate this morning. It’s not agreeing with me.”

One of the Pareto crewmen appeared, no doubt having been sent to find out what the delay was.

Paula repeated her story and said, “I don’t think I can go on the—” she interrupted herself by conjuring up a less than delightful topping for the pizza. Margot retreated into the airlock, and the Pareto took a step back to avoid getting any splashes on his immaculate gray flight suit.

“What about you?” he asked me.

“I had what she had,” I told him, then started convulsively swallowing, as if fighting a losing battle to hold back a copious torrent. No doubt fearing he could end up wearing my breakfast all over his neatly pressed coveralls, the Pareto retreated inside the airlock.

“Bad luck,” the professor’s wife said as the airlock doors closed.

Although I wasn’t throwing up, I felt as sick as Paula.

CHAPTER 18

01000011010010000010000010101000001010100010001010101010010

Burning Bright

"I'M SORRY," I SAID TO PAULA AS WE LEFT THE JETPORT.

"What for?"

"This wouldn't be happening if I'd accepted Doug MacDougall's death at face value."

"You were right not to, so there's no need to apologize."

I couldn't fault Paula's logic, but that didn't stop me regretting my actions. "If we're right about all this, not boarding the flight has just earned us a stay of execution rather than a reprieve," I told her. "The Ecosystem will make another move, and it'll be against you as well as me because of the probability—" I'd never hated that word more—"that you know as much about Doug's death as I do."

"I know," she said. "Look, Ben, this isn't your fault any

more than it was Doug MacDougall's."

We stood there between the ghostly ruins of the old city and the gray blocks of the community. I didn't know which way to turn. Ironically, given that I'd uncovered the whole mess in the first place and had spent so long trying to convince Paula there was more to it than met the eye, I was the one who went into denial. "Do you think we might be reading too much into all of this?" I said. "Could we be inventing a conspiracy that doesn't really exist?"

"That possibility's looking ever more remote. And if the Faradays and the two doctors don't come back from Niagara safe and sound. . ."

"I still don't really understand what's going on," I said, not worrying about losing face. The point-scoring games we used to play belonged to another lifetime. "I can see why the Ecosystem viewed Doug as a threat, but surely what Heather Adams is on the verge of uncovering is for the greater good."

"For the good of mankind, not the Ecosystem."

"Aren't they one and the same?"

"They were, but it looks like the Ecosystem program got corrupted somewhere along the way."

"How could that happen? The whole thing about the Ecosystem is that it's incapable of acting out of self interest."

"Not any more, apparently. It might be possible to believe there's another explanation for MacDougall's death, and that your number coming up on the lottery is a coincidence, and Heather Adams' number coming up as she's on the point of making her breakthrough is another coincidence—but that still leaves the professor, and I can't believe his number came up by chance."

That was how caught up I'd been in our plight; it had slipped my mind that the man with the pipe had apparently answered one of the most profound questions ever asked. "How did he do it?" I asked. "How did he prove the existence of God?"

"By taking a new approach to the ultimate cosmological mystery: namely, the fact there's not enough matter in existence to hold the universe together."

I don't have a great grasp of science, but I remembered enough physics from my schooldays to have a rough idea what she was talking about. Matter exerts gravity, and apparently there isn't nearly enough of it to stop the cosmos from catastrophically flying apart. In other words, the universe shouldn't exist. The discrepancy has led to decades of postulating about 'dark matter' and the hunt for exotic particles, but they've never been found.

"Faraday thinks he knows the answer to the puzzle," Paula said. "He thinks what's holding the universe together is the will of God. If the jetliner goes down, it suggests the Ecosystem has come to the same conclusion and feels threatened by the notion of word getting out that there is a greater power than its logic."

I couldn't have imagined in my wildest dreams or worst

nightmares that getting the empty syringe from Doug MacDougall's flat analyzed would lead to all of this.

"Put the pieces together and they make a compelling case," Paula said. "First of all, the Ecosystem felt threatened by MacDougall's observation about *immaculata solaris* because it undermined The Search for Meaning—and man's reliance on computer processing power to further that search and have any hope of reaching a conclusion. . .

"Then it was threatened by you when you showed signs of finding out what MacDougall had learned."

"And Heather Adams?"

"Her enzyme discovery takes away the need for genetic engineering, so reducing the Ecosystem's ability to create life in its own image.

"Then there's the professor, offering proof of the existence of a higher power; a power that people—Names, anyway—might start putting their faith in, rather than putting their trust in the Ecosystem."

"I still don't see how the Ecosystem could go from pure logic to this."

"Maybe all these years of exposure to the most powerful expressions of human thought and feeling in The Search for Meaning corrupted its program in some way, warped its logic and imbued it with the very human characteristics it was analyzing—things like the desire to be needed, to feel important, to create life in its own image."

A piece I hadn't even realized belonged to the puzzle

fell into place: why there seemed to be more Paretos than there used to be.

Other things followed, like the possibility Slo-Mo and Rush had been formulated by the Ecosystem rather than by a naughty lab technician. Given that Numbers would avoid something which gave them pleasure but destroyed them, and Names lacked the logic to resist such temptation, the drugs would be an ideal way to deplete the pool of illogical thinkers.

And then there was the notion that the author of *The Pet Shop* had been killed for writing a story that was too close to the truth, or simply offended the Ecosystem's sensibilities. Maybe Tim McCann started writing the story on his computer, like he'd always done before. The Ecosystem didn't like what he was writing and wiped it out, so he started writing with pencil on paper in an Olden Days diary—and never finished because the Ecosystem sent a Pareto to wipe him out.

Just as it would send one to wipe *us* out, if we were right about all this.

"What are we going to do, Paula?" I asked.

"If the Faradays and the doctors don't come back from Niagara we've got to assume we're next on the list that started with MacDougall. That leaves us with a choice of fight or flight."

Which meant a quick death in the community or a lingering death Outside.

Paula put it in more clinical terms, but it came down to the same thing: "Our chances of being able to live for any length of time Outside aren't great, but they're a whole lot better than the odds of beating the Ecosystem and the Paretos who embody it."

"You think we should make a run for it?"

"I don't think we have much choice," she said. "We better start preparing ourselves mentally and physically for life Outside, Ben."

I nodded, unable to speak. You tend to think of your future in terms of years. It's not easy to suddenly be confronted by the knowledge that what's left of your life can be measured in days and weeks at best, hours and minutes at worst. Yet Paula's words and manner suggested she'd already made the adjustment. She seemed so very different from me as she stood there weighing probabilities, calculating odds and formulating options that I wondered if things could ever have worked out between us, even if we'd had the luxury of time.

"We should fill a couple of packs with anything that'll be of help on the Outside, so we're ready to make a run for it if the jetliner doesn't come back from Niagara," she said. "Agreed?"

I nodded. Things weren't turning out like they do in books and movies, where the strong hero takes charge when the going gets tough, and adversity draws you closer to whoever you're facing it with.

It wasn't turning out like that at all.

We headed up the deserted street toward Haven Nine. I looked over my shoulder every ten or twenty steps, expecting to see a Pareto in pursuit, and each time we approached a street corner my pulse quickened and my steps slowed in expectation of an ambush.

"Relax," Paula said. "They won't come at us in the open, where we can take them out with our knockdowns, or in a public place where it'll cause a scene. They'll either wait until we're sleeping, like they did with MacDougall, or make it look like an accident—sending a lift plummeting out of control, something like that."

"Remind me to take the stairs from now on."

"Something tells me I won't have to."

"I'm not being paranoid, they really are out to get me."

She managed a smile, which was more than I could have done if someone had just cracked such a feeble joke.

A small food distribution freighter approached us. I reached for my knockdown and didn't take my hand off the butt until the hoverjet was past. I only realized I'd been holding my breath when it came out in an audible sigh of relief.

When we got to Haven Nine I half expected my card to set off an alarm as I inserted it into the reader, but the doors opened without a sound.

I gave the elevator a hateful look, as if it had already tried to kill me, and made my way over to the stairs with Paula at my side. "Your place or mine?" I asked. I'd always wanted to say that to her but hadn't imagined doing it in circumstances quite like this.

"We'll go to your apartment first," she said. "You can pack a holdall, then we'll head up to mine and I'll do the same. It's best if we stick together."

That was fine by me. I'd never felt less like being alone.

The first thing I did when we got to my flat was ditch the camera from my daypack. Taking photos didn't seem all that important any more. If I pointed my camera and said 'smile' to Paula after a couple of days' scavenging in the ruins I was pretty sure she would bring out her knockdown and take a shot at me before I could take a shot of her.

I packed a spare coverall and some changes of underwear, then looked around the apartment for anything else that might be of use Outside.

"Better leave plenty room for food and water," Paula said. "We might as well max out our credit cards at the store before we head off."

I nodded, and was on my way to join her at the door when I remembered something we might be very glad of a little way down the line.

Paula watched curiously as I rummaged in my desk drawer. When I found what I was looking for I slipped it in my pocket before she could see what it was.

"What's that?" she asked.

"Just something we might need later on."

"Travis. . ."

Before she could press me further I walked past her, slotted my card, and did an 'after you' to show her out the door.

When we were halfway down the corridor I couldn't resist stopping again and pretending I'd forgotten something else.

Paula tutted loudly and didn't see the funny side when I said, "Just kidding."

"I think we'll end up going our separate ways within a couple of days, Travis," she told me.

"I think you'll come to treasure my impish sense of humor," I told her.

This was more like it: laughing in the face of adversity. I'd like to think it was a natural resilience shining though, but I suppose it was simply resignation setting in.

"Isn't humor supposed to be funny?" Paula asked.

I couldn't think of a witty retort, and force of habit had me reaching up to rub my nose, like I used to do when she bested me. I stopped myself just in time, covering my mouth and faking a cough because I couldn't think what else to do.

"Now *that* was funny," Paula said, reading me like a book.

We laughed together, which was fine, but it would have been even better if we hadn't both been laughing at me.

I thought I'd packed quickly but Paula put me to shame. She didn't even pause to look around her apartment. I did. It was my first time in her flat. It held a big surprise, in the form of a well-filled bookcase. Most Numbers don't feel the need to collect anything. Clutter is anathema to them, and once they've finished with something they discard it. Besides, when it comes to books they prefer the electronic versions, regarding the old printed editions with disdain. It's as if they find the yellowed paper too unclean to touch, the foxing too distracting, the taint of damp and mould too unpleasant. Those things aren't outweighed by the satisfaction of being able to hold something in your hands, as they are for us; of turning pages and listening to the sound they make, as if the words are being whispered down the years by whoever wrote them; of feeling the draught from the moving paper and smelling with it something other than the antiseptic sterility of the haven.

So it came as a surprise to see a bookcase in Paula's apartment.

I was even more surprised when I saw the books that filled it. Numbers prefer hard fact to fiction, however Paula's bookcase had works by the Brontes and Jane Austen. There was *Message in a Bottle* and *True Believer* by Nicholas Sparks, and *The Bridges of Madison County* and *A Thousand Country Roads* by Robert James Waller. Each had no doubt been bought at great cost from The Book Store, because Perfect Paula hadn't been to the old city before our trip to the library. Looking at those books I realized how much of an act she'd been putting on when she played the ice maiden. I could only guess how hard it must have been for her.

Paula came out of the bedroom and I straightened up guiltily. In a bid to make up for my prying I said, "Do you want me to carry some books for you in my pack?"

"I won't need any love stories about noble, courteous heroes, Travis; I'll have you."

"Maybe I better pack six or seven just in case."

That earned me a smile and broke the awkwardness.

Paula didn't take a last look around before leaving, but she did hesitate in the doorway and go back for something from her desk, as I'd done. She tried to hide the object, like I had, but it was too big for her hand to conceal. It was a cube with lots of tiny multicolored squares, like on Olden Days Rubik's puzzle but infinitely more difficult to master. As if unable to make up her mind about something, she stood perfectly still for much longer than I'd ever seen a Number do before—they usually know exactly what to do in any given situation. Then she put the logic puzzle back in the desk and walked over to the bookcase. She knelt down and her slender fingers unerringly found what she was looking for.

I thought she'd never looked more beautiful than she did in that moment, kneeling in front of the bookcase of love stories from a lost world. The crush that had turned into a fondness turned into something else, something I'd only experienced once in my life and thought I'd never feel again. I felt it as a tightness in my chest, a lightness in my stomach and a weakness in my knees. Watching Paula take her chosen book from the shelf I wished she'd opted for the logic puzzle instead, because that would have added to the feeling I'd had outside the jetport that maybe the differences between us were too great to overcome, no matter how much time we'd had together. It would have made the knowledge that in all likelihood I'd soon have to watch this woman die just a little bit easier to bear.

"So you were joking about not needing a book with a noble hero in it," I said.

"It's not a love story, Ben, and it's not for me, it's a present for you."

She handed me the book and my eyes blurred when I saw what it was: John Steinbeck's *Burning Bright*, a song of praise for the human spirit.

"Oh, Paula," I said, and took her in my arms. I rocked her from side to side, glad she couldn't see my face because there were tears streaming down it. From the small movements of her shoulders I knew she was crying, too. I think she was maybe crying for the same reason as me—helpless frustration that something was happening between us and we'd never know how beautiful it could have been.

One thing led to another and. . .

Let's just say that if the Paretos had come for us in the next four hours, none of the positions they'd have found us in included any that would have left us able to defend ourselves.

The first hour was about desperation and need; about time running out and having to make the most of every moment; about fear of what we were facing, and the need to hold someone so we didn't face it alone. It was about pent-up desire and the need to release it with someone. And only a little of it was about love. It was an hour of raking nails and clutching hands and breathlessness, of pleading and pleasure that came close to pain because it was sought and given with such urgency.

The next two hours were about recovering; a time with her arm draped across my chest, the smoothness of the inside of one of her thighs lying across mine.

The last hour was about discovering: stroking and caressing and tracing with fingertip; touching and being touched, and being moved without moving; coming together and drawing apart over and over again, and always coming together one more time than we drew apart. It was a time of whispers spoken and listened to and understood; of wordless moans that said more than the whispers, some of them hers and some mine and some so much a single sound they couldn't be separated.

That last hour was about love, and at the end of it Paula asked, "Do I still seem like one of *them*?"

And I said, "No, you seem like a part of me."

CHAPTER 19

01000011010010000100000101010000010101000100010101010010

The Paretos

Afterward—once we'd maxed out our credit cards and filled our daypacks in the imaginatively named Food Store—we headed to the canteen. The afterglow of loving meant our Last Supper felt more like a honeymooners' late breakfast. Paula kept giving me knowing smiles accompanied by the hint of a blush, and her feet playfully sought out my legs and teased me almost as much as her expression.

I ended up doing lots of swallowing even when there wasn't any food in my mouth.

The fact we were sitting across from each other, that we were so obviously *together*, drew disapproving looks from other tables. Everybody knows Names and Numbers sometimes get it on, but public displays of cross-genetic affection are literally frowned upon. Knowing we had an audience, I couldn't resist spearing a synthesized vege-stick with my fork and offering it to Paula.

She threw her head back and laughed in a way I'd never heard a Number laugh before. More heads turned, but I don't think Paula was caring about the disapproving looks any more than I was. I'm sure she realized, as I did, that this was the only chance we'd ever get to act like carefree lovers.

And then, inevitably, the mood turned somber. The canteen was emptying and it was time for us to leave, too. The sobering thing was that we didn't have the prospect of a relaxing night in comfort and security ahead of us like everyone else did. The chances were we'd never have another night like that again.

"The news'll be on soon," I said.

Paula nodded, all trace of laughter gone from her eyes.

"Where do you want to watch it?" I asked.

"Your place is closest."

We didn't say anything as we climbed the stairs. Halfway up the second flight we heard a distant roar in the sky.

The Niagara Falls jetliner.

We raced to the next landing like a couple of children. From the small stairwell window we watched the lights grow in the sky and listened to the roar get louder, and nothing had ever looked or sounded so good.

"Just because the jetliner came back there's no saying

its passengers did," Paula said, but she wasn't quite able to keep her voice emotionless.

"I feel like running down to the jetport to see if the Adams Family and the Faradays are there," I said.

"I know what you mean, but it'd be simpler to watch the news," Paula said.

So we did.

Every minute that passed without mention of a Niagara mishap raised my hopes a little higher.

Which made it all the more crushing when, right at the end of the broadcast, the newsreader said, "It is with great regret that we report a tragic accident which has claimed the lives of four valued citizens."

I felt like the ground had opened up beneath my feet and I was falling into a bottomless pit. My heart thumped as if it was trying to shatter my ribs, and the blood was pounding so loud in my head that I barely heard the newsreader. It was as though the words were coming from a lot further away than the wallscreen.

"The good luck of a lottery win turned to the ultimate misfortune for four day-trippers to Niagara Falls when they plunged to their death after a viewing platform gave way. Dr Heather Adams and her husband Jonny, also a doctor—"

Paula switched off the screen.

I kept staring at the blank wall, numbed by the implications of what I'd just heard; trying to come to terms with the fact my life was about to change forever, and that 'forever' wasn't likely to last longer than a few weeks or months.

Paula had the same adjustment to make but made it much sooner. "There's no point wasting any time, Ben."

I nodded dumbly.

There was an air of unreality about it all as I followed Paula to the door. I hesitated and took a last look around. It was hard to believe I wouldn't be coming back to the place that had been my home since the academy.

"Ben—" Paula prompted, and with that I turned my back on the apartment and my old life.

I half expected to find a Pareto walking down the corridor or coming out the lift to confront us, but we didn't see anyone as we headed for the stairwell. What we were doing was so drastic that, despite all the evidence, I couldn't help but wonder if we were fleeing from a phantom enemy that was a product of imagination rather than a reflection of reality.

All of that changed when we reached the bottom of the stairs. Any lingering doubts I'd had about whether we were really running for our lives were blown away by the most innocuous of sounds. Paula heard it first, and it stopped her in her tracks, hand poised on the handle of the door to the foyer. She stopped so abruptly I nearly banged into her. I was about to ask what was wrong, but she pressed an upraised forefinger to her lips. She cocked her head, ear to the door, and I did likewise.

I couldn't hear anything except white noise and the hammering of my heart.

Then I heard something else: *click.*

A couple of seconds' silence.

Another *click*, slightly louder this time.

A silence lasting exactly as long as the last one.

Click. Definitely louder than the last time, telling me the source of the sound was getting closer.

Paula made a silent gesture with thumb and index finger. Even before her mimed finger-clicking I knew there was a Number heading toward the door.

It could be an ordinary citizen, I told myself. But then the soft clicking stopped and was followed by a louder, metallic *CLICK-CLICK* from no more than a meter or two away.

A weapon being cocked.

Paula mouthed '*knockdown,*' and I nodded.

The first *CLICK-CLICK* was followed by a second. There were two people on the other side of the door.

Moving so slowly she wouldn't make a sound, Paula unslung her daypack and placed it on the stair at her back. By the time I'd done likewise Paula had raised a fist in front of my face and was unfolding a finger, initiating a silent countdown. I knew the drill. I'd seen it often enough on Olden Days cop shows, when two partners are getting set to go through a door. The drill hasn't changed since those shows were made, because it can't be improved on.

Paula unfolded another finger.

I drew my knockdown and she drew hers and we both took a deep a breath.

Her third finger went up and so did her right knee and my left.

The soles of our feet slammed into the doors in simultaneously executed front thrust kicks.

The black-clad Pareto standing on the other side of Paula's door couldn't have been more perfectly placed—the edge of the door hit the point of his chin hard enough to knock him off his feet and put his lights out.

I wasn't quite so lucky; the other Pareto was almost out of range of my swinging door, and all the frame made contact with was his knockdown. It dislodged the weapon from his hand, but he recovered his wits before I recovered my kick. Before I knew what was happening his foot was crashing into my hand and my own knockdown was flying through the air.

By the time my knockdown hit the floor the Pareto had stepped forward into a follow-up kick with his other leg, and the foot at the end of it was flying at my chin. I barely managed to step back from a blow that would have broken my jaw and maybe my neck. Avoiding the kick was good, but the fact I tripped over the unconscious Pareto in the process was bad. What was even worse was that I took Paula down with me. The dull thud as my head landed on the fallen Pareto's forearm was followed by a sharp crack as Paula's skull hit the stairway door.

From the corner of my eye I saw Paula blinking and shaking her head, and knew she wasn't seriously hurt.

I turned my attention to the Pareto above me just in time to see him raise his knee and chamber a stamping kick. I rolled away and his heel flashed down past my ear. There was a snap like a crunchy protein bar being broken in two as his foot slammed into the forearm of his fallen partner, right where my head had been resting a fraction of a second earlier.

As the Pareto recovered his kick I used the momentum of my roll to get to my feet, and we squared up to each other with only the fallen assassin's body between us.

The man I was up against might have been the same Pareto who'd mocked me in the gym a few nights earlier when I couldn't keep up with him on the exercise bike. He might have been any one of a hundred Paretos who'd mocked me in a thousand different ways over the years. Whatever, he was looking at me the way you do when you've got someone at your mercy and don't intend showing them any.

I glanced around for a weapon, knowing I needed one to have a fighting chance.

The nearest knockdown was closer to the Pareto than to me. He obviously thought he didn't need it because he was making for me and not the weapon. While I'd stolen a glance at the knockdown, the Pareto had stepped over the body of his fallen partner. Now there was nothing separating us at all.

I'd only squared-up to a Pareto once before, in close-quarter-combat training at the academy. It had been once too often and left me bruised from head to foot for a week—and broken in spirit for a lot longer than that. You couldn't have called it a fight because it barely lasted a dozen seconds and I didn't lay a finger on him. He'd goaded me with the kind of sneer you can't be taught, then suckered me with a feinted punch to the face. When my hands came up, he'd hooked me to the floating rib. As I doubled over he grabbed my nearest hand and in one flowing movement went from wrist lock to elbow lock to shoulder lock—and I went from my feet, to my knees, to flat on my face. If my life had depended on moving a single centimeter I couldn't have done it because each wave of pain from my overloaded joints was more paralyzing than the last.

All of that was going through my mind as the Pareto closed to striking distance. He knew he had the beating of me, and he knew that I knew it. The mockery on his face made that clear. I'd never hated anyone as much as I hated him, and I'd never felt more helpless and afraid. Not a good combination.

Then the sneer froze on his face, and his glassy blue eyes flitted to my left. I thought it was an attempt at misdirection, and was surprised he'd resort to such a crude and obvious tactic.

But his eyes actually focused behind me. The next

thing I knew there was the *WHOOSH* of a knockdown being discharged. Unfortunately Paula must have been seeing double. She must have seen two Paretos about to attack me and, as luck had it, she fired at the wrong one. The gel sac flew past the Pareto and hit the foyer door with a cross between a *THUNK* and a *SPLATTER*, leaving a vivid green stain. The next sound was the clatter of a knockdown falling to the floor; the effort of firing it had been too much for Paula.

The sneer returned to the Pareto's face, bigger than ever. I tried desperately to think of a way to wipe it off. I couldn't hope to match his strength, let alone his reactions. He'd block or evade whatever I threw at him, and counter so fast I couldn't do likewise. A fair fight would be anything but fair—so instead of fighting fair and throwing a punch or kick I raised my hands as if in surrender. . .

And then I spat at him.

Numbers hate that even more than Names do; they're obsessive about cleanliness.

His hands instinctively came up to his face and I stepped in with a right hook that landed so solidly I felt his jaw dislocating and my arm jarring all the way up to the shoulder. I had a brief, nightmarish vision of the Pareto shaking his head, holding his jaw in his hands and clicking it back into place, and that awful sneer reappearing. With that in mind I followed the hook with an elbow strike. Such techniques don't look nearly as spectacular as a punch to anyone watching, but they do a dozen times the damage. The Pareto in front of me was living, barely breathing, proof of that; he pitched forward, reaching out for the nearest thing to grab hold of. The nearest thing was me, but I wasn't about to be grabbed. I took a step to the side and the Pareto clutched at thin air, then went down so hard I knew he wouldn't be getting up again until long after we were gone.

I hurried over to Paula, who was shakily getting to her feet.

"You okay?" I asked.

She nodded, and blinked a few times. It must have cleared her head, because her eyes were a lot more lucid after the last blink than the first one. We grabbed our packs and ran for the foyer doors.

I rammed my card in the reader and waited for the doors to slide open.

They didn't.

Paula looked at me and then we both looked at the reader. We were just in time to see it swallow my card.

More in hope than expectation I watched Paula take out her card and slot it in the reader. The doors remained firmly closed, and my hope disappeared along with the small plastic rectangle as it was swallowed by the reader.

My first impulse was to try the same thing on the airlock that I'd done on the stairwell door. However the airlocks are built to withstand a superstorm, and I knew that even if by some miracle I kicked down the inner door without breaking my foot, I'd shatter my leg on the more substantial outer one.

Even after a blow to the head, Paula is a whole lot sharper than me. She proved it by running over to the nearest of the fallen Paretos and taking the card from the ID pocket on the sleeve of his black coveralls.

I gave her a 'That's my girl smile,' but she didn't smile back. There was an Olden Days saying about counting chickens. I couldn't remember exactly how it went, but I knew it was meant for situations just like this.

Paula took a deep breath, then slid the card home.

Nothing happened.

Then, just as my shoulders sagged, the doors slid open.

A little light flashed and there was a beep, reminding us to take some filtermasks from the dispenser beside the reader. Paula took four, and then the supply dried up. I considered running back for the other Pareto's ID in a bid to free up more filtermasks, but didn't want to give the reader time to change its mind about the validity of the card. And, anyway, all the filters in the dispenser wouldn't be enough to let us live happily ever after. So I followed Paula into the airlock.

The doors closed behind us with a hiss. For a horrible moment it seemed like the outer doors weren't going to open, and the airlock would imprison us until more Paretos came to finish the job the other two had started.

But seconds later there was a louder hiss. My ears popped as the pressure changed, and the warm, tainted air of the Outside washed over us. I'd never thought toxic air could be so good to breathe. I slapped on a filtermask. Paula did likewise, and we ran out into the dusk.

We didn't stop until there were ruined buildings on either side and a cracked and pitted road ahead of us.

CHAPTER 20

010000110100100001000001010100000101010001000101010100 10

The Enchanted Forest

We didn't know where we were going, but knew we had to get there before night fell; in the darkness it would be a matter of 'when,' not 'if,' one of us had an ankle-breaking accident. Once the filtermask Paula had given me ran out I didn't bother replacing it. Paula didn't say anything, but I know she felt the same way because she didn't bother replacing hers when it fell off a few minutes later.

After a little while we saw a sign saying HOTEL up ahead. It seemed like as good a place to stop as any. Actually, it said H T L in letters that were meant to light up but wouldn't have had anything other than toxic rainwater running through their circuits for the last half a century.

It should have been romantic—two runaways, off to

see the world—but we were quickly disabused of any such illusions. The first five or six bedrooms were overrun with cockroaches, and they'd turned each mattress into a breeding ground.

We didn't bother checking out any more bedrooms after that; we went to the dining room and made a table our bed, with our daypacks as pillows. It was so hot we didn't need blankets, which was just as well because all the ones we'd come across were filthy beyond belief. We did, however, need air-conditioning, not only to purify the toxins, but to moderate the temperature. In its absence all we could do was lie there and sweat.

Paula fell asleep quite quickly. I suppose that's one advantage of not having an overactive imagination.

I just lay there with her head on my shoulder, and my hipbones digging into the hard tabletop. My coverall already felt loathsome and dirty, and so did I. I longed for a cold drink and a hot shower; for cool, clean air and a soft mattress. As I listened to the scurrying of rats, the scuttling of cockroaches and the whine of flies, a voice inside me asked the same question over and over again: *How long can we live like this?*

I finally fell asleep in the hour before dawn. . .

And woke up at first light, stiff and sore, with something tickling my ear. Unfortunately it was a cockroach, not Paula, nibbling my lobe. I swatted it away and it was so big it fell onto the table with a metallic *CLINK.* It lay there on its back, coppery and hideous, with its legs thrashing at the air as it frantically tried to right itself. The only thing more disgusting than the top of a cockroach is the underside of one.

Not the ideal start to the day.

I don't know if it was my swatting movement that woke Paula, or the sound of the falling cockroach, or the weak gray light filtering in through the broken windows. Whatever, she stirred and moved against me. I'm guessing that in those first few moments she'd forgotten where she was because she smiled when she felt the length of my body against hers. Then she opened her eyes and the smile died as she took in the squalid surroundings. All she could say as our situation sank in was, "Oh, Ben!"

I couldn't say anything at all.

We were so filthy by the next day that we raided the first chemist we came to for shower gel and headed down to the river, even though the water was probably so full of toxins it wasn't safe to bathe in, let alone drink.

Our skinny dip cleaned away the sweat but left our skin horribly itchy.

I asked Paula the question I'd put to myself earlier: "How long can we live like this?"

Practical as ever, she said, "We'll have a better idea when

we've seen how much food and drink there is in the ruins."

As it turned out, we couldn't find anything to eat and drink at all. Too many people, no doubt every bit as desperate as we were, had beaten us to each house and shop by forty or fifty years.

While we didn't find food or drink we found plenty of other things, and at first the novelty of them distracted us from our thirst and hunger. Everywhere we looked there was something we wanted to examine more closely, either because it was particularly quaint or poignant: mailboxes with letters addressed to people who'd long since died; garden furniture for sitting Outside; playparks with swings and roundabouts; rockeries with foot-tall plastic gnomes; and cars vandalized in every kind of way—windscreens smashed, tires slit, doors dented and scratched. Some were burnt out, others covered with paint that had been flung from pots or sprayed in angry aerosol attacks. Words like *Mass Murderer* and *Planetkiller* appeared over and over again.

And, inside the houses, we came across countless unusual things that told of a bygone age:

A collection of costume dolls, an album of stamps, and bundles of football cards.

Photos of newly-weds sharing their first kiss as man and wife; proud parents christening babies; retired couples posing on vacation in faraway places. I couldn't help but wonder what had become of all those people; of their hope and love, their joy and pride.

And then there were the other buildings:

A courthouse and jail block with unlocked cells and graffiti scratched on the bare plaster walls.

A filling station which had been burned almost to the ground, probably by eco-terrorists rather than by accident.

A boutique full of moth-eaten clothes that hadn't been in fashion for over half a century, from trousers with flared bottoms to striped halter-tops.

A museum with golf clubs and fishing rods and other reminders that the Outside had once been viewed as a healthy place to be.

A bus station with timetables for coaches that hadn't run for sixty years.

And a church that had fallen victim to every conceivable form of sacrilege. Despite all the signs of abandonment by God, someone had apparently sought refuge there; a perfectly articulated skeleton clad in disintegrating clothes was spread out on a duvet near the altar, as if somebody had simply lain down and died.

As always in such situations I felt like a cross between a tomb raider and an archaeologist.

"I wonder who it was," Paula said, looking at the bones.

Something in those words and the way she said them made me look from the skeleton to her.

Aware she was being watched, Paula met my gaze and asked, "Why are you staring at me like that?"

"Because of what you just said—about wondering; and

the way you said it—wistfully."

Paula looked back at the skeleton, and said, "The past's never seemed so immediate."

"What about that first time you were Outside, when we went to the library?"

"I suppose I knew on a subliminal level that what I was seeing had nothing to do with the reality of my life, and so I made no effort to engage with it. But now I know this is my world, I'm starting to wonder about it."

"Looks like we're not as different as we thought," I said, but she didn't seem to hear.

"In the museum I found myself wondering about the games people once played," she said, as if thinking aloud.

"In the courthouse I began wondering about the people who'd scratched their names into the cement of the cellblock walls.

"In the bus station I got to thinking about where the buses had gone to, and who'd stood in line waiting for them.

"Everywhere we look, I find myself thinking about something to do with the past, whereas before I never gave it a second thought."

"Looks like you have a sense of wonder after all, Paula. It just never had a chance to come out in the community."

"I'm starting to feel like a different person," she said. "I still can't identify with the past like you do, but I want to find out about it. I *wonder* about it. There are thoughts filling my empty moments, thoughts of vanished lives."

She looked up from the bones in front of the altar, and said, "The downside is that some of those thoughts that fill the empty moments are about our future, as well as other people's past—and those thoughts are ones I'd rather not be having." She looked back at the skeleton.

I knew exactly what she meant.

We exhausted our food in four days and, despite rationing our drinks to the point of being permanently thirsty, our bottles were as dry as our throats by the day after that. My throat was raw as well as dry, as if something in the air was burning it, and I developed a wracking cough. Paula was the same and, like me, her voice became croakier by the day. As if things weren't bad enough our skin got steadily itchier, and contact with water only made things worse.

That night, our fifth Outside, there was a colossal thunderstorm. We were so thirsty we ran out of the house we'd made our home for the night—a luxury bungalow that was no longer luxurious—and stood on the patio with our mouths wide open and our arms outstretched.

But the rainwater tasted vile on our tongues and left our faces burning. We boiled some of it in an old pot, on a fire of ripped up cardboard boxes and broken chair legs, lit with a scavenged cigarette lighter. But, after twenty minutes of bubbling away, the water was still so foul we couldn't make ourselves drink it.

It was as good a time as any to bring out what I'd taken from my desk back in the haven: a syringe full of clear liquid.

Paula looked at it for a very long time. Then she looked at me and said, "Ben, what's in that?"

"Promise not to turn me in if I tell you," I croaked.

She almost managed a smile.

"It's Slo-Mo," I told her. "I found it on a callout a few weeks ago. When you were being a good cop I was being a bad cop—I never bothered handing it in."

"Why not?"

"I thought it might be fun to try a few drops of it some day."

Paula looked from me back to the syringe.

"We can watch each other die a lingering, miserable death," I told her. "Or we can take some of this and die in each other's arms after what seems like a lifetime of love."

"That's what they used to call a no-brainer, isn't it?"

We shared out first laugh in more than a day.

There was nothing funny about the silence that followed.

Paula reached for my hand and gently closed it around the syringe, saying, "Not here, Ben. Let's find somewhere special to. . ."

She wasn't able to finish the sentence. She didn't have to. I knew how it ended.

"I can think of the perfect place," I said.

Jen had taken me there once, but it was such a long walk we'd only had a few minutes to look around, and even then our filtermasks were used up before we got back to the community.

"What sort of place is it?" Paula asked.

But I wouldn't tell her. I wanted to surprise her with it, the way Jen had surprised me. I was helped by the same toxic haze that was slowly killing us, for it hid the tell-tale shapes from view until we were nearly upon them. They appeared as if by magic in front of us, dark and unmoving amidst the swirling pearlescence. I watched Paula as she looked at these shapes, which must have been so unlike anything she'd come across before.

"Trees," she said, disbelievingly.

"It's the relic of a forest," I told her. Then I didn't say anything, because I was too caught up in the excitement of being in the presence of something that was almost as alien to me as it was to her. I just stood there with a tightness in my chest and throat that had nothing to do with the ill-effects of the toxic haze.

I could tell Paula was feeling the same things, too, because she said, "It's. . . It's. . ."

I picked a word for her: "Amazing."

She nodded. "If only we'd come across this place earlier," she said.

I knew what she meant—the light was fading fast. The darkness closed in all around us like a physical thing. As it did, we drew closer together.

It should have been eerie but I didn't feel frightened, and when I stole a glance at Paula I saw she wasn't scared, either. Her eyes were glowing with something I'd never discerned in them before, something that couldn't be reflected light, not in the fast approaching darkness.

She led me deeper into the forest with a tug of the hand, wanting to explore.

Instead of growing more hesitant as the darkness deepened, we walked faster and faster. And then we were running, laughing with wild, carefree abandon like a couple of children, discovering a strangely beautiful world that was dramatically different from the only one we'd ever known. It was a world where there was give in the ground beneath our feet; where every texture felt with our fingertips was different from the last, and not a single one was perfectly smooth.

Finally, inevitably, I tripped over a tree root. Paula fell down next to me. The darkness was complete by now, and rather than get up we crawled on hands and knees until we came to a place comfortable enough to lie down in: a make-do mattress of what I took to be pine needles, softened by time and the elements so they were no longer jaggy.

I flipped over onto my back and Paula settled on her side next to me, head resting in her palm, the fingers of her other hand tracing my cheekbones.

My thoughts turned to the syringe in the pocket of my

coveralls, and I said, "Paula—"

She knew me well enough by then to read my mind. "Not now," she said. "Not yet. Let's just spend a night here. All I've seen of the Outside is what remains of the worst of it; I want to experience what remains of the best of it.

So we lay there silently appreciating the place and each other. I waited for her to get bored and restless like a Number should in such a situation, but she snuggled up to me contentedly. In this place, Paula truly was a different person—and, with her beside me, so was I.

After a time I'd no way of measuring—we'd long since abandoned our i-bands—she fell sound asleep with her head resting on my chest.

Moments later, emotionally drained, I was sleeping, too.

I dreamed of birdsong high above, and wind whistling through the branches.

And woke up in the middle of the night to find I hadn't been dreaming, at least about the wind. All around me I heard the creak of trees swaying and branches bending in something much stronger than a breeze. I don't know how long I lay there with my eyes closed, listening to those unfamiliar, evocative, strangely beautiful sounds: the roar of the wind as it roamed the skies far above; the howl it made passing through the high branches; the creaking of trunks straining against their roots; and the rustle of small things I could only guess at moving all around us on the forest floor.

When I opened my eyes I found I was looking into Paula's. I don't know if my waking had woken her, or if it was the other way around. Her expression was one of awe. "Paula, what is it?" I asked, intrigued by what had put that look on her face.

She didn't answer, and I thought she hadn't heard. Then she turned to me, and it was as if she'd returned from somewhere very far away. "Ben," she said, with the same bewilderment in her voice that I'd seen in her eyes, "I think I just had a. . . I think I just had a dream."

I'd rarely seen anyone, let alone a Number, look so intensely moved.

"What did you dream of?" I asked, sharing her wonder.

"I can't remember details, just a feeling. I just remember that things seemed different while I slept."

"In what way?"

She struggled to find words, another thing I wasn't used to seeing a Number do. Finally she said, "The world was young, not old, and we had time enough for love."

Reaching into the thigh pocket of my coveralls and bringing out the syringe of Slo-Mo, I said, "The world might not be young, Paula, but we do have time for love."

She looked at the syringe and I looked at her. I wondered if she was anything like as afraid as I was. I wanted to say something that would make things easier for her. Given the situation, it should have been almost impossible to think of what to say. But the words came to me unbidden: "I won't let you die without making sure you believe in love, Paula, and I'll tell you everything I know about the way the world was when the wind had many names."

EPILOGUE

0100010101010000010010010100110001001111010001110101010101000101

TIME LOST ALL MEANING FOR THE TWO OF US. THE earth might have turned once or made a thousand revolutions, the sun might have stopped rising, the moon might have fallen, and the brightest star might have burned itself out. Paula and I could have been the first people in the world, or the last, or the only two who ever lived. We talked until our thoughts turned into feelings, and then discovered just how many things can't be put into words: the secrets and mysteries; the beauty that's more than skin deep, and the magic that makes people so much more than a sum of their parts.

Only once did anything intrude into our world, a light so bright it was like every sheet of lightning that's ever flashed across the sky.

After that I didn't see or feel or hear anything.

Until a sound that was vaguely familiar yet somehow very strange. I couldn't pin down what it was. There was a word for it, but I'd forgotten it long ago.

Then I remembered that the word was 'language,' and I listened to the sound.

The language was strange but familiar, like the sound had been before I realized what it was. I felt like I should have been able to understand it. I thought that on some level I did, and yet I had no idea what was being said.

I opened my eyes and looked into two pools of blackness that were full of secrets I understood, mysteries I'd solved, memories I shared. Each black pool was set in silvery blue, and they were so beautiful I could have looked into them forever. I felt like I already had looked into them forever, and it hadn't been long enough.

There was a pinprick on my arm. Suddenly time accelerated and I could barely breathe. I was lying on the forest floor next to Paula, looking into her eyes and seeing my own confusion mirrored there. The world was spinning so crazily that, even though I was lying down, I felt like I was about to fall over. I held onto Paula and she held onto me as though we might be flung off into opposite corners of the universe at any moment.

Looking up to see what was happening, all I could make out was a spiral of pink and brown, white, and blue. A wave of nausea rose in my throat. I swallowed it back and closed my eyes.

When I opened them the spinning had slowed and the colors were resolving themselves into the faces of people looking down on us; the branches of trees; and the beautiful blue of a sky streaked with pure white clouds.

Someone spoke, and the language I hadn't been able to understand suddenly made sense now that I was no longer hearing it in slow motion.

They explained what had happened, or at least what they knew of it. A tremendous coronal mass ejection—a solar flare in common parlance—had engulfed the Earth, burning out electronic circuits, erasing hard-drives and databanks; disabling the Ecosystem and resetting mankind's technological clock to the year zero in the blink of an eye.

It did something else, that flood of charged particles that swamped the Earth: it ionized the toxins in the atmosphere, burning off the leaden haze that had blighted the planet for so long.

Some of the shell-shocked people who emerged from the crippled community had found Paula and I lying in the forest. They thought we were dead because the Slo-Mo had virtually put us into stasis. But then a faint whisper or a moan told them we were still alive, and they'd given us some Rush to bring us back to the world.

To a new world.

We ate some of the food they'd brought from the community, and slaked our thirst with rainwater they'd collected earlier that morning—water that was sweet and safe to drink without being boiled, just as the air was good to breathe without being filtered. We told them our names and our story, and they told us theirs, and we sat with them at the river's edge and watched the sun disappear behind the distant havens. It was something they said they'd seen many times now, but still it awed them. The setting sun streaked the blue of the sky with fire and turned the river to a shimmering sheet of liquid gold and amber. There had to be a hundred people in that foraging party but not a single word was spoken, such was the reverence for sky and sun and river, for the difference between day and night, and the magical transition between the two.

As the fire died in the sky we built one with driftwood on the land. The people who'd found Paula and I told us the rest of what they knew, and we did likewise, and together we tried to make sense of what had happened to us and to the world. Ideas and explanations leapt from our collective imagination like sparks from the burning wood as we confronted the past and considered the future.

Many things were beyond our comprehension—perhaps more than we understood—but of one thing we felt sure: there had to be a greater power than man at work in this. I don't know how we knew; we just did. It had used computers to save us when we lost our way, and taught us that we must put our faith not in technology but in ourselves and each other. It had taught us how bad it was when greed came to be seen as good, and how much was lost along with coral reefs and butterflies and rainbows, the pull of far horizons and the names of the wind. It had taught us that the true god is nature.

And now it was down to us to start anew and make a world where we could learn to live, to laugh and to love again.

Then once more there was silence around the fire because above us—impossibly far above us—the stars were coming out one by one, and it was a humbling sight. I put my arm around Paula and we counted stars until we ran out of numbers, and then gave names to constellations until we ran out of words.

The tide turned and with it came a wind. It was stronger than a breeze but gentler than a storm, so nobody knew quite what to call it. There was nothing acrid or tainted about it; instead, it carried the salty tang of the sea. It was a smell so fresh we wanted to breathe it in deeply—and, in doing so, were reborn.

I know that in time the wind will carry other things: the earthy promise of freshly turned soil and the scent of rising sap; the perfume of blossoming flowers and the sweetness of ripening fruit. I know that in years to come it will carry the sound of leaves rustling in dark green forests, and stalks of wheat swaying in golden fields; the call of birds in high branches, and the laughter of children as they dance barefoot with carefree abandon around fires such as this. It will be a song of Mother Earth that sounds different from place to place and one moment to the next—and, in listening to this song of things long-forgotten and yet to be found, people will be enchanted by the singer, and they'll rediscover wonder and wisdom and give wildly romantic names to the wind once more.

THE END

01010100011010000110010100100000010001010110111001100100

Escape *Tomorrow's World* of names and numbers and explore the stunning beauty of

DAVIE HENDERSON'S

WATERFALL GLEN

When Kate Brodie inherits Waterfall Glen it seems like the start of an exciting new life. Full of romantic notions, she swaps her dull routine in San Francisco for life as a Highland lady.

But the stunning beauty of the glen belies a troubled history and uncertain future, and Kate's imposing new home, Greystane House, is full of disturbing revelations about her family's past. Each portrait on the ancient walls tells an un-nerving story, while the empty rooms echo with rumors of a centuries-old curse that takes on new significance when unsettling events threaten the small community whose fate lies in her hands.

The only person Kate can turn to is a man haunted by equally troubling events, a man she has every reason not to trust. Only with his help can she find a way to defend old values against the materialism of the modern world. Only together can they lay their ghosts to rest.

The Piaras Legacy

Scott Gamboe

LONG AGO, SO THE LEGENDS SAY, THE NECROMANCER VOLNOR invaded the continent of Pelacia. His legions of undead soldiers ravaged the land unchecked, until the three nations united and pushed their evil foes back into the Desert of Malator.

But that was centuries ago, and few people still believe the tale. Other, more worldly matters occupy their time, such as recent attacks by renegade Kobolds. But Elac, an Elf who makes his way as a merchant, is too concerned with his business affairs to become involved in international politics. Until a marauding band of Kobolds attacks Elac's caravan and he finds himself running for his life.

Befriended by an Elven warrior named Rilen, he travels to Unity, the seat of power on the Pelacian continent. There he is joined by a diverse group of companions, and he sets out on an epic quest to solve the riddle of his heritage and save the land from the growing evil that threatens to engulf it.

ISBN# 9781933836256
Trade Paperback / Fantasy
US $15.95 / CDN $17.95
APRIL 2008
www.scottgamboe.net

DARK PLANET

CHARLES W. SASSER

KADAR SAN, A HUMAN-ZENTADON CROSSBREED DISTRUSTED BY both humans and Zentadon, is dispatched with a Deep Reconnaissance Team (DRT) to the Dark Planet of Aldenia. His mission: use his telepathic powers to sniff out a Blob assault base preparing to attack the Galaxia Republic. Dominated by both amazing insect and reptile life forms, and by an evil and mysterious Presence, Aldenia was once a base for the warlike Indowy who used theirsuperior technology to enslave the Zentadon and turn them into super warriors to deploy against humans.

The DRT comes under attack not only from savage denizens of the Dark Planet, but also from the mysterious Presence, which turns team member against team member and all against Kadar San. The Presence promises untold wealth and power to any member of the team unscrupulous enough to unleash the contents of a Pandora's box-like remnant of Indowy technology. The box's possessor poses a greater threat than the entire Blob nation, for he is capable of releasing untold horrors upon the galaxy.

Kadar San finds himself pitted against a human killer, an expert sniper, in a desperate struggle to save both the Republic and the human female he has come to love. Like all Zentadon, however, Kadar San cannot kill without facing destruction himself in the process, and he has no choice but to kill. In order to save the galaxy, Kadar San must face the truth . . . No one will leave the Dark Planet.

STEPHEN HENDRY

LEAPFROG

A SCIENTIFIC EXPEDITION HAS GONE TERRIBLY AWRY. Highly advanced aliens decide to test the human race by offering free secrets that will enable universal space travel without time or distance constraints. Earth snaps at the challenge and collectively musters resources to develop the most advanced starship ever built on earth, which is appropriately named Leapfrog for the technological jump over existing science.

Unfortunately, corrupt secret services, greedy politicians, and overly wary generals condemn the mission from the start. Instead of arriving at the designated rendezvous with goodwill and an intent to share, the joint military contingent mutinies, plunders, then destroys the site to prevent possible access from any other species.

Returning with their plunder and while in cryo-sleep, the ship encounters a disastrous meteor shower that destroys the main engines. Thousands of years pass while the stricken ship slowly meanders its way back to earth with two hundred and seventy-five humans solidly frozen in deep suspended animation.

While they sleep, earth becomes embroiled in a disastrous DNA/RNA holocaust. The perpetrators use a crocodile-bred virus to alter the human genetic code and reverse human evolution, thereby eliminating their enemies.

Once the plague damages the human sexual organs, nothing can be done in time to save the human race, and human beings eventually reverse back to soulless Neanderthals. However, the crocodiles benefit immensely from this ill-fated experiment. Their evolutionary cycle goes into high gear, and they soon surpass humans as the dominant creature.

Seeking clues as to what has happened, the survivors encounter enormous wolf spiders hidden in a long-abandoned pressurized dome on the moon. Barely escaping with their lives, the explorers are forced to abandon their derelict starship and return to earth to face horrifying battles among cannibal Neanderthals and highly evolved crocodiles.

ISBN# 9781933836508
US $15.95 / CDN $17.95
Trade Paperback / Science Fiction
NOVEMBER 2008
www.stevehendry.com

TOLTECA

K. MICHAEL WRIGHT

His name is Topiltzin. He is the son of the Dragon, a blue-eyed Mesoamerican hero. He is also a godless ballplayer, a wanderer, a rogue warrior. He will become known as the Plumed Serpent, the man who became a god, who transcended death to become the Morning Star.

In the world of the Fourth Sun, Topiltzin is the unconquered hero of the rubberball game. When he comes with his companions to a city to play, children flock to meet him, maidens cover the roadway with flowers for him to tread on, and people gather to watch the mighty Turquoise Lords of Tollan. They are the undefeated champions of the ancient game of ritual, a game so fanatically revered that spectators would often wager their own children on its outcome. To lose meant decapitation. The Turquoise Lords of Tollan never lost. At least until now.

The Smoking Lord, descended from Highland Mountain kings, has come with vast armies. He has learned of the splendid Tolteca from a priest who tried to teach him the true way of the one god. After offering the old man up as a sacrifice to the midnight sun, Smoking Mirror has now come north to see if the legends are true.

An army has come, and a new age. Topiltzin witnesses its horrors. He finds cities destroyed, villagers raped and ritualistically slaughtered by sorcerer priests sent as heralds to offer up human sacrifice. Unable to stop the blood slaughter of innocents, realizing the vast armies of the Shadow Lords will annihilate even the mighty Tolteca, Topiltzin becomes obsessed with one final objective, one last move in the rubberball game: the death of the Smoking Mirror.

ISBN# 9781932815467
Hardcover Adult / Paranormal
US $26.95 / CDN $35.95
Available Now

shinigami

django wexler

Shinigami: In Japanese folklore, a spirit that collects the souls of the dead.

At age fourteen, Sylph Walker died in a car accident. That turned out to be only the beginning of her problems. . .

She and her sister Lina awake to an afterlife, of sorts — the world of Omega, ruled by cruel, squabbling, and nearly all-powerful Archmagi. When Lina finds a magical sword of immense power, she becomes the unwilling epicenter of the conflict. The sisters are forced to join the Circle Breakers, rebels sworn to prevent the tyrants from expanding their rule.

Lina, bearing the ancient artifact, is hailed as the Liberator — the latest in a long line of heroes expected to destroy the Archmagi. Sylph finds herself at the head of the rebel armies fighting to take back the land and the lives of its people. But what kind of a land is it? Is Omega really the world that lies beyond death? And who is the legendary Lightbringer, a being greater even than the Archmagi?

From the author of NIGHT BIRDS' REIGN and CRIMSON FIRE

HOLLY TAYLOR

The Coranians have won the war, Kymru is defeated. For Havgan, however, the victory is not complete. Cadair Idris, the hall of the High Kings, remains closed to him. To gain entrance he must locate the Four Treasures—the Stone, the Spear, the Cauldron and the Sword—and bring them to the Guardian of the Doors. Only then can he proclaim himself High King of Kymru.

But the Treasures were hidden long ago, after the death of the last High King. To find them Gwydion the Dreamer must locate a long-forgotten song, and the clues it contains. Following the dictates of the song, he persuades Rhiannon, her daughter Gwenhwyvar, and his nephew Arthur to set out with him on the dangerous quest.

Dogged by Havgan's soldiers they race against time to find the artifacts. But the difficult journey is made even harder by the distrust they have for each other, as well as the necessity to face their own worst fears in order to succeed and gain entrance into Cadair Idris—only to watch helplessly as Arthur risks his life, and his very soul, on the next move in the deadly game.

ISBN# 9781933836263
US $15.95 / CDN $17.95
Trade Paperback / Fantasy
JUNE 2008
www.dreamers-cycle.com

DAVIE HENDERSON

photo by
Davie Henderson

I'm a forty-year-old journalist with a love of writing, travel, and photography. I like to find out about the people and places of the world at first hand, living out some little dreams along the way. For many years I combined my interests in the form of travel articles, but long wished to write a story set in my native Scotland.

The result was *Waterfall Glen*, published by Medallion Press in April 2006. The idea began with two characters and a wildly beautiful place that changes their lives forever. The story wrote itself, driven by the fact that the people are at turning points in their lives, and the place is under threat from dangers old and new.

In this novel, I wanted to write about what's happening to the world, what we're in danger of losing, and how much we'll miss it when it's gone. Issues like global warming and genetic engineering form the backdrop for a murder mystery and the relationship between two very different people trying to solve it.

www.daviehenderson.bravehost.com